For America's Wounded Warriors

Printed in the United States of America.

Publisher's note
This is a work of fiction. The people, events, circumstances,
and institutions depicted are fictitious and the product of the
author's imagination. Any resemblance of any character to any
actual person, whether living or dead, is purely coincidental.

The publisher is not responsible for websites (or their content)
that are not owned by the publisher.

Library of Congress Cataloging-in-Publication Data

Williams, Terrence L.
Cooper's revenge : a novel / by T.L. Williams.
p. cm.
ISBN: 978-0-9884400-0-5
1. United States. Navy. SEALs—Fiction. 2. Improvised explosive
devices—Fiction. 3. Iran—Fiction. 4. Terrorism—Fiction. I. Title.
PS3623.I5639 C66 2013
813—dc23

Epigraph

"What enables the wise sovereign and the good general to win victories, to achieve successes more than others, is that he possesses beforehand information regarding the enemy.

This information cannot be obtained by offering prayers to gods and spirits; nor by inductive thinking; nor by deductive calculation. It can be obtained only from men who have a thorough knowledge of the enemy's conditions."

Sun Tzu on the Art of War

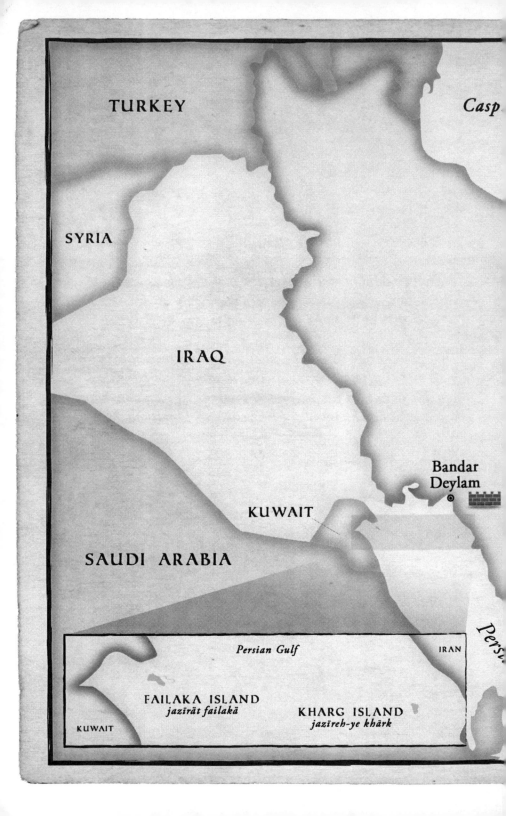

TURKEY

Casp

SYRIA

IRAQ

Bandar
Deylam
◉

KUWAIT

SAUDI ARABIA

Persi

Persian Gulf

IRAN

KUWAIT

FAILAKA ISLAND
jazīrāt failakā

KHARG ISLAND
jazīreh-ye khārk

Sea

TURKMENISTAN

 Tehran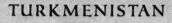

Esfahan

AFGHANISTAN

IRAN

PAKISTAN

Gulf

Strait of Hormuz

Chapter 1

Lieutenant Logan Alexander flexed his toes and then pushed off from the upper rack of the metal bunk bed. Forward Operating Base Spin Boldak wasn't Montpelier, but for Afghanistan, it was pretty good, he thought, as he landed softly on the converted conex storage container floor. His platoon of twenty Navy Seals had flown into the dusty encampment a few hours before from Kandahar. They'd taken a quick tour of the post and then grabbed a couple of hours of shut-eye before dinner.

Seal Team 8 was going to be operating outside the wire for the next several nights in a push to drive out a band of Taliban fighters who, just the week before, had launched a successful attack against the residence of the former provincial governor. The cunning bastards had used a remote-detonated bomb carried up to the gates of the governor's fortified compound on the back of a camel. Two of the official's sons had been killed in the freak attack.

There was a knock on the door, and Chief Petty Officer Chico Martinez stuck his head inside. "Sir, time to get up. The chow hall's open and we still have our Intel briefing before we head out tonight. The J-2's got that laid on for 1900 hours."

Logan looked at his watch and saw that it was already six o'clock. "All right, Martinez. Thanks for the wake up. Tell the men I heard they do a respectable surf and turf at Old Bill's on Fridays. It's worth doing because it's going to be MREs once we're outside the wire."

"Yes, sir. They already know about it. Most of them were over in the gym the last time I checked. They've got a pretty good setup over there; free weights, an elliptical, and some other cardio machines."

1

Martinez closed the door and Logan stared after him. Martinez was a little guy but he was one tough bastard. He'd grown up in Juarez, Mexico, dodging bullets in the street battles between warring drug cartels. His parents had shipped him out of there at the start of his senior year in high school to live with a sister who'd gone to UCLA and settled there after marrying a lawyer from Los Angeles. Martinez had taken advantage of a little known program that grants U.S. citizenship to foreigners who honorably serve in the U.S. military. He'd enlisted in the Navy and then had been selected for Seal training.

Logan poked his head into the welfare and recreation center on his way over to Old Bill's. The building housed several pool tables, a movie library, big screen TV and a library. After dinner Logan walked over to the briefing room and introduced himself to the J-2, Major Mike Campbell.

"Lieutenant, you've got your work cut out for you. The Taliban's been pretty resilient in these parts. The International Security Assistance Force hasn't been able to shut them down, despite our best efforts. They're like those damn zombies in that horror show, the 'Night of the Living Dead.' They just keep coming back." He looked at his watch. "If all your men are here we can get started."

Logan looked around the room, counting noses. While he and Major Campbell had been talking, his men had filed in and had taken their seats. "That's everybody, sir."

"All right. Let's get started." He walked to the front of the room and turned on an overhead projector. "I'm Major Mike Campbell. I'm the J-2 at FOB Spin Boldak, and the following briefing is at the Secret level." He dimmed the lights and then brought up the first slide.

"Spin Boldak is key in ISAF's effort to defeat the Taliban, largely because of our proximity to the Pakistan border." Using a laser pointer on the on-screen map of Afghanistan, Campbell highlighted the road from Kandahar to the border of Pakistan. "Highway 4 links the provincial capital of Kandahar to the north with Chaman and Quetta, Pakistan, to the south. It's a rough and tumble piece of real estate, crawling with smugglers, drug lords, corrupt officials, and an ever-changing political landscape.

"All the shifting political alliances and old tribal rivalries have made it very difficult for ISAF to keep the Taliban from operating in southern Afghanistan. They're targeting not only U.S. and coalition forces but also Afghan villages that the Taliban suspects are sympathetic to President Karzai, and by extension, the U.S. and our allies. Most of the people in this area are Pashtuns. They're from the Noorzai and Achakzai tribes."

"Sir, is it true that the Taliban can cross in and out of Afghanistan through that border area you just highlighted, at will?" Logan looked over at Petty Officer Garrison Peters, a big rawboned sniper from Great Falls, Virginia, who'd posed the question.

"That's one of the biggest obstacles we face. Pakistani and Afghan Border Police are mostly corrupt and have divided loyalties. So, to answer your question, yes, the Taliban has figured out how to slip through the cracks. That border is like a sieve. It's out of control. And until our good friends in Pakistan decide to crack down and stop providing safe haven for the Taliban, this problem isn't going to go away." Campbell paused and looked around the room.

"Consider this. The Quetta Shura is the Taliban's top military leadership organization. It's been based in Pakistan for over a decade. It's not as though this is some big secret. They are there with the full support and recognition of Pakistan's military and political leadership."

"What's the Taliban doing over there?" Peters followed up.

"They're plotting their comeback, and staging cross-border operations. Remember, before 2001, the Taliban was running Afghanistan. After 9-11, when we came in here, they were defeated, but their founder, Mullah Omar, slipped across the border and set up his Shura in Pakistan. He's been running Taliban military operations out of there ever since."

There was a muffled explosion and the men in the room fidgeted, looking jittery over the unexpected sound of detonating ordnance. "Easy, men," Major Campbell said. "One of the ISAF patrols, I believe it was the Canadians, captured a suicide bomber outside the gates this afternoon before he could detonate his vest. I know the forensics unit was examining it over in their area earlier. Normally after they've had a chance to look at these things they turn them over to the bomb disposal team for disposition. I suspect that's what the explosion was all about."

After Campbell had wrapped up the Intel briefing, Logan's team filed over to their staging area and began to get ready for the night patrol. An hour later they had loaded up their vehicles and were on the road. There were no Afghan National Army troops deploying with them tonight. Aside from the platoon, there was only an Afghan interpreter, Rahmat Niazi. She was from Kandahar, and had been working for ISAF in Spin Boldak for two years.

Seal Team 8's objective was Wesh, a village of 10,000 located five miles south of Spin Boldak. The three-man Desert Patrol Vehicles they drove are capable of moving out, with top speeds of eighty miles an hour. The DPVs have a range of about 210 miles, but with an extra fuel bladder attached, that can be extended to over a thousand miles. The road from Spin Boldak to Wesh can best be described as third world. It is a single lane, with a mixed gravel and asphalt surface and is poorly maintained.

Logan leaned forward and spoke to his driver on the tactical radio. "Jake, keep an eye out. Major Campbell pulled me aside before we left and said he had forgotten to mention that there's a lot of run-off through this area, and at last count there were something like forty collapsed culverts on this road between Spin Boldak and Wesh. We don't want to be driving into any of those tonight."

"Roger that, sir."

Logan keyed his radio and passed the same information on to the other vehicles. He shivered in the night air. Spin Boldak was situated at an elevation of 4,000 feet, and after sunset it cooled off pretty fast. Or was it the sense of foreboding, that hair standing up on the back of the neck feeling he always experienced just before going out on patrol? From what the J-2 had said, the Taliban was definitely trying to make a comeback, and they'd had some success too. That would just embolden them. Well, bring it on.

Logan fingered the 50-caliber M-2 Browning machine gun mounted to the DPV and scanned their approach to Wesh. They were carrying some pretty heavy firepower: M-60 machine guns, 40 mm MK-19 grenade launchers, and AT-4 anti-armor weapons. He squinted at his watch and could just barely make out that it was going on ten o'clock. There hadn't been any traffic on the road, and it had been quiet, except for the howling of a couple of mongrel strays they had just passed.

Up ahead he could see the glow from a spotlight shining onto the road. We must be coming into Wesh, he thought. A platoon of Royal Canadian Dragoons had been attacked in this village two weeks ago. The assault had taken place in broad daylight on the fringes of the village bazaar. The Dragoons had managed to retreat, shooting their way out of it without losing anybody. A couple of their men had sustained non-life-threatening injuries in the skirmish.

Logan nudged Jake as they approached a dusty cemetery on the outskirts of Wesh. "Let's go left past the cemetery, Jake. I want to check the southern perimeter of the village, without driving right through the middle of town. The Taliban's supposed to be holed up south of here, according to reporting the major shared with us."

As they made the turn past the cemetery, Logan looked to his right and could see the outline of a slim octagonal minaret rising from the village mosque. Under the pointed roof, where the mullahs called the people to prayer five times a day, he thought he detected movement. Straining to see into the dark recesses, he could just make out the barrel of a heavy machine gun.

"Jake, sniper in the tower on the right!"

As Logan shouted his warning to Jake and the others, the sniper opened up and the chatter of what sounded like a 14.5-mm spitting lead disrupted the night quiet.

"Fan out!" He looked back and could see Jackson Towers swinging the big M-60 into position and, in seconds, ball and tracer rounds were slamming into the tower. The sniper hadn't done any damage yet, but if they didn't get off the dime he just might get lucky. Towers' heavy fire was not having much effect; the sniper was still laying down lead.

"Peters, this is Lieutenant Alexander. See if you can lay a grenade into that fucking minaret."

A few seconds later Peters' MK-19 began lobbing its lethal M-430 grenades. At a rate of sixty rounds a minute, it didn't take long to silence the enemy fire.

They had continued south of the mosque and were coming up to a small park on the east side of the road. Without warning, RPG rounds began raining in on them. The distinctive whoosh and concentration of fire led Logan to conclude that there were at least five Taliban fighters manning the RPGs. As Seal Team 8 fanned out along the west side of the park, Logan could hear the blast of explosives detonating, and glancing back towards their route in, he could make out two burning vehicles blocking the road. Bastards have us pinned down, he muttered.

"Shit, it's almost like these suckers were expecting us tonight. We need to get the fuck out of here. There's no place to dig in, and going forward would be a suicide run."

They were returning fire, but it didn't seem to be having much impact. That's when the mortar rounds started coming in. It would just be a matter of minutes before the Taliban attackers dialed in their position.

"Damn, we need tactical air support." Logan keyed his radio. "Base, this is Alpha one. Do you read me?"

"Alpha one, this is Base. Read you loud and clear."

"We've been ambushed. We're boxed in. Most of the fire seems to be coming about 400 meters east of our position. We're exposed right here and our egress has been blocked off by burning enemy vehicles. Not sure we can tow them out of the way. Right now we're taking heavy fire from RPGs, mortars, and machine guns. Request tactical air support."

"What's your position, Alpha one?"

As Logan relayed their position, Chico Martinez's DPV took a direct hit from a mortar round. One moment they were there returning fire and the next their DPV was dead in its tracks. Logan cringed as the gas tank blew and the DPV was engulfed in flames. Martinez and his men would be consumed by the fire, the concussive force of the mortar round making it impossible for them to move.

Martinez shrieked as the flames raced through the crippled DPV. Logan leaped out of his seat and ran towards Martinez's vehicle. The heat from the burning transport was melting the seats and he had a last look at the horrified expression on Martinez's face before the flames enveloped him. The sound of incoming rounds was punctuated by the cries of the dying men, at first shrill, and then growing silent.

As Logan turned back to his own vehicle, the sound of machine gun fire broke a momentary lull in the attack, when without warning, a round tore into his left leg. His feet flew out from beneath him and he hit the gravel road hard. He tried to stand up but his left leg was useless and he collapsed on the road. Looking up, he could see Jake rushing over to him, and as he began to lose consciousness, he could hear the roar of Apache Longbow attack helicopters unleashing their Hellfire missiles on the Taliban positions. The reassuring chatter of the 30 mm M-230 chain guns answering the enemy onslaught was the last thing he heard before passing out.

Chapter 2

"Lieutenant, can you hear me? Squeeze my hand if you can hear me."

Logan opened his eyes and looked into the face of a Navy corpsman bent over him. From the movement and sound of the chopper, he could tell that they were airborne.

"Where am I? Where are my guys?" He tried to sit up, but could tell from the tug across his chest that he was restrained. As he labored to focus he could see that he was hooked up to an IV and another corpsman had stripped off his bloody pants and was working on his left leg. "What's happening?" He didn't recognize his voice. It sounded distant and foreign to his ears.

"You were injured, sir. You must have taken a machine gun round to your knee. We came in right after the air cavalry cleared the way. Looks like you and the three guys in the DPV that took the direct hit were the only casualties. Everybody else got out all right, and they're headed back to Spin Boldak. Oh, and your interpreter was missing."

"How are ..." Logan choked as he tried to form the question that had been plaguing him.

"I'm sorry, sir. None of the guys in the DPV made it."

Logan swallowed and closed his eyes. Fucking Taliban, he raged to himself. "Where are we headed?"

"Kandahar. We've got you stabilized. All your vitals are looking good, but we're not equipped to deal with this kind of leg trauma. We can do triage out here, but you're going to need some serious surgery to deal with that injury. That machine gun round pretty much took out your left knee. That sucks, Lieutenant. But look at the bright side. You're getting out of this shit hole."

A few minutes later the helicopter landed at Kandahar, and Logan was rushed into surgery. As he drifted into a morphine-induced haze, he could still smell the gunpowder and hear the rounds from the AK-47's and SVD Dragunov rifles. The memory of rounds biting into flesh and ricocheting off of metal prompted an involuntary shudder.

Several hours later, Logan awoke from his surgery. He felt disoriented from the anesthesia. His mouth was dry and as his eyes focused he noticed a doctor standing by his bedside. "So, Doc, how long's it going be until I'm cleared for active duty?"

"Ah, you must be feeling better. I'm Doctor Gregory, your surgeon." The doctor stared down at Logan with a thoughtful look. Clearing his voice, he consulted a chart in his hand. "You're quite lucky, Lieutenant. I would say that you should be happy just to be alive. You have a long road to recovery ahead of you though. Your tibia's shattered and your knee is damaged, almost beyond repair. If it'd taken you any longer to get here there's a good chance we wouldn't have been able to save your leg.

"I'll be brutally honest with you, Lieutenant. Walter Reed has a lot of experience dealing with lower limb traumas. You'll get the best care available anywhere today, but how quickly, and to what extent, you recover really depends on you."

Logan looked up at the British surgeon. He was around his age, maybe a little older, but he looked exhausted, probably from the hell he had to deal with day in and day out. Logan swallowed, and responded in a more serious tone. "So what are my chances, Doc?"

Doctor Gregory placed his hands on the bedrail and stared down at Logan before replying. "You know, since the U.S. has been in combat missions in Iraq and Afghanistan, we've performed over 1,100 major limb amputations. We've learned a lot in the process and we're much better than even a couple of years ago. You were fortunate. The nature of your injury and the quick response on the battlefield means that you'll be able to keep your leg."

"We'll get you home in the next couple of days. They'll schedule knee replacement surgery right away. I can't say for sure, but what they'll likely do is make a plastic artificial joint that they'll attach to your thigh and shinbone with a kind of medical super-glue. Eventually the muscles and ligaments in your leg will bond with the new joint. Once it's healed, say in a couple of weeks, you'll be able to begin physical therapy."

Logan thought about what the surgeon had said and then grunted in pain as he tried to shift his weight in the bed. "Thanks, Doc. Thanks for all your help."

As he drifted off into a fitful sleep, one image continued to haunt him; the tortured look on Chico Martinez's face as he burned to death on that godforsaken road in Wesh, with Logan standing there, helpless to save him.

Chapter 3

MacDill Air Force Base juts into the southern interbay peninsula where the Manatee and Hillsborough rivers lap at its edges. The Little Manatee and Alfia rivers empty into Hillsborough Bay to the east and old Tampa Bay to the west, making Tampa Bay the largest estuary in Florida. Congress did something right for the good old U.S.A. when they made Tampa Bay a national protected estuary back in the early 1990s, Logan thought as he wound his way along the crescent-shaped bay on Dale Mabry Highway towards the main gate.

Hertz had cut him a deal on the convertible; the clerk had a soft spot for Navy Seals. Logan soaked in the warmth of the mid-afternoon sun. A reluctant breeze barely stirred the listless flag, poised at half-mast in front of the MacDill gate. He flicked a bead of sweat from his brow and returned the security guard's salute as he drove on base.

Glancing at his dive watch, he saw that he was early for his 1630 hours meeting. The American Airlines flight from Reagan National yesterday afternoon had been on time for once and the Mainsail Suites on Eisenhower Boulevard had a good bar. He smiled briefly. That redhead in the Jacuzzi had been tempting, but he had more important things on his mind.

He had just completed an eighteen-month rehab program at Walter Reed Medical Hospital, and was exhausted from the physical exertion. He'd been skeptical about going to Walter Reed initially because of a *Washington Post* editorial that had depicted substandard conditions at the hospital. Heads had rolled, but by the time he got there a special commission's recommendations were already being implemented.

"We've done everything we can for you here, Lieutenant," his doctor had said last Monday, handing him a copy of his medical records. "Next week we want you to report to MacDill AFB to stand before a Medical Evaluation Board. They already have your medical file, as well as a recommendation from our medical panel here. Go ahead and take your copy of the records with you, just in case they're missing anything."

"So, what's the purpose of meeting with the medical board at MacDill?"

"They're going to decide if you're fit for continued active duty status."

Revisiting that conversation had kept him up a good part of last night, but after a hot shower, a mug of java, and a workout in the pool he was ready for anything.

Logan turned into Special Operations Command's 6th Medical Group Clinic parking lot just off of Bayshore Boulevard and nosed the rental into a parking space. As he walked into the clinic he stopped before a poster on the wall depicting Special Forces troops in action. The bold caption read: Unconditional Medicine for Unconventional Forces. Well, he sure couldn't complain about the treatment he'd received from the Navy since he'd been airlifted off the battlefield to the combat field hospital in Kandahar, and on to Walter Reed eighteen months ago.

"Lieutenant Alexander?"

Logan stirred from his reverie and looked in the direction of the voice. The redhead looked a whole lot different in her starched whites with Navy ensign insignia than she had in the Jacuzzi last night. She blushed as recognition set in. "I'm sorry about last night, sir," she stammered. "In your civvies I didn't realize you were Navy. I just got into town yesterday and reported for duty this morning."

"At ease, sailor." Logan chuckled at her discomfort, but decided not to rub it in. "So, what's the drill here, Ensign?"

"Sir, the panel's almost finished reviewing your file, and they'll be ready for you in fifteen minutes. Admiral Sylvester's the senior officer in charge. You can wait here and I'll come get you when they're ready." She started to move away but paused. "I just wanted to wish you good luck, sir. You know, with the panel."

"Thanks, Ensign. I have a feeling I'm going to need all the luck I can get."

Logan folded his six-foot-two frame into a nearby chair and noticed a few admiring glances from passing nurses. Well, they hadn't seen his Texas Two-Step yet, he grinned to himself. He decided to check his voicemail while he was waiting.

"Hey, big brother, it's Millie. I'm due in court in an hour, but I wanted to let you know that I'm pulling for you. Call me when you're through."

Logan smiled. Of the three siblings, Cooper, Millie and himself, Millie was by far the most talented, and beautiful to boot. Yale Phi Beta Kappa and Harvard Law Review. She was already a rising star at the prestigious Boston law firm O'Reilly, Page and Stewart, just two years out of Harvard, and was on the fast track to make junior partner. Their kid brother, Cooper, was in Iraq, an Army Ranger working out of a base camp up near Fallujah. He clicked on his next message.

"Logan, hope you get this before you go to your meeting. Mom and I asked Father Pat to say a special mass for you Sunday. It was really nice, Logan. Everyone came up after mass and asked us to give you their best. We love you, son. Give us a call when you know something. Your mother's worried sick."

The hospital hummed with activity as he reminisced about his family. Nurses bustled by with purpose, clutching clipboards and lab samples. Doctors made their rounds, signature white coats flagging their approach. A triage team rushed to the emergency room exit as an ambulance sped to the door.

"Lieutenant, they're ready for you."

Startled, he looked up. Ensign Harris, a picture of efficiency, was standing before him. She led him down the corridor to a conference room, and left him at the door. Logan took a deep breath, squared his shoulders and entered the room.

The wood paneled room was richly decorated. The Stars and Stripes and the various service flags on standards flanked the mahogany conference table. Six leather executive chairs stood around the table. An antique ship's clock was mounted on the wall, and a small side table held mugs and a coffee service. To the right was a window, slightly ajar, with partially drawn dark blue drapes, stirred by a restless breeze.

"Lieutenant Alexander reporting, sir." He saluted Admiral Sylvester and then took his seat, placing his medical file on the table in front of him. Three other doctors seated around the table acknowledged Logan as he sat down.

Once he was seated, Admiral Sylvester addressed him. "Lieutenant, just to make certain that you're clear on the process we're undertaking, I'd like to go over the actions this board has taken to date, the recommendation we're prepared to render, and the options available to you. Are you clear?"

"Yes, sir."

The admiral shuffled through the papers in the file folder before him. "Following your injury, the Navy has thoroughly documented your progress, charting your convalescence and rehabilitation at Walter Reed. Last month three doctors there convened a Military Medical Board to review your medical condition, the progress you have made, and your fitness as it relates to suitability for continued service as a Navy Seal. Any questions thus far?" he asked, looking up.

"No, sir." Logan shifted in his seat. The old man was old school Navy. He had been a ship's doctor in Vietnam, and had managed to land in a few other hot spots over the years. He hadn't gotten that far by being wishy-washy. Logan liked it served straight up. He wouldn't want it any other way.

"I have that board's recommendation before me. After having read it in great detail, and having reviewed your medical records thoroughly, this board has unanimously agreed to accept their finding. Let me just say, Lieutenant, that the board acknowledges the tremendous strides you've made over the past eighteen months."

"When you initially returned from Afghanistan, there was some question about how successful knee replacement surgery would be. Quick acting triage on the battlefield made you a good candidate, and the surgery was successful. You embarked upon a rigorous and ambitious rehabilitation program. Are you with me, Alexander?"

Agitated, Logan looked directly into the admiral's eyes. The impassive steel gray eyes looking back at him echoed the question. "I'm sorry, sir. My mind must have wandered. It took me back for a moment, to Afghanistan. I was thinking of the three men from my team that didn't make it that day – Jake, Chico and Mike."

Admiral Sylvester pushed the file away from him and massaged his brow. He studied Logan for a moment before speaking. "More than forty years after Vietnam, not a day goes by that I don't think of the men I served with who didn't make it back home. I think of their families. The wives who find no comfort in their lonely nights, the children who never shop for a Mother's or Father's Day card, the mothers and fathers, who, in their anguish, feel that surely this price was too much to pay. I ask myself, why them? Why not me?

"The burden of surviving, Alexander, is not only the physical challenges you have faced. It's also about being mentally strong, acknowledging your losses, honoring your fallen comrades and moving forward with your life."

The admiral returned to the file in front of him and withdrew a single sheet of paper. "Lieutenant, it is the finding of the Military Medical Board that, based upon the injuries you sustained, surgeries and rehabilitation notwithstanding, you are no longer able to meet the physical requirements for continued service as a U.S. Navy Seal."

"It is the recommendation of this panel that your file be forwarded to the Navy's Physical Review Council for final adjudication. They will make a determination on the percent of disability the Navy will award you and facilitate your separation from the service."

Logan sat in stunned silence. There must be some mistake. He'd worked so hard, and the rehab therapists at Walter Reed had been so encouraging.

"Sir." He clenched his hands, and fought to keep his voice from trembling. "I know I can do it. I just need a little more time."

"Alexander, the case made by the medical board is very compelling. You have the right, under this process, to rebut their findings and we in turn will have an opportunity to address your rebuttal. I'll be frank with you though. I've seen any number of cases, not unlike yours, where the board has recommended separation and it's been unsuccessfully rebutted. In the vast majority of cases, all that happens is that the process gets dragged out. I cannot compel you to accept the recommendation, but in your case I feel it's the right decision." He put the sheet of paper down in front of him and waited for Logan to respond.

"Sir, I ..." Logan's voice cracked as he began. He thought back over the last year and a half. Despite the injury, he'd stayed fit during his time in rehab. He had been able to increase his swimming distance to three miles, and had spent hours in the weight room to build up his strength. He had not, however, been able to handle any distance running and he felt uncomfortable running off track where he might twist an ankle or re-injure his knee.

Deep inside he knew that the medical board was right. He just hadn't wanted to face the truth. Inwardly he had been brooding over what he would say or do when faced with this moment.

"Sir, being a Navy Seal is the best thing that ever happened to me." Logan glanced at the clock behind the admiral and was surprised to discover that it was almost 1700 hours. They had been meeting for nearly thirty minutes. "Ever since I graduated from high school, the Navy is all I've known. I got a great education at the Academy, and then got into the best special operations outfit in the military. I never really thought about being anywhere else. In my mind I saw myself as a lifer, putting in twenty-five, maybe thirty years.

I didn't see this coming. I didn't plan for this. In Seal training we learn to plan our dive and to dive our plan."

"Lieutenant, it's impossible to plan for every contingency. We know in our line of work that we'll face adversity but we cannot know when or how it will manifest itself. We steel ourselves and as warriors accept that injury or even death may come calling at any time. It's how we respond to those challenges that defines us," Sylvester said.

"Maybe this will shed some light." He pulled a worn black notebook from his pocket and began to read, "I will never quit. I persevere and thrive on adversity. My nation expects me to be physically harder and mentally stronger than my enemies. If knocked down, I will get back up, every time. I will draw on every remaining ounce of strength to protect my teammates and to accomplish our mission. I am never out of the fight."

He slipped the notebook back into his pocket. "I think that part of the Seal Creed, never being out of the fight, means both on and off the battlefield. It's a way of life."

Logan remained silent for a moment. His heart pounded in his chest, and the finality of what he was about to say pierced him. "If I'm out of the Seals, the next best thing for me would be to put that Navy education to good use. I'm trained as a naval architect, and with my special ops background, maybe I can get involved designing boats for the Special Warfare Command. Kind of a way to keep taking care of my guys."

"You just might be able to do that, son," the admiral said.

Logan bowed his head, fighting to keep his composure. The poignant sound of a solitary bugle playing taps drifted through the window. The soothing words of old washed over him as he heard them in his mind:

Day is done, gone the sun, from the lakes, from the hills, from the sky. All is well, safely rest, God is nigh. Fading light dims the sight and a star gems the sky, gleaming bright from afar, drawing near falls the night. Thanks and praise for our days 'neath the sun, 'neath the stars, 'neath the sky. As we go, this we know. God is nigh.

Logan looked up, stood, and positioned his cover firmly on his head. He squared his shoulders and saluted the panel. "Request permission to be dismissed, sir."

"Permission granted, sailor."

Logan turned on his heel, his head held high. He didn't look back, but marched crisply to the door and exited the U.S. Special Operations Command Headquarters.

Chapter 4

Logan shivered as he stepped off the Delta flight into a crisp fall Boston afternoon. It'd been a whirlwind week since his meeting with the board in Tampa. The Navy's Transition Assistance Program had been painless, and personnel at Fleet and Family Support Center had expedited his processing. His exit interview with the Navy shrink, Captain Brennan, had given him a lot to think about. He sighed in exasperation. What he couldn't shake was the lingering sense of loss he felt.

"Look, Lieutenant." Brennan had peered at him over steel-rimmed-glasses. "Your identity shouts out Navy Seal. Everything about you, from the way you dress, where you report for work in the morning, who your friends are, your core being is Navy. The prospect of involuntarily separation often causes depression. It's not unusual to experience a sense of lost identity.

"Hell, lifers who're thinking about retiring are encouraged to begin the process two years before they get out. You're dealing with all these emotions in real time."

"I felt that when the admiral read me the board's decision," Logan had confided. "Intellectually, I understand that it takes time, but leaving the Navy isn't like anything else I've ever felt. Now it's Mister instead of Lieutenant, business casual instead of BDUs, a wave instead of a salute. It's that feeling that you're not doing anything meaningful. You know, being a Seal's not just a job, it's a passion." He exhaled slowly. "I know it's supposed to get easier after awhile, but right now it hurts."

"You're going to do just fine, Alexander," Brennan had said. "You're a survivor."

"Hey, big brother." Logan stirred from his reverie. He registered the familiar voice and looked up to see Millie waving from the arrivals area, a broad smile on her face. He reached her in two strides and enveloped her in a big hug. Millie Alexander was a small package at five feet six inches and 120 pounds, but what she lacked in stature she more than made up for in good looks and smarts.

Logan studied his little sister. "So, it wasn't enough to sweep top honors at Yale and Harvard? Mom tells me you're already making a big name for yourself at your law firm."

"You know Mom, she's prone to exaggeration. But hey, it's probably the best place to be in Boston for someone who wants to practice international trade law. Some of our clients are pretty big on the international scene."

Navigating the throng of arriving passengers, Logan and Millie reached the baggage claim area where Logan retrieved his olive green duffle bag. A K-9 bomb-sniffing dog paused briefly at Logan's bag and then moved on. Slinging the duffle onto his shoulder, Logan trailed Millie onto Massport's covered walkway to the central parking garage.

Logan chuckled as he noticed male heads swiveling to gape at his little sister. She took after their mother, another French-Canadian beauty; raven haired with hazel eyes and smooth white skin. Beneath that soft exterior, though, Millie was one tough cookie, evidenced by her convincing record of legal wins in just two short years of practice.

"Are you interested in doing dinner in Little Italy tonight? I want you to meet Ryan, and then we can drive up to Montpelier early tomorrow morning."

"Ryan. Isn't that the poor slob who's currently the object of your affections?"

Millie glared at him in mock anger. "Come on, Logan. I told you about him. We were in a torts class together at Harvard. He's an ADA in the DA's office here. He's already won a couple of high profile corruption cases, so he's on the fast track. Back to dinner, I thought we'd try Ristorante Fiore on Hanover Street. Zagat gave them rave reviews and some foodie bloggers have said the food is scrumptious. They have a new sommelier who specializes in small West Coast wineries. Apparently she's acquired some amazing vintages."

"Sounds cool, Mills." Fifteen minutes later they pulled into the underground garage at Millie's north end loft on Stillman Street. They rode the elevator to the top floor and Logan let out an appreciative whistle as they walked into Millie's apartment. "Wow! What a view! I can't believe you can see the Zakim Bridge and Bunker Hill from your living room. Isn't that the Old North Church over there?"

"Yep. I know. It's pretty incredible. It's the best place to just chill out with a glass of Chablis after work."

"Mills, this place is awesome. How'd you find it?"

"Poring through *The Globe* real estate section and Sunday open houses. It helped that I'd already narrowed it down to the North End, but I still wore out a pair of flats walking around town." As Logan admired the exposed brick walls and open beams she continued, "It's almost a hundred years old. Got converted to condos ten years ago."

Later, over a dinner of antipasti and saltimbocca, Logan studied Ryan Cook. He was quiet, not like the Alexander brood when they were all together. Which reminded him, "Hey, Mills, have you heard from Cooper lately?"

"I had an email from him a couple of days ago. You know Cooper. He's always so hush-hush about what he's doing. He said he was being deployed with the Ranger 2nd Battalion to Ramadi, and would be out on patrol for several days, so not to worry about him if we don't hear anything. I looked up Ramadi when I got home. It's in the Sunni Triangle area west of Baghdad. I'm worried about Cooper, Logan. That place has been crazy with Sunni militants ever since we got into Iraq."

"He'll be all right, Mills," Logan murmured quietly. Damn, he thought. Ramadi, Fallujah, Tikrit, Sammara. He ticked the names off in his head. Some of the worst fighting in Iraq had taken place there. As usual, Cooper was in the thick of things. A pensive look crossed Logan's face.

The Alexander family was close knit. Logan smiled as he pictured them all. Dad's lumber business had provided a comfortable living while they were growing up. Their 1800s-era home in Montpelier's Center City historic district had been a warm gathering place for family and friends. The house had always been filled with laughter, even during that dark period when Cooper was in fourth grade and got leukemia. Thank God, it had gone into remission. Mom and Dad had believed in a good public school education, and all three of them had graduated from Montpelier High School. They had all skied competitively and Logan had been an All-State quarterback for the Solons, Montpelier's varsity football team.

"Maybe we should call it a night," Ryan spoke up. "You two have to get up early and I've still got loads of preparation for a murder trial next week. We're doing jury selection Monday morning, and I have a lot of homework to do." He rose and gave Millie a peck on the cheek. "Give me a call when you get back into town."

He waved to Logan. "Nice meeting you, Logan. Next time maybe we can hit this new cigar bar that just opened around the corner from here. It's supposed to be pretty good."

"Sounds right up my alley, Ryan. Talk to you later." Logan watched Ryan make his way through the restaurant. Nice guy, he thought, and perceptive too. He had picked up on the bummed out vibe from the discussion about Cooper and had gracefully called it a night.

Chapter 5

Logan and Millie were on the road by eight o'clock the next morning. No matter how many times he made the trip, Logan was always surprised by the sense of anticipation he felt exiting Route 93 onto I-89 north and crossing over into Vermont. The air felt brisker, green-cloaked mountains rose up out of nowhere, and bustling Boston faded away.

They had been channel-hopping on the radio all the way north, one classic rock station after another. Fleetwood Mac, Van Halen, Beatles, Rolling Stones. Logan and Millie howled with laughter, belting out the verses to the Stones, "You Can't Always Get What You Want," as they rolled through White River Junction and took Exit 8 towards Montpelier.

"Look, there's Dad," Millie nodded as she turned into the driveway of the sprawling historic Federal building on Main Street that had been home for as long as any of them could remember.

Harry Alexander's face broke into a broad smile as Millie and Logan drew near. He dropped his rake and enveloped both of them in a bear hug as they stepped out of the car and started up the walkway. "Aren't you two a sight for sore eyes? How was the drive up? Any traffic?" Taking Millie's overnight bag, he called out towards the rear patio, "Lise, Logan and Millie are here."

"Dad, let me get that." Logan reached for the bag.

"I can handle it. I may be getting AARP membership applications in the mail, but I'm not quite ready for the nursing home."

Logan shook his head, a bemused look on his face. "I didn't mean you couldn't handle it, Dad. I was just trying to help you out."

Harry gave his eldest son an appraising look as Lise Alexander rounded the corner, swinging a basket of purple and white New England asters. She stopped short and broke into a smile when she saw the three of them standing together. A Northern flicker began a staccato tat, tat, tat in the brilliant orange maple tree to her right. She glanced that way to look for him, as she walked toward her family.

"Logan, I swear you look more and more like your father every time I see you. Big, handsome Alexander men." She enfolded them in her arms, inhaling deeply to take in their scent. Turning to Millie, she winked and squeezed her daughter's hand. "How's that beau of yours, darling? I thought he might come up with you for the weekend."

Millie blushed and protested. "Mom, we're going out but I wouldn't call him my beau. I mean, I like him and all but ..." Her voice trailed off.

Taking Millie's hand, Lise looked into her eyes. "You'd be a catch for any man. Have I told you how much I love you?" Walking towards the rear of the house she added, "I thought we could have lunch on the back patio. It's warmed up, and we can enjoy the maples. Why don't you two go in and wash up and we'll eat in about fifteen minutes."

Meals were never a simple affair in the Alexander household. Lise Alexander loved creating culinary delights for her family. In no time at all they were feasting on creamy pumpkin soup, grilled trout and a maple-apple-cranberry tart.

Harry turned to his son. "I know this past week has been difficult for you with the medical board decision and all. Have you thought about what you're going to do next?"

"It was a shock, Dad. I really thought I'd made enough progress in rehab to be certified for active duty. When Admiral Sylvester read me the decision, it was like a sucker punch to the gut."

His dad studied him. "We know you did everything you could to get your medical clearance back, son. But I understand how tough the Seals are, and you know they have to be able to count on every man when the going gets tough. I'm sure they hated to lose you just as much as you hated to go."

"One of the things I've been thinking about doing is setting up a consulting business in Boston using my naval architecture background. You know, maybe design special operations craft for the Seals. Take the Mark V SOC for example. It was originally built in the mid-1990s, but was re-engineered thirteen years later because Seals were getting injured operating it. A company in Maine got the contract to improve the design and they came out with a new model using advanced composite materials, carbon fiber and Kevlar. I could see myself doing that sort of thing."

"Let me know if you want some recommendations on how to set up your business, Logan," his sister said. "You may just need an LLC. Depends on whether or not you'll have employees. If you decide to incorporate, some of my legal buddies in Boston practice corporate law and could get you set up." Millie looked thoughtful as she went through her mental Rolodex.

There was a distant chime from the front door, and Lise jumped up. "That must be Father Pat. I told him you'd both be home this weekend and he said he'd try to come by to say hello."

She hurried into the house while Millie and Logan exchanged noncommittal looks. They had both been active at St. Augustine's, the oldest Catholic Church in Montpelier, when they were growing up, but after going away to college they had gradually drifted away from the church. Mom and Dad were always trying to nudge them back into the fold. It had been years since Logan had set foot in St. Augustine's. He could still picture its gray Vermont granite, its slate roof and the three stained glass windows high above the altar of a hand, a lamb and a dove, portraying the three persons of the Holy Trinity.

Father Pat and his predecessors had ministered to Montpelier's mainly French-Canadian parishioners for over a century. It'd been a good parish for the Alexander family, especially since they were half Canuck on Mom's side. But after Annapolis, Logan had kept away. He pursed his lips. Nowadays he'd probably be called a lapsed Catholic at best. Still, he was touched that the folks had asked Father Pat to say a mass for him.

A piercing shriek from the front of the house brought them all to their feet. Hearts hammering, Logan and Millie charged into the house with Harry trailing behind to find Lise slumped against the stairs.

"Mom, what's wrong? Are you all right?" The front door was slightly ajar; without waiting for an answer Logan jerked it open.

Standing in the afternoon sun were two U.S. Army National Guard officers dressed in Class A blue uniforms. Logan felt his throat tighten as the meaning of their presence dawned on him. Harry pulled up short and clutched his chest as he caught sight of the two. Millie had a somber, questioning look on her face.

"Mr. and Mrs. Alexander, I'm Captain Avery, and this is Major Forrester from the Army Chaplain Corps. We're from the Vermont National Guard's Camp Ethan Allen Training Facility. May we come inside?"

Logan was the first to recover from the shock of seeing the officers, and held the door open for them.

"This is about Cooper, isn't it?" he whispered as the two officers filed inside. Lise was gasping for breath and Harry moved over to comfort her as they faced them.

"Yes, sir. Lieutenant Cooper Alexander, Ranger 2nd Battalion, deployed to Iraq six months ago, is that correct?" Captain Avery regarded them with concern.

"Yes, that's our son, Cooper," Harry confirmed.

Captain Avery cleared his throat. "Mr. and Mrs. Alexander, the Secretary of the Army has asked me to express his deep regret that your son Cooper was killed in action in Ramadi, Iraq, on October 3rd. He was on a nighttime patrol and his platoon was ambushed. During their retreat and the ensuing firefight, Lieutenant Alexander was hit by an IED detonation. He was killed instantly. The Secretary extends his deepest sympathy to you and your family in your tragic loss."

Millie clutched Logan's arm and began to cry. Lise and Harry held onto each other as Major Forrester began to speak.

"We have a personal letter from the battalion commander, Lieutenant Colonel Brighton, that we'll leave with you. It has additional details of the specific circumstances surrounding the attack that you will want to read in private." He handed the envelope to Logan, whose hand trembled as he took it.

"Before we go, we're going to leave you contact numbers for the Army's Casualty Assistance Program; you'll have questions in the days ahead that they can help you answer. Within the next few days, your son's remains will be transported by military aircraft from Iraq to Dover Air Force Base, Delaware. Depending upon your specific wishes, the remains will then be accompanied by an honor guard on a commercial or military flight from Dover to an airport closest to his final resting place."

"Burlington International is the closest commercial airport," Logan said. "Sugarbush has a smaller, public airport, but I'm not sure what size aircraft they can handle."

"We'll ask the Casualty Assistance Liaison to coordinate that with you tomorrow. They'll contact Sugarbush authorities to determine what size aircraft they can accommodate, and whether they have regularly scheduled commercial flights.

"Your son's sentimental personal effects, like a wedding band or a Bible, will be delivered to you by the honor guard accompanying his remains. His other items will first be processed at DOD's Joint Personal Effects Depot. They'll log everything in and prepare it for shipment to your home." Forrester paused briefly. "Is there anything that we can do for you right now before we leave? Is there anyone we can call?"

"You've been very kind, Major," Harry said, his voice shaking. "I think just those couple of things you mentioned, checking on flights into Sugarbush, and contact information for the Army Liaison will be all." He made a futile gesture toward the family beside him. "I don't think this has sunk in for any of us."

"May I pray with you then, before we go?" Harry nodded and Major Forrester bowed his head.

"Lord, we ask at this time of great sorrow for the Alexander family, that your grace come over them and give them comfort in this, their darkest hour. Cooper Alexander was a warrior, Lord, but he was a righteous young man, fighting to end this plague of terrorism, and gain some measure of peace for the people of Iraq. God bless Cooper Alexander; watch over his earthly remains as he makes his final passage home to Vermont. Lord, if there is any certainty in this world, it is our belief that Cooper now rests in peace in your loving arms. We ask that you give this family the strength and courage they will need in the days and weeks ahead. We ask this in the name of our Savior Jesus Christ. Amen."

After the two officers had departed, the Alexanders returned to the back patio in shocked silence. Logan creased the envelope in his hands and looked around. His parents leaned into each other, holding hands and staring at a distant point on the cold stone floor. Millie slumped in a chair, one hand supporting her head in abject disbelief.

"If you're all up for it now, I'll read Lieutenant Colonel Brighton's letter." Harry nodded his assent and Lise and Millie looked up in trepidation.

Logan tore the envelope open and began to read.

"Dear Mr. and Mrs. Alexander, it is with a heavy heart that I sit down to write these words. By now you will have heard from the Casualty Notification Officer, the tragic news regarding your son Cooper. I have personally spoken with the men in Cooper's platoon while receiving their after action report, and know that some of them have expressed the desire to reach out to you separately, so I am certain that you will be receiving condolence messages from them as well.

Cooper made his mark in the six months that he was in Iraq. He had a unique quality. I would call it quiet compassion. It allowed him to go about the business of fighting a war without losing his sense of humanity and compassion, not only for his men, but for the Iraqi people."Logan could feel himself tearing up. He paused to wipe his eyes and then continued reading.

"On October 3rd Cooper volunteered to lead a night-time patrol in the vicinity of Ramadi in an effort to root out insurgents that had been sniping at our patrols. His platoon, accompanied by Iraqi forces, engaged the enemy on the north side of Ramadi at circa 05:00 hours. There was a heavy exchange of gunfire for about forty-five minutes, and it became clear that our troops would have to retreat because the enemy had commandeered the rooftops of several buildings from which they were firing automatic weapons. It was impossible to call in air support because of the risk to civilians in nearby homes. Their route in was cut off, and Cooper's team was forced to back out through an area that had not been cleared."

Images of the firefight brought back memories of combat in Afghanistan and Logan's voice halted for a moment. Then he went on.

"Cooper was leading the way out, but insurgents had mined the road with a remote-controlled Improvised Explosive Device. The triggerman got anxious and set it off early, sparing most of the platoon from what would have been certain carnage. As it was, Cooper was close enough that the primary blast from the IED resulted in a severe brain concussion, and instant death. Several men in the platoon were injured from the secondary blast, but they retrieved Cooper's body and fought their way out of the ambush.

"I know it is of scant consolation in your grief, but I can tell you that Cooper did not suffer when he was killed. I send you my most sincere condolences. The loss of soldiers under my command is an unfortunate reality in war, but it is never easy to accept. I get down on my knees and pray to God everyday for my men and their families. May you find peace and comfort in the knowledge that Cooper died doing what he loved and in what he believed."

The letter was signed, Thomas Brighton, Lieutenant

Colonel, U.S. Army.

Logan dropped the letter on the table in front of him. Fucking IEDs, he raged to himself. Cooper didn't have a chance. In an ambush like that everything is moving at lightning speed. They didn't have time to use tactics like robotics, imaging, or radio jamming to neutralize the IED. They were just running like hell to get out of a bad situation. He knew one thing though. Somebody had to do something about the IEDs. Somebody had to pay for what had happened to Cooper.

Chapter 6

The Army Casualty Assistance Program has extensive experience helping families cope with their losses. Logan had been impressed. ACA had managed the flight details from Dover to Burlington, had coordinated on the Montpelier end with Perry and Son's Funeral Home, and had been working together with the Montpelier VFW chapter on a special recognition for Cooper. In addition to all of that, they had called the family every day to check in and provide updates.

"Logan, I'm glad we were both here to help Mom and Dad deal with all of this. I mean, it's all I've been able to do to hold it together, but at least we're here for them." Millie bit her lip as she moved over to the hangar entrance to get a better view of the runway.

Logan joined her there and put his arm around her shoulder. "Yeah, I know what you mean. This hasn't been easy for anyone."

It was Wednesday afternoon and the Alexander family was standing in a cordoned off area at the Army Aviation Support Facility at Burlington International Airport. Jason Perry had picked them up in one of the funeral home's limos an hour earlier, and it was now parked next to the hearse that would carry Cooper's body back to Montpelier. Meanwhile, Jason had just stepped out of the facility manager's office and was walking over to where Harry and Lise stood.

"There it is." Logan pointed to the C-23 Sherpa military aircraft in the distance. It banked to the right, sunlight reflecting off the nose, and began its final approach to the runway. Moments later it rolled to a stop in front of the hangar and the pilot cut the engines. After a short wait, the front hatch opened and a gangway dropped down to the tarmac.

"Those two are the honor guard," Logan said, as two soldiers dressed in blue Class A uniforms emerged from the plane. They moved down to the tarmac and then walked to the rear cargo area of the plane. There was a brisk wind blowing, and it was all they could do to keep their covers from blowing off. In just a few minutes the silver transfer case bearing Cooper's remains emerged from the hold. As it came to rest at the end of the ramp, the honor guard snapped to attention and executed a slow salute.

Jason's son got into the hearse and drove it over to the plane, backing it up so that the rear door faced the ramp. The honor guard draped an American flag over the transfer case and then helped Jason Junior roll it onto the bed of the hearse, gently closing the door once it was secure.

Before beginning the drive to Montpelier, the two honor guard members walked into the hanger where the Alexander family was waiting. Removing their covers, they introduced themselves as Lieutenant Erickson and Captain Peters. After expressing their condolences, Captain Peters presented Harry with a small carton about the size of a shoebox.

"These are your son's personal effects, sir. His Bible, a diary, and a few other personal items."

Harry took the box from him, and handed it to Lise, who clutched it to her chest.

"Thank you, Captain. We're grateful to you for all the Army has done to help us out. It means a lot to our family."

"It's an honor to be here, sir. Lieutenant Alexander made the ultimate sacrifice, and we're proud to be with him on his final journey home." He looked expectantly toward Lieutenant Erickson.

"Mr. and Mrs. Alexander, the captain and I will ride with Mr. Perry," he said, gesturing towards the younger Perry. "We'll escort Lieutenant Alexander to the funeral home and then we'll be returning to Dover later this evening."

"Thank you, Lieutenant," Harry said, grasping Erickson's hand. "Thank you for all you've done."

Moments later the limo, trailing the hearse, departed from the airport. Traffic was light once they merged onto I-89 south. An occasional eighteen-wheeler headed for Burlington sped by, but inside the limo everyone was quiet, lost in his or her own thoughts. Forty-five minutes later, as they entered Montpelier and turned off of Memorial Drive onto Main Street, traffic slowed to a crawl.

"Must be an accident," Harry sighed, gazing out the window.

Logan opened his window, craning his neck to make out what was going on. What he saw brought a lump to his throat and tears to his eyes. "You'll want to see this," he said, turning back towards Millie. "This is how Montpelier says goodbye to one of its own."

Up ahead, both sides of Main Street were lined with the men, women and children of Montpelier. Most were wearing yellow ribbons as they paid silent tribute to Cooper Alexander on his final journey home. A young girl held a sign that simply said "We Love You Cooper" while an old-timer clutched a placard that read "American Hero."

Now all the Alexanders had their windows down and were looking out. The only sound was the crisp fall wind blowing through open windows and the hum of the limo's tires on the pavement as they glided forward. There was an ethereal quality to the crowd's silence, almost as though this homage of theirs was deeper, more meaningful, in its utter stillness.

"This must be what the VFW was planning," Logan said, leaning forward to gently squeeze his mother's shoulder. "I had no idea they were going to get the whole town involved."

He recognized many of the people they passed by. None waved, but instead maintained an attitude of quiet respect. One little girl stood with her hand over her heart and a couple of young soldiers in uniform saluted the hearse as it drove by.

Lise, looking back gratefully at Logan, broke her silence. "Cooper was always an inspiration to people. From the time he was a little boy and we had that awful scare with his leukemia. He was so brave and determined to fight it. Who would've thought as sick as he was, that he would grow up to play sports in high school and go on to be an Army Ranger." She gazed out at the silent mourners as Harry held her hand.

"He was an inspiration to all of us," Harry agreed, shifting in his seat to look back at Millie and Logan. "I couldn't believe he wanted to go out for lacrosse in high school. It'd only been five years since he got leukemia, and I know I for one was still feeling very protective."

"Yeah, and then he went on to make high school All-American in his senior year," Millie reminisced. "When Cooper made up his mind he was going to do something, there was no holding him back."

A couple of minutes later Jason turned into their driveway. "Mr. and Mrs. Alexander." He opened the back door for them. "We'll come get you in the morning, so the family can have some private time before the visitation. We're going to take Cooper over to the funeral home now and make sure everything's just right. We got his dress uniform from the Honor Guard folks." He inclined his head toward the waiting hearse at the end of the drive.

"That's fine, Jason," Harry replied. "We'll see you, say around ten o'clock?"

Pulling Logan aside as the family moved into the house, Jason said, "Look, Logan, I know your folks are settled on an open casket tomorrow, and the Army mortuary fellows I talked to yesterday seemed to feel like it would be all right, but I want to make sure before we go there. I'll give you a call after I've had a chance to get him fixed up proper."

"Thanks, Jason. Whatever you can do. Do him proud." Logan shook Jason's hand and then turned to follow the rest of the family into the house, stopping to check the mailbox on his way in. Mom and Dad had been receiving dozens of condolence cards and calls since word of Cooper's death had gotten around.

Amongst the cards today he spotted a letter with a New York APO address that he recognized as being from Baghdad. It was from one John Gomez, a medic in Cooper's platoon. Moving into the family room, Logan settled into a leather armchair next to one of the long windows flanking the carved chestnut fireplace. He turned on a table lamp, one with those hand-sewn shantung shades Mom was so fond of, so that he could read the letter in the fading light.

"Dear Mr. and Mrs. Alexander,

I'm writing to tell you how sorry I am about your son Cooper. I worked for him here in Ranger 2nd Battalion. He talked about you all a lot. He had a picture of you two and Millie and Logan that he had in his pocket all the time. I feel like I know you all from the number of times I've seen that picture in his hands. I guess he wrote to you regular, but I don't know if he had a chance to tell you about someone special in his life. Her name is Zahir. Zahir Parandeh. Zahir was an Army contract linguist embedded with our battalion. Her family was originally from Iran, but her parents left in the '70s when the Shah got run out of there. They ended up settling down in Virginia."

Logan shifted in the chair and held the letter closer to the light as he tried to make out Gomez's scrawl.

"Zahir grew up American, but her family is very conservative Muslims. She spoke Persian at home and when she went to college she studied Arabic too. She was planning on being a college professor, but I think she felt like she wanted to help when the Army said it had a shortage of Arabic speakers to work in the badlands. So she signed up.

"She got here around the same time Cooper did, and they hit it off from the get go. She spent a lot of time on patrol with our platoon, and made a huge difference when we were trying to talk with the locals. She was making a real impact. She was with us that morning when Cooper was killed, and it just tore her up. Later that morning when we got back to battalion headquarters, our commander,

Lt. Colonel Brighton, called her on the carpet. Before you knew it her bags were packed and she was on her way out. I don't know what happened in there, but I think she's on her way back to the States.

"I just want to tell you again how sorry me and the men here are about Cooper. He was a regular guy, and we sure do miss him.

"Sincerely,

"John Gomez

"Sergeant, U.S. Army

"PS – My enlistment is up this week, and I'll be returning Stateside. I'm going to try to make Cooper's funeral."

Millie came into the room just then and Logan wordlessly handed her the letter. She sat down opposite him and began to read.

"I wonder why Cooper never mentioned Zahir in any of his letters," Millie said, looking up from the letter when she was finished. "Gomez seems to hint that there was something romantic going on between them. You think Cooper would've said something."

"I don't know, Mills." Staring out at the fading daylight, he spoke quietly. "Strange things happen in war. People are thrown together in really intense situations. Stuff happens so fast, sometimes you don't even get a chance to react emotionally, let alone understand what went down. When you do, everything seems twice as complicated.

"Remember when I got hurt in Afghanistan? We were on a night patrol and got ambushed. I found out later that our interpreter, who was an Iraqi contractor, was bad. She was working with the insurgents. Information she provided to them set us up for an ambush that night. She disappeared during the attack. Probably went over to the other side." He stood up and stretched.

"I don't know what to think about Zahir Parandeh, but I plan to find out why Colonel Brighton sent her home." He looked at his watch and saw that it was already seven o'clock. "What do you say we get something to eat?"

Logan and Millie moved into the kitchen. Their parents had already gone upstairs to their room for the night, so they heated up a shepherd's pie that Mrs. Patterson from next door had dropped off, and had a quiet dinner by themselves, talking about Zahir and wondering what had happened to her.

As promised, the next morning Jason Perry sent a car over to pick them up. He had called Logan the night before to let him know that everything was all set, and that Lise's desire to have an open casket for the visitation could be accommodated.

At the funeral home, a florist, touching up an arrangement of Vermont fall flowers, eased past the family when they entered the parlor. Jason led them over to the flag-draped bronze casket and stepped back.

Cooper Alexander lay in repose in his dress blue uniform. The polished Lieutenant insignia gleamed on his epaulets and campaign ribbons and medals adorned his left breast. Lise clutched the edge of the casket for support and she trembled as she fixed her eyes on him. "Oh, Cooper," she sobbed.

With that, Harry and Millie broke into tears, holding onto one another for support. Only Logan remained dry-eyed. Standing slightly apart he stared down at his brother, jaw clenched and fists balled up.

The Alexanders kept vigil there throughout the day, alternately spending time with Cooper, and sitting together, sometimes quietly, and sometimes telling stories about Cooper. They were emotionally spent, but as the time for the evening visitation approached, a calm had settled over them.

Somehow they got through the two-hour visitation. Cooper had gone to the University of Vermont, and many of his friends and professors drove down from Burlington to pay their respects. The Alexander family had been in Montpelier for several generations and they were liked and respected by nearly everyone.

A large contingent from St. Augustine's was there; Monsignor Pat, who would be presiding at the funeral on

Friday, came by to offer his condolences and conduct a short service. A generously proportioned man at 300 pounds, the French-Canadian priest's normal jovial demeanor was muted. Cooper had been an altar server at St. Augustine's for over fifteen years, even when he was in college, and had been a favorite of his.

Logan saw a number of their old teachers and coaches from Montpelier High School. Even old man LaFleur, who owned the Main Street Deli where Cooper had worked part-time in high school, shuffled by, wheezing from the emphysema that was slowly killing him. Ryan Cook had come up from Boston that afternoon and was in deep conversation with Millie off to one side. Ryan was staying with the Alexanders through the weekend. When all the visitors had left, the family returned home, where they had a quiet supper and then retired to their rooms.

Friday dawned as one of those rare Vermont Indian Summer days. The cold frost from the preceding week had given way to milder temperatures, and the sumptuous Norway maples along Main Street that had begun shedding their yellow leaves, held sway beneath the sapphire sky.

St. Augustine's was filling up quickly before the ten o'clock funeral mass. As mourners took their seats, the musicians began playing one of Cooper's favorite Kenny Loggins' songs, "Celebrate Me Home." The mournful notes filled the church and the vocalist gave a haunting rendition that left Millie clutching Logan's arm.

Logan scanned the pews as they waited for the six pallbearers to bring Cooper's casket into the entryway. He recognized almost everyone, and estimated that there were close to three hundred people. One couple sitting midway up the center aisle that he didn't recognize caught his attention, a muscular Latino male in his early thirties and a slender woman in her mid-twenties who was talking in a hushed, but urgent manner to her companion.

Monsignor Pat gathered the family around the casket just inside the main gathering area. He blessed Cooper's remains with holy water, and then Jason covered the casket with a white velvet pall. The family trailed behind the pall-bearers as they carried the coffin to the front of the church. The somber entrance hymn reverberated throughout.

The rhythm of the mass was like a salve, soothing an open wound. Logan felt himself let go, the ancient rituals washing over him. Monsignor Pat's homily was both heartfelt and inspirational. He had known Cooper since childhood, as priest, confessor and friend.

Afterwards, Ed Johnston, Cooper's best friend since elementary school, got up and spoke about friendship. He told how, as a young child, his mother had unexpectedly passed away, and he had felt isolated and lonely. Cooper had befriended him during those dark days, persisting even when Ed, in his pain, had given him no encouragement. Cooper, even at that young age, had grasped the depth of Ed's despair and had instinctively reached out to him. They had been inseparable ever since.

And then suddenly it was over. Monsignor Pat was reciting the benediction, and they were trailing the pallbearers out of the church. Logan made eye contact with the young woman he had noticed before and was startled by both her stunning beauty and the look of grief on her face. She averted her eyes as they walked by.

It was a short drive to the St. Augustine's Catholic Cemetery, located on a plot of terraced land just off of Lincoln Avenue. It was fitting that Cooper was being interred at St. Augustine's, given its all-encompassing view of the city that he had loved so much.

Gathered around the gravesite, Monsignor Pat spoke the ancient words from Genesis 3-19. "By the sweat of your face will you earn your food, until you return to the ground, as you were taken from it. For dust you are and to dust you shall return." He made the sign of the cross and offered a final prayer in closing.

Turning away from the grave, Logan was surprised to see the couple from church that he hadn't recognized, standing off to one side. The interment was supposed to be private, only for family and close friends. They were probably from out of town and didn't know. As he approached them, the man stepped forward with an outstretched hand.

"Logan, I'm John Gomez, from Cooper's platoon in Ranger 2nd Battalion. I sent you a letter from Baghdad last week, right after..." He paused, searching for the right words and then continued, "Anyway, I'm really sorry about your brother. Like I said in my letter, I worked real close with Cooper during the six months he was in country, and I considered him a good friend."

"John." Logan grasped Gomez's outstretched hand. "It's nice to meet you. Thanks for your letter and for coming today. It means a lot to our family to have you here. You're probably one of the last few people to see Cooper alive. Are you able to join us for lunch at the VFW? We're all getting ready to head over there right now."

"I'd like that." He turned to the woman standing next to him who, up to this point, had remained silent. "I'd like you to meet another friend of Cooper's. This is Zahir. Zahir Parandeh. She's the friend of Cooper's that I mentioned in my letter." Upon hearing Gomez mention her name, Zahir looked up at him with a reproachful protest on her lips.

Logan appraised her with cool detachment as he recalled Gomez's letter, in which he had described Zahir's relationship with Cooper. His initial impression of her attractiveness was reinforced as he sized her up. She was tall for a woman, with long black hair and green eyes that, today, were dulled with grief. She was slender, with firm breasts pressing against her dress. A single strand of pearls was her only jewelry. Logan took all of this in straight away, but his impressions were overshadowed by memories of the ambush in Afghanistan. Was Zahir like the woman who had set up his Seal team? Had she betrayed Cooper's platoon?

Millie, who up to this point had been silently assessing Zahir, stepped forward and embraced her. "I'm Cooper's sister, Millie, and these are our parents, Harry and Lise Alexander," she said, gesturing to where Harry and Lise stood. "Please join us for lunch too. It would be very special for us to be able to talk with both of you since you were with Cooper when he died."

Zahir shook her head. "I'm afraid that won't be possible," she whispered. "I must go."

"Are you going back to Ramadi?" Logan probed.

"No. I've been relieved of my interpreting duties in Iraq," she responded, raising her head and holding his gaze.

"Isn't that unusual, Zahir?" Logan pressed. "You were only in Iraq for about six months. Most of those tours are for a year."

"I had no other choice. I'm very sorry." As she turned to go, Logan grasped her arm, and pulled her around so that she faced him.

"What happened on that patrol, Zahir? Why did Brighton pull you out of Iraq?"

"I can't talk about it," she sobbed. Yanking her arm free, Zahir turned and fled down the cemetery pathway to the street.

Logan started after her but Gomez grabbed his arm.

"What the hell?" Logan said. "Something's not right with her. I need to find out what she knows. Did Zahir have anything to do with that attack, Gomez?"

Gomez released Logan's arm. "I wanted to say something before, but I didn't want you to find out in a letter. Cooper told me about your injury in Afghanistan. How your interpreter set up your team, so I can understand how you feel. But it wasn't like that. Cooper and Zahir had a thing for each other. Despite the Army's non-frat policy, Cooper and Zahir were seeing each other."

"So are you telling me she got pulled out of Iraq for violating the non-frat policy? Come on, John. First time offense, everybody gets a warning. They don't get sent home. It has to be something more serious."

"Oh it is," Gomez said, studying Logan. "Zahir's pregnant. She's pregnant with Cooper's child."

Chapter 7

Barzin Ghabel considered his reflection in the mirror. Wiry, with short, curly hair and the faintest hint of a beard, the Qods Force colonel liked what he saw. Just thirty-seven, he was one of the youngest officers in his class to command an operational training facility in the Republic, the secret Improvised Explosive Devices Research and Training Facility. The Qods Force had enjoyed unprecedented success against the American soldiers and their proxies in Iraq and Afghanistan, and his unit had played no small role in that.

According to his spies in Iraq, their IED attack against a U.S. Army platoon in Ramadi just ten days ago had resulted in the death of the platoon leader. This had also been reported in the international press. That fool Al Qaeda triggerman had been impatient though. If he'd only waited one more minute, the number of casualties could've been much higher.

"Barzin?"

Ghabel turned at the sound of his wife's voice. Azar Ghabel's name had been aptly chosen. Azar meant "fire" and also stood for the ninth month of the Iranian calendar. She was all he could ask for in a wife; obedient, a good cook and usually willing to indulge his sexual fantasies. The only area where she had let him down was in her failure to produce a son. Hell, at this point even a daughter would be welcome. This morning when he got up to wash his face he had told her that he wanted her to seduce him. There she was now like a little whore, languishing against the doorway in a sheer nightgown. He had to admit that she was as beautiful as the day they had married fifteen years before. The outline of her breasts against the fabric roused him as she led him into the bedroom, and mounted him. Their frenzied lovemaking left them both gasping.

"I was at the bathhouse yesterday, Barzin, and all of the women were talking about how frightened they are that the U.S. is going to attack us. They are blaming us for all of the bombings that are killing their soldiers. How long can we continue to attack America before they retaliate against us? Even though these attacks are happening in Iraq and Afghanistan, by now they have surely figured out that Iran is behind them."

Ghabel considered Azar's question before responding. He had always made it a point not to talk about his work at home, but Azar was college-educated and even though she was a woman, she was very smart.

"We are safe, my fire maiden. America is over-extended in its military commitments. They've spent billions of dollars and sent hundreds of thousands of their troops to fight these wars. Now they're worried about the Arab Spring, and what it means for their lapdogs in Egypt and Saudi Arabia. No, the Americans have no stomach for more than saber-rattling in the United Nations."

Ghabel paused as he turned on his side and traced the outline of a nipple on his wife's breast. "Besides, we have been very careful to conceal our role in this. We do all of our training on the base. I imagine the Americans know about Bushehr Province because of the nuclear plant near Bushehr City, but I seriously doubt that Bandar Deylam is on the American radar."

Azar sat up in bed and looked down at her husband.

"You know best, Barzin. Still, I worry sometimes."

Looking at his watch Ghabel saw that it was almost eight o'clock. "I must leave soon. What do you have for breakfast?"

"I went to the bazaar yesterday afternoon. We have *noon-o paneer-o moraba* bread, cheese and jam. It's fig jam and the bread is a fresh Barbari loaf just coming out of the oven. I'll put the tea on while you dress." Azar pulled back her hair, slipped on a sweatsuit and left him to his uniform.

An hour later Ghabel arrived at the entrance to the Qods Force Research and Training Facility. The base was fairly spartan, set on forty hectares northeast of Bandar Deylam. A barbed wire fence ran around its perimeter. Inside there was a basic classroom building, administrative building with laboratory, a bombing range and barracks/mess large enough to accommodate twenty trainees at one time. Behind the Administrative Building there was a small warehouse with materiel and a motor pool/garage where mechanics worked on the camp's vehicles. The gate guard inspected his identification, returned it, and saluted. Ghabel returned his salute and drove over to the Administrative Building. Getting out of his car he saw Tahmouress Samadi, his Chief of Operations, who had just returned from Iraq, where he had been debriefing the Al Qaeda in Iraq team that had mounted the successful IED attack in Ramadi.

"Major Samadi, in my office at nine o'clock. I'm very interested in your report on the Ramadi operation."

"Yes, sir. That pig-for-a-mother triggerman robbed us of greater glory. He was so anxious that he almost pissed his pants. Of course he did not reveal this to me, but three others on the team sought me out separately to convey this. We will not use him again. It's only by the grace of Allah that they were able to kill the American platoon leader."

Ghabel clasped Major Samadi's shoulder. "Easy, Tahmouress. We've had some setbacks. It's true. Usually the Al Qaeda IED cells are reliable and can be counted on to get the job done. For this reason we did not train this team. We only provided the explosive package and the operational scenario for the attack. We took their word that they knew what they were doing."

As they entered the building, Samadi said, "I will be with you in just a couple of minutes. I want to retrieve the notes that I made when I met with those incompetent bastards. I don't want to leave anything out."

As he continued walking towards his office, Ghabel reflected on the fact that over half of the American combat casualties in Iraq and Afghanistan could be attributed to

IED attacks. Now, granted he couldn't take credit for all of them. In Iraq, most of the work was being carried out by Sunni Iraqis, although they'd also had some success importing foreign fighters from Syria, Kuwait and Saudi Arabia. Where he hoped to make the biggest impact now was in the new IED technology his men were developing in the lab. He'd have to press them to step up production. He wanted to get these new devices into the hands of as many IED cells as possible."

Ghabel entered his office. It, like the rest of the camp, was furnished modestly. The only concession to informality and a hint of his life off-base was the large red and brown Shiraz carpet with geometric designs and the customary pole medallion in the center. A silver-framed picture of Azar astride the outsized bay Az Arab horse she loved to ride caught his eye as he sat down.

Moments later, Major Samadi knocked on the door, and Ghabel signaled to his orderly to bring in tea and sunflower seeds. Ghabel offered Samadi a cigarette, which the latter inhaled deeply before beginning.

"Almost as important as the IED package was the operational planning that went into this attack. Do you remember several years ago when we discovered that the Americans were jamming the radio frequencies our cells were using to remotely trigger the IEDs? They even documented this tactic in a report put out by the Congressional Research Service for the American Congress. But we were able to outfox them in Ramadi, by forcing their patrol to retreat along a route that had not previously been cleared; we gained the upper hand.

"It is unfortunate that we had not deployed one of our new passive infrared electronic sensors with this package. Still, the Americans were unable to make use of their countermeasures because they were too busy retreating."

Ghabel took a sip of his tea and then commented. "It's true that we've been able to stay one step ahead of the Americans because of the work that we're doing in our labs and the tactics we're using. We will continue to rain fire on their heads.

Not only are we killing their soldiers, we're maiming them. America calls them 'Wounded Warriors' and, praise Allah, we will fill America's streets with them."

Samadi went back to his report, focusing on the great strides the team had made recently – their refinement of shaped projectiles, the so-called explosively formed projectiles, or EFPs.

"It's because of these that the American president will rethink his commitment to this war," Samadi said. "America does not have the stomach to see its soldiers torn to shreds, filling the bellies of their C-130s with body bags."

"God willing."

Chapter 8

Ghabel stood, and walked over to the window that looked out on the grounds. A group of eight men was walking from the barracks in the direction of the classroom. This was a group of foreign fighters from Kuwait that had arrived last week. They would be here for another two days, training on a new infrared device for a planned car bomb attack.

"Tahmouress," he gestured to the group of men, "This is what we cannot afford to ignore – training. If we had trained the cell in Ramadi ourselves, I'm certain that we would've killed more than just the platoon leader."

"Sir, as you know, there are complications. Many of these cells depend upon family or tribal connections that have been in place for decades, if not longer. They don't trust outsiders, even though they don't hesitate to take our equipment and targeting packages." Samadi joined Ghabel at the window.

"Do you see that one, there, the young one? He's a nephew of one of the sheikhs from the House of Al Subaie, a prominent family in Kuwait. It would be a diplomatic disaster if his parents knew that he was here."

Returning to his seat, Ghabel stubbed out his cigarette. "We're fortunate that the Supreme Leader has been supportive of our efforts and has directed the government to do likewise. In the President's UN General Assembly speech, he lambasted the Americans and their fawning allies for accusing us of supplying insurgents in Iraq and Afghanistan. They may have suspicions, but they have no proof."

Turning from the window, Samadi walked over to Ghabel's desk and picked up his report. "Indeed, ever since the American Embassy was taken in 1979 and that nest of spies was captured, they have had no intelligence capability in Iran. They have no idea what is going on. Anyway, they are so focused on our nuclear program that our work here is under their radar."

"I agree with your assessment." Ghabel ran his hand through his hair. "Still, we cannot afford to be sloppy. I would like you to review our security procedures, just to make certain that we have not become complacent. With biometrics and access to travel manifests, the Americans may be able to identify people coming here for training. Of course, they could then target them for recruitment, or worse yet, neutralize them before they have a chance to execute their operations."

They spent an additional twenty minutes reviewing the agenda for an upcoming training class when the phone on Ghabel's desk rang. Samadi turned to excuse himself but he halted when he heard Ghabel's sharp reply.

"When? How many? I'll be right there." Ghabel replaced the receiver and stood up with a grim look on his face. "Tahmouress, grab your hat and come with me. There has been an incident at the range."

"What happened?"

"I didn't get all the details, but apparently our Kuwaiti visitors finished their classroom exercise and then went to the range to test a prototype infrared device that they plan to use as a detonator in the car bomb attack. Somehow, the explosives package detonated while it was being placed in the test vehicle. I do not have a report on casualties."

"My God!"

Moments later Ghabel and Samadi arrived at the bombing range. Downrange they could see billowing flames erupting from the remains of a four-door sedan, whose wreckage spread out across the grounds. An emergency crew was already on the scene, spraying chemical foam on the blaze. The Kuwaiti foreign fighters and range personnel were clustered beside the blockhouse one hundred meters up range from the fire.

The range master, Sergeant Major Tehrani, approached Ghabel and Samadi as they exited the vehicle, and snapped to attention. "Colonel, Major."

"At ease, Sergeant Major," Ghabel said, returning his salute. "What do we know?"

"Sir, the emergency responders arrived a few minutes ago, and have been attempting to extinguish the fire but, as you can see, they're still working on it." He gestured towards the group of Kuwaiti fighters. "I ordered the men to remain here at the blockhouse until our emergency responders get the fire under control. Our standard protocol when we test a vehicle detonation is to empty most of the gas from the tank, to minimize risk, but in this case we were attempting to determine the incendiary effect that the gasoline would produce. The gas tank was three-quarters full."

"How about casualties? Anyone injured?"

"One of the students and an instructor went downrange to place the IED in the car. They were just getting out of the vehicle when it exploded. A ball of fire erupted when the gas tank blew up. At a minimum, they were seriously injured, but I'm afraid they may have been killed. There are no signs of survivors."

"Who are they?"

"The instructor is First Sergeant Ghorbani. He has been here for three years and is one of our most experienced explosives experts. He fought in the Iran-Iraq War in the late 1980s and was one of the first enlistees when the Qods Force was created. It will be a tremendous blow to our program if we lose him."

"Do you know if Ghorbani has any family?" Major Samadi asked, shifting his gaze from downrange to Tehrani.

"Yes, sir. He has a wife and three sons. I believe they are all high school age or younger."

"Damn," Ghabel exclaimed. "How about the Kuwaiti?"

Tehrani looked over at the group of Kuwaitis who had been listening to the exchange. One of them came forward and said, "It was Mohammed … Mohammed Al Ateeqi."

"My God," Samadi exclaimed, pulling Ghabel aside. "That's the young one that I pointed out to you in your office. He's a relative of the Al Subaie family, that wealthy family in Kuwait. This is bad. Very bad."

Looking downrange, Ghabel could see that the fire was still ablaze. Motioning to First Sergeant Tehrani, he said, "Get the students back to the classroom. Make sure that there is no outside communication. I want to find out what we have here and keep a lid on it until we decide what to do." Turning to Major Samadi he said, "Let's get down there and find out what we've got."

Returning to their vehicle, Ghabel and Samadi sped towards the smoldering wreckage. The emergency responders looked grim as they poked through the debris. Car parts, twisted beyond recognition, were scattered hundreds of feet from where the vehicle had been parked. As they pulled up and parked some distance from the wreckage, Ghabel could see that the first responders had found the two victims. They were lying on the ground, charred beyond identification. One body was little more than a torso, with the arms, legs and head gone. The other was a skeleton with bits of blackened flesh clinging to bone.

Ghabel looked away. He was no stranger to death. When their IED cells were operational there was always a cameraman along to record the carnage so that it could be posted on the Internet. He turned back to face his Chief of Operations.

"Tahmouress, we must get to the bottom of this. Of course, there can be no question of a cover-up. One of our own men and a student who was in our charge are now dead. I want you to drop everything you are working on right now. Put together a team and go over everything. I want to be briefed on your preliminary findings in forty-eight hours."

"Yes, sir, of course. We'll interview everyone who was at the range this morning for eyewitness accounts, and then take it from there. I don't anticipate anything sinister coming out of this. It appears to be the result of human error, not subterfuge."

"Keep an open mind, Tahmouress. While I agree with your assessment, we owe it to our dead comrades to investigate this incident thoroughly. As you say, it is probably no more than human error. But if there is something more insidious at play, we must ferret it out."

"One other thing, Colonel." Samadi gestured towards the charred bodies on the ground, as they returned to the car. "How are we going to play Al Ateeqi's death? If word gets out to the Kuwaitis that he was training here with a Kuwaiti foreign fighters' cell, there could be hell to pay."

"Ah, my friend. As in our chess matches, I am already two moves ahead of you. As soon as I return to my office I'm going to set up a meeting with our liaison officer to the Foreign Ministry. I don't want to do this on the phone. Even with a secure line, it's too sensitive.

"I don't plan to go into any great detail. I will stress the sensitivity of the family connection, but will hold off providing a full account until after we have completed our investigation. The government will not be able to claim that we did not keep them informed, should this come out. I may have to travel to Tehran this evening, if I can set up a meeting for tomorrow morning."

After calling Tehran, Ghabel called home and told Azar to pack an overnight bag for him.

"Barzin, must you go? I have something special planned for you this evening," she sulked.

Ghabel felt a spasm of anger. Why couldn't Azar just do what she was told? He chose not to show his irritation. "Ah, my sweet. Perhaps there will be time before my flight. I will be home within the hour."

Chapter 9

The Alexander family and Ryan Cook sat in uneasy silence in the family room as Zahir Parandeh came out of the adjacent bathroom and sat down. John Gomez had caught up with her after she had run away from Logan at the cemetery, and convinced her to join everyone at the VFW Hall, and then come home with the family. Millie had tried to draw Zahir out during lunch, but she had been noncommittal.

Gomez had excused himself after lunch and promised to stay in touch with Logan. He was flying out to California to spend a couple of weeks with his parents, and wasn't sure what he would be doing after that.

Zahir took a deep breath and, brushing her hair away from her face, began to speak. "I don't know where to begin, really. I had not planned to contact you. I guess I was too ashamed. I thought that I would be able to go to Cooper's funeral and then just disappear in the crowd. I didn't know that Gomez was going to be here. When I saw him, all of these feeling came pouring out and I ended up telling him that I was pregnant. I had no idea that he would say anything to you."

There was an uncomfortable moment and then Lise moved over to sit next to Zahir. Putting her arm around her shoulder she said, "You're carrying Cooper's child. How could you think that we wouldn't want to meet you, and welcome you into our family?"

Zahir began sobbing. "You don't even know me. How could you care?"

Lise looked thoughtful for a moment and then walked over to the mahogany Colonial secretary and picked up a worn book. She returned to her seat next to Zahir. "It's true

Cooper never told us about you. Maybe your relationship was so special that he did that on purpose. He wanted to keep you all to himself. But I now know he loved you deeply and felt that he had found his soul mate." She thumbed through the book.

"This is Cooper's diary. The honor guard brought it back from Iraq." Finding what she was looking for she began to read:

"September 13th. Zahir and I have been together for three months now. It's getting harder and harder, with the non-frat policy, to keep our feelings for each other under wraps. Brighton would have a cow if he knew what was going on. She's the most remarkable person I've ever met. She's so strong. Growing up in a traditional Iranian family was hard for her because she's smart and doesn't buy into all of that subservient bullshit the Muslim clerics lay on their women. When we get out of here I'm going to ask her to marry me. I feel whole when I'm with her."

Looking up, Lise said, "Cooper was a good judge of character. He wasn't the kind of person to give his heart away easily. He loved you, Zahir."

Zahir stared at the floor, motionless.

"Have you thought about what you're going to do?" Millie asked, breaking the silence. "Have you had a chance to talk with your family?"

Zahir looked up with a grimace. "Oh, we had this discussion last week, when I returned from Iraq. My parents were so upset they asked me to leave their house. My brother was so angry he ran off without saying goodbye to me. A couple of days later he phoned me and left this message." Zahir searched her cell phone messages and then played the message from her brother on speakerphone.

"You're a whore. You have brought disgrace to our family. You have destroyed Mom and Dad. All Mom does is cry in her bedroom, and Dad stays outside working in the yard. You are dead to us, Zahir. Don't bother calling or trying to come back. We never want to see you here again."

"Whoa," Millie said with concern. "Your brother sounds

like one of those Taliban fundamentalists in Afghanistan. I thought you guys grew up in the States and were pretty much American."

"We did," Zahir agreed. "But we were raised Muslim. Ali, that's my brother, got involved with a pretty conservative circle at the mosque. Since then it's like I don't even know him. He's turned into a different person. We were barely talking before this, and now ..." Zahir made a futile gesture with her hands.

Millie moved over to take a seat on the other side of Zahir and gave her a hug. "Why don't you come stay with me in Boston, while you sort things out? I have plenty of room. Logan's going to be there for awhile too until he finds an apartment." She looked at Logan with arched eyebrows.

Logan was lost for words. He felt bad about the harsh way that he had treated Zahir at the cemetery, but at the same time was struggling with old prejudices he hadn't been able to put aside. He was about to say something when Ryan Cook spoke up.

"Millie, I have plenty of room in my apartment too. If it's going to be tight at your place, Logan is welcome to stay with me until he gets squared away."

"Ryan, that's too much," Logan began, but Ryan interrupted him.

"No, I mean it. I've got three bedrooms. It's a great place up on Beacon Hill. It's yours if you want it."

"That would work," Millie added. "Plus Logan is such a neat freak you won't even know he's there."

Logan took the bait, even though he could see that she was smiling. "Come on, Mills. Just because I don't have a week's worth of dirty underwear lying around on the floor, makes me a neat freak?"

Millie pouted, but let it go.

Zahir looked at Millie. "Are you sure? I've been seriously considering moving to Boston anyway, so that would be perfect. There's a program at Boston University, the Academy for Arabic Teachers, that offers a professional development course for Arabic teachers. I've been in touch with them and they're interested in hiring me to teach while I work on my PhD at BU. I think I would only need a couple of weeks to find an apartment."

Zahir looked around the room. "Thank you all. You've shown more care than even my own family." At that she burst into tears, her body wracked with sobs.

Harry, who up to that point had listened in silence to the discussion, got up and went to Zahir. He and Lise helped her to her feet. "Let's take a walk outside," Harry suggested. "There's not much that some fresh air and a little walk won't do to improve one's outlook."

It was a week later and Logan and Ryan were having lattes at a small coffee shop on Tremont Street. It was the only coffee shop in Boston that served Stumptown Coffee, a Portland, Oregon, roast that is arguably the best coffee in the world.

"So how's the consulting idea coming along, Logan? Millie told me that she had hooked you up with a couple of our law school buddies who specialize in corporate law."

"Yeah, she did, and they were helpful. From what they told me, I think, at least initially, an LLC is going to cover my situation." Logan sipped his latte with pleasure. "You know when people used to say Bean Town you knew they were talking about Boston. But some people call Portland Bean Town now because the coffee there is so unbelievable."

"Yeah, it's interesting how the coffee industry has changed. I have a friend who works at Starbuck's corporate headquarters in Seattle. He says the coffee industry is now in what they are calling the Third Wave."

"What's that mean?" Logan set his mug down.

"Well, the First Wave was everything pre-Starbucks. The basic cup of coffee Mom and Dad used to drink. Then along came Starbucks and they started the Second Wave, delivering a high quality beverage you can buy just about anywhere. Now, we're into the Third Wave. Places like Stumptown take what Starbucks did to a whole new level. They treat coffee roasting and brewing like a craft."

"Kind of like what happened with beer, isn't it?" Logan grinned. "It used to be pretty basic, but then we started having microbreweries that bring out beer more like hand-crafted batches." Logan raised his latte cup in a mock toast to Ryan.

"Anyway, getting back to your question, it doesn't look like it'll be that big of a deal to set up the LLC. I have to file a certificate with the Secretary of the Commonwealth, send them $500 for the filing fee, execute an operating agreement, and then take care of local licenses, registration and back accounts and I'll be in business. And if I decide to expand later on I can always rethink the idea of incorporation."

Glancing at a neighboring table, Logan glimpsed a *Wall Street Journal* article describing a bomb attack against Shiite Muslims in Iraq the day before. Logan felt himself break into a cold sweat.

"Are you OK?"

Ryan's question registered, and Logan looked away from the paper. "I just can't get over what happened to Cooper. I know it's only been a week since the funeral, but there are reminders everywhere." He tilted his head toward the newspaper on the neighboring table.

"Before I went to Afghanistan, the Navy had me take an introductory course on Islam. So in a nutshell, Mohammed established Islam in the seventh century in Medina, Saudi Arabia. Pretty soon after he died, the religion split into two branches – the Sunnis and the Shiites. Most Muslims are Sunni; I think only roughly ten percent are Shia."

"I know I should probably know more about Sunnis and Shiites given how much they're in the news. I guess with law school some of this international stuff took a back seat. I mean, obviously I know about the two main branches of Islam, but I don't have the context for when and how they split up. How would you characterize it?"

"The Sunnis all believe that the first four Caliphs, the religious leaders who came in after Mohammed, and all of their heirs, were the rightful leaders of Islam. These guys ruled Islam until the end of World War I, when the Ottoman Empire was dissolved. The Shiites didn't believe in, or support the first three Caliphs. They only believed in the fourth one."

"So, they split off at some point?" Ryan leaned forward in his seat.

"Pretty much. There was a lot of violence during the succession period right after Mohammed's death. The key event though was when Shiite supporters of Mohammed's son-in-law, Ali, killed the third Caliph. This pissed off the Sunnis and they went after Ali's son, Hussain. After he was killed there was a lot of violence, but it pretty much settled down after the Sunnis won. There has been a kind of truce between the two factions until recently.

"Anyway, my point is that there's plenty of fuel to throw on the fire in Iraq. I don't know if the Iranians had anything to do with this attack." He inclined his head towards the neighboring table. "It just doesn't make any sense because they're ninety percent Shia. I wouldn't put it past them, though, just to create chaos."

Ryan looked at his watch and jumped up. "I've got to run. Today's our last day of jury selection on this murder trial, and I'm the lead prosecutor. Thanks for the history lesson. Hey, I'm having lunch with Millie at twelve-thirty near the courthouse. Do you want to join us? I think Zahir is going to be there too."

"Thanks for the invite, but I've got some work to do. Maybe next time." Actually he wouldn't mind having lunch with Ryan and Millie, but he wasn't that keen on spending an hour with Zahir. She was still staying at Millie's place and, in the week she had been there, had already been over to BU for some meetings. She had told Millie that BU was in the middle of the semester and couldn't use her full time until January. Her PhD coursework wouldn't begin until next fall. Meanwhile she was looking for an apartment.

Logan decided to walk the two miles to the Boston Public Library on Boylston Street. Walking through Boston Common brought back childhood memories of rides on the swan boats on the lake in the Public Garden. Some of those boats were over a hundred years old.

Turning into the library, Logan found the reference

section, located an available computer and typed in *improvised explosive device*. The number of hits that came up, almost two million, staggered him. There were photos of IEDs, newspaper accounts of IED attacks, and DOD websites like the Joint IED Defeat Organization, research papers by the Congressional Research Office and on and on.

"Sir?"

Logan was startled by the question and looked up. The angular visage of one of the reference librarians peered down at him. Horn-rimmed glasses and a bad haircut accentuated his appearance.

The librarian repeated his question. "I asked if you were almost finished, sir. We're getting ready to close."

Logan stretched and groaned. He had been hunched over the computer all day and realized that he was famished. "Sorry. I got so wrapped up in my reading that I lost track of the time." He looked at his watch and was astonished to see that it read a quarter to five. He had been reading nonstop for almost seven hours. "What time do you close?"

"We close at five on Fridays." Bad haircut pursed his lips and hovered over the desk until Logan logged off and took the stairs to the first floor exit.

Chapter 10

As Logan made his way through Copley Square, he couldn't stop thinking about what he had read. DOD had so many people working on IED countermeasures, it was a wonder they were getting anything else done. The national labs, universities, all the uniformed services, and other government agencies like the Department of Energy, all were trying to solve the problem. And there was probably some rag-head splicing wire in the Iranian desert that was just one step ahead of them, he thought to himself.

Logan's cell phone rang. "Hey, Mills. Sorry I missed lunch with you guys today. What's up?"

"Do you feel like stopping by for a glass of wine? Ryan's working late tonight and Zahir is out looking at apartments. One of my clients is stopping by. We had meetings at the office today and we talked about Cooper. That's when he told me a very interesting story, one that I think you'll want to hear."

"Sure. That'd be great, Mills. I'll be there in about fifteen minutes."

Logan flagged a cab, gave the driver Millie's Stillman Street address, and settled back in his seat with a sigh. His curiosity was piqued by what Millie had said. He felt bad that he hadn't seen much of her in the week since Cooper's funeral. He had to admit that it was because he was avoiding Zahir. At some point he was going to have to deal with it, but not tonight.

Ten minutes later Logan paid his taxi driver and walked up the steps into a stylish lobby. After identifying himself to the concierge, he went to the elevator and punched the button for the top floor. As the door was closing a voice shouted out.

"Wait, please!"

Logan reflexively stuck his good foot out and the elevator door jerked back open, revealing an urbane looking, foreign male about forty-five years of age. He was slim, had dark eyes and a pencil-thin mustache. He was slightly out of breath from running to catch the elevator.

"Thanks for waiting. I'm running a bit late." He reached over to punch the button for his floor but halted when he noticed that it was already lit. He looked at Logan and said, "Are you Millie's brother, Logan?"

When Logan nodded in the affirmative, he said, "I'm Nayef Al Subaie, a client of hers. We met today on a trade issue she's handling for our family, and she told me about your brother, Cooper. I offer my sincere regrets for your loss." Nayef paused, reading Logan's face.

"Thank you. It's only been a week and I'm afraid we're all still dealing with the shock."

The elevator stopped and opened into Millie's foyer. Her loft occupied the entire top floor. "Oh, you two have already met," she exclaimed, coming forward to greet them. She led them into the living room where a coffee table held a lead crystal wine decanter, glasses and hors d'oeuvres. "I have a nice pinot noir that should be just about ready to pour. Logan, do you want to do the honors?"

"Sure, Mills." He gave Nayef a questioning look and the latter chuckled.

"Yes, I suppose you are surprised that a devout Muslim would consume alcohol. Alas, I formed the habit as an undergraduate student at Princeton. In Kuwait, it is forbidden to purchase alcohol. Of course it can be found on the black market, but it would be embarrassing for our family."

"Are you related to the Al Subaie family that's very prominent in Kuwaiti political and business circles, by any chance?" Logan asked.

"Ah, yes. Guilty as charged," Nayef conceded, settling into his chair and taking a grateful sip of his wine.

"Millie mentioned that you had business with her firm."

"Yes, we're importing a wide range of American products – things like telecommunications equipment and electrical power systems. We enjoy very favorable trade relations with the U.S. on the policy side, but sometimes there's a breakdown with individual manufacturers or exporters, and we find it useful to have local counsel to resolve those issues. But that's not what I wanted to talk to you about."

"So, what's on your mind?" Logan reached over to refill Nayef's glass.

"Two days ago my nephew was killed by an IED in Iran."

Logan almost dropped his wine glass upon hearing Nayef's statement. "What! I don't understand. What was your nephew doing in Iran? Was this a personal attack against him?"

"We're still gathering details," Nayef explained. "As you may or may not know, my family controls the security and intelligence services in Kuwait. We have been concerned in recent years over the radicalization of Kuwaiti youth and are working with international partners, including your country. One of the most troubling phenomena for us has to do with Kuwaiti foreign fighters, radicalized Kuwaiti citizens going on Jihad in Iraq and Afghanistan."

"We'd run into them occasionally in Afghanistan," Logan commented.

"Well, apparently my nephew was on such a mission. The boy had everything going for him, but something changed after he made his pilgrimage to Mecca last year."

"The Hajj," Logan said.

"Yes. When Mohammed came back he didn't seem to be himself. His outlook was much darker. He disappeared last week. We didn't know where he had gone, until by chance we discovered that he had joined a group of Kuwaiti foreign fighters who went to Iran to get training."

"How'd you find that out?"

"Ah, this is where it gets interesting." Nayef reached over to take an olive from the tray. "It turns out that our intelligence service has been watching this group for some time, and had actually infiltrated it. They have an asset who has been masquerading as a foreign fighter, and he and Mohammed were on the same team that traveled to Iran. These fighters are not supposed to use their real names with each other, but somehow he must have figured out Mohammed's connection to the Al Subaie family."

Millie got up to turn on some lights.

"Anyway, two days ago there was an accident at this training facility in the south of Iran. Mohammed was killed trying to test an IED for a remote car bomb attack. The intelligence asset was there and saw the whole thing happen. He took a great risk to report this because the Iranians immediately shut down communications. As soon as he could, he broke away to make a phone call to his handler." Nayef sighed and swirled his wine in the glass. "My sister, who is Mohammed's mother, is devastated."

Logan slammed his hand down on the table. "Damn the Iranians. This whole issue with the Iranians and IEDs has been tearing me up ever since Cooper was killed. I mean, it's been a big deal for the military for years, but it gets personal really fast when someone you love dies like that. The thing that really pisses me off is that the Iranians pull off these attacks and get off scot-free. They get their surrogates to do their dirty work and no one even knows they were involved."

"You seem very angry, and rightly so." Nayef put his wine glass down on the table and stood up. "I must go, but I will say this to you. We, as a family, sadly are unable to take any action, or even acknowledge Mohammed's death. It would be too much of an embarrassment to reveal that a member of our family was a terrorist in training. But, if there were, how shall I put it, like-minded individuals who wish to send a message to the Iranians, certain support could be afforded to them."

He pulled out a card and wrote on it. "That is my personal cell phone number. I will be in the U.S. for a couple more days before returning to Kuwait. Please feel free to give me a call." Nayef shook hands with Logan, and Millie walked him to the elevator.

Millie sat back down, kicked off her shoes, and tucked her feet in. "Nayef's family is worth billions, and they're a political powerhouse. It must be a shock to have something like this happen. It just goes to show you how impressionable some of these young Muslim men are, when a kid who has everything going for him, drops off the face of the earth and ends up dead in a terrorist training camp in Iran."

"Look at Osama Bin Laden," Logan pointed out. "The Bin Laden family fortune is worth billions and they're in tight with the Saudi royal family. All that came out after September 11th, when Bin Laden and Al Qaeda became household names. I'm sure he was a source of embarrassment for the Saudis and his family. That is, until the Seals waxed his ass in Pakistan. Hoorah!"

After a moment he continued. "Al Qaeda likes to take credit for its terrorist attacks. They always come right out and claim responsibility. With the Iranians it's different. They're all about deniability. Even though we know they're behind a lot of these attacks, Washington hasn't done much about it other than blast them in the United Nations."

Looking at Millie with a hard glint in his eyes, Logan said, "Maybe it's time that changed."

Chapter 11

Barzin Ghabel deplaned at Imam Khomeini International Airport, and flagged down a taxi. "Take me to the Kazemi Garrison," he ordered the driver.

The Garrison, near the Joint Command Center for the Islamic Revolutionary Guard Corps (IRGC), was located on the former American Embassy compound in Tehran. The irony of that fact did not escape Ghabel as he settled into his seat. He had been summoned there to meet there with Brigadier General Salehi, the Qods Force Commander, in anticipation of Ghabel's meeting with the Foreign Ministry liaison later in the day.

Ghabel had been unable to get a flight out of Bushehr Airport the previous evening and had been forced to take an early morning shuttle. Just as well, he thought, for Azar indeed had something special waiting for him when he had returned home last night. She had greeted him at the door, wearing an aqua silk harem outfit, billowing pants and a tie top that left her midriff bare. She was barefooted and had led him into the living room as he had reached for her. Guiding him to the Kilim rug pillows on the floor, she had put on a belly-dancing CD and then proceeded to seduce him with her exotic movements. Still playing the seductress, she had stripped off his clothing and they had merged there on the carpet moving rhythmically until their union left them both sated.

Persian women, Ghabel had mused. In public they look sexless, particularly after the Revolution, when the imams required women to wear the *chador* and a headscarf in public. But at home. Ah, that was another matter.

"Here we are, sir."

Looking out the window, Ghabel saw that they were at the intersection of Taleqani and Khalil. After paying the driver, Ghabel walked through the gates of the former Den of Spies. A mural on the wall depicted the Statue of Liberty with Liberty's face portrayed as a skull against the backdrop of a U.S. flag. Once inside Ghabel presented himself to General Salehi's aide de camp, who was set up in a small alcove just outside his office. He offered Ghabel tea, which he declined, and five minutes later ushered him into the general's spaces.

"Colonel Ghabel. Thank you for coming in. Please take a seat. Do you care for tea?"

General Salehi was not much older than Ghabel. In his mid-forties, he was one of the most influential generals in the IRGC, having made a name for himself in Kurdistan during the Iran-Iraq war. Legend had it that in 1987 he had rallied Iranian troops and Iraqi Kurdish rebels to surround an Iraqi garrison at Mawat, in northern Iraq, imperiling Iraqi oil fields. His appearance belied his fame. An unassuming personage, he was short in stature, thin, with curly black hair and a slight beard tinged with gray. Only his penetrating gaze and confident manner gave credence to rumors that he was not a man to cross.

"My General. Thank you, but no."

"We received your report about the incident at Bandar Deylam. It's a pity about First Sergeant Ghorbani. I did not know him personally, but I understand that he was one of our best explosives experts. Please give my regrets to his wife and children."

"Of course, sir."

Walking over to a side table that held an antique Russian samovar, Salehi added hot water to his cup, and returned to his desk. "I'm somewhat concerned about fallout from the other victim." Scanning the report on his desk he looked up. "Mohammed Al Ateeqi, who is apparently related to the Kuwaiti ruling family."

"Yes, sir. According to the other Kuwaitis in Al Ateeqi's training class, he was somebody's nephew. We are still trying to track that down."

"Ah yes, of course. We look forward to your full report." Sliding a sheet of paper off the top of the file, Salehi perused it briefly and then continued. "When we received your telex yesterday, we sent a message to our man in Kuwait and asked him to look into the matter. He informed us that Al Ateeqi's mother is the sister of Nayef Al Subaie of the ruling Al Subaie family.

"Al Subaie is a big time player in the telecommunications and electrical power generation industries in Kuwait, but as far as we can tell, he plays no active role in government. He may have connections in the Kuwaiti security and intelligence apparatus, but appears not to have any great influence there."

"I wonder how Al Ateeqi got involved in Jihad," Ghabel mused. "He wouldn't seem to have the profile of a Jihadist."

"The usual way," Salehi retorted, shrugging his shoulders. "According to this report he was initially identified by one of our recruiters at the mosque he attended in Kuwait City. Another facilitator in Mecca approached him last year when he made the Hajj, and the rest just fell into place. He almost recruited himself."

There was a knock on the door and Salehi's aide stuck his head in. "I am sorry for interrupting sir, but this just arrived and is marked urgent." He entered the room and handed Salehi an envelope.

"Thank you, Captain Saatchi." Salehi tore the envelope open and scanned the single sheet of paper. "So, it appears that word travels quickly. This is a follow-up account from our man in Kuwait." Waving the sheet of paper, he continued. "It seems that the Al Subaie family is already aware of Al Ateeqi's death, and is seeking additional details. Naturally, they are being circumspect, because of the political fallout should this become public knowledge."

"I'm shocked that this is already out there." Ghabel leapt to his feet and paced back and forth in front of Salehi's desk. "I gave strict orders yesterday that there was to be no communication about this outside of the camp until we had conducted our damage assessment and come up with a strategy for minimizing any political fallout."

He halted in front of Salehi's desk. "I take full responsibility for this unauthorized disclosure, sir."

"At ease, Colonel. I don't blame you personally for this getting out. You did everything by the book, and showed good political instincts. I initially shared your thinking that we could ill afford to have this incident leak to the press, especially if it were to be picked up by the international press. It would just be another weapon that the Zionists and Americans could take to the UN to discount Iran. But now we see that the Kuwaitis are even more concerned than we are."

Ghabel returned to his seat. "Sir, if I may be so bold ..."

Salehi nodded for him to continue.

"This development gives me an idea for a strategy going forward. First, aside from our ongoing forensics investigation into the explosion, I plan to initiate a counterintelligence investigation immediately, to see if we can discover the source of this leak. Who informed the Al Subaie family about Al Ateeqi's death? While my initial thoughts turn to the Kuwaiti foreign fighters, I can't discount the possibility that we have a mole within our ranks."

"Excellent, Colonel. This mirrors my own thinking. This breakdown in discipline must be dealt with immediately. If we find the serpent we must cut off its head!"

"And then, General, how do you propose we handle the matter with the Kuwaitis?"

"What I am thinking, Colonel, is that we must keep this matter in intelligence channels for now. Cancel your visit with the Foreign Ministry liaison. We'll bide our time to see if the Kuwaitis make any overtures to us through official intelligence channels. If they don't reach out, maybe it will just go away."

"Then there is the matter of the body," Ghabel pointed out. "It's mutilated beyond recognition." Brightening, he continued. "Perhaps we could fabricate a plausible story for how Al Ateeqi came to be in Iran and met this unseemly end. Maybe a car crash?"

"We'll consider that as a possibility, Colonel. For now, take whatever measures are necessary to keep the body at the military mortuary at Bushehr. Impress upon the personnel there that the utmost discretion is in order. Until then, I believe that will be all."

Before departing for the airport, Ghabel placed a call to Major Samadi and advised him of the security breach. He suggested that Samadi begin interviewing the Kuwaiti trainees.

The flight from Tehran to Bushehr was uneventful. Ghabel reviewed his meeting with Salehi as he flew over the infinite expanse of desert visible from twenty-five thousand feet on a cloudless day. From that high up he could make out the dark blots on the desert floor leading to *qanats*, the underground channels conveying water from *karst* aquifers that for millennia had been a critical source of water for the country's desert dwellers. The quanta system was a vast complex of linked underground aqueducts crisscrossing the desert plane. The first ones may have been built as early as 800 BC.

Less than three hours later, Ghabel was in his office.

"So, how was the trip?" Major Samadi stood in the doorway. "Did the Foreign Ministry liaison whine that we were making his job more difficult?"

"Ah, Tahmouress, come in please. No, alas, I was spared their sorry-ass complaining." Ghabel filled him in on the rest of his meeting with General Salehi.

"Probably a better strategy to keep this in intelligence channels anyway," Samadi offered. "The Foreign Ministry would screw it up through ineptitude and cowardice. Those diplomats have no stomach when it comes to playing hard ball."

Ghabel smirked at the image of ineffectual bureaucracy that came to mind. "Have you had a chance to begin interviewing the Kuwaitis?"

"Yes, Colonel. As you ordered, we called them all in individually and had Base Security conduct the interviews. As expected, there were no admissions. To a person they denied having any contact with the outside world since they've been here. While they were being interviewed we conducted surreptitious inspections of their personal belongings. Three out of the group had cell phones, which we were able to exploit. That data is being evaluated even as we speak."

There was a knock on the door and a young civilian whom Ghabel did not recognize entered the room.

"This is Reza Farhadi. He is a security specialist with the Telecommunication Company of Iran. We asked him to come over as soon as we got your message. Reza, tell Colonel Ghabel what you discovered."

"Sir, as you may or may not know, for internal security purposes, we have special screening capabilities enabled by the various cell phone manufacturers and through our own network. This is sometimes referred to as a law enforcement capability," Farhadi said. "This technology lets us conduct a wide range of functions – intercepting calls, monitoring cellular traffic, network diagnostics, etc.

"When Major Samadi contacted our office I came over immediately with two of my technicians and we examined the cell phones retrieved from the foreigners. We determined that only one phone had any outgoing calls in the last forty-eight hours."

Ghabel gave Samadi a grim look. "Have we identified the owner of this phone?"

"Yes, Colonel. We don't really have much information about him. His name is Jaber Behbehani. He is twenty-four years old and is from Sabah Al-Nasser. But there is more. Reza?"

"Yes. Colonel, after we narrowed our search down to this phone we conducted reverse directory checks for the number called. That number corresponds to an address in Kuwait City."

"And that location," snapped Samadi, "happens to be a known address for the Kuwait Security and Intelligence Service. I confirmed it with our counterintelligence people."

"Hm. That will be all, Reza. Thank you for your help. You have performed an important service and we will be certain to pass that on to your superiors."

After Farhadi had left, Ghabel turned to Samadi. "Have we confronted Behbehani yet?"

"No, all he knows is that everyone in the group was brought in for individual questioning. They are all in class now. I have put extra security around the camp in the event any of them are thinking of making a run for it."

"I wonder what the Kuwaitis are up to," Ghabel murmured. "And, how sloppy is that? Calling a known intelligence service number from inside Iran. Whoever this poor fool is, he was ill prepared for his mission. Have him brought to my office immediately."

"Yes, Colonel."

Ten minutes later, Samadi escorted Jaber Behbehani into Ghabel's office. He was slight in stature, with bushy eyebrows, closely cropped black hair and a finely trimmed goatee.

"Yes, Colonel? Major Samadi said that you wished to see me."

"Please come in, Mr. Behbehani." After he was seated, Ghabel came right to the point. "So, let's not beat around the bush. After the accident yesterday, I ordered that there be no outside calls until we had figured out how we were going to handle matters. You violated that order."

Behbehani began to protest, but Ghabel cut him off. "In fact, Mr. Behbehani, it appears that you are acquainted with someone at the Kuwait Security Intelligence Service."

Behbehani rose from his chair, but Samadi pushed him back down.

"What are you doing here, Mr. Behbehani? And why are you in contact with Kuwaiti Intelligence? Are you a spy?"

"There must be some mistake, Colonel." Behbehani licked his lips and cast a look around the room.

"You dare to lie to me!" Ghabel leapt from his seat and struck Behbehani a blow across his cheek. Turning to Samadi he said, "Bring them in."

Two security officers, who had been waiting outside Ghabel's office, entered and grabbed Behbehani, who began kicking and screaming. They gagged him with a strip of white cloth and tied his hands behind his back. Then they stripped him and threw him to the floor.

"Now, Mr. Behbehani. Perhaps you will understand the merits of being truthful."

One of the security officers held Behbehani down, and the other began to beat his feet with a short strip of cable. Behbehani writhed in pain, but the gag prevented him from crying out loud. After a few minutes the soles of his feet turned bloody and began to swell.

Yanking the gag down, Ghabel shouted at his petrified captive. "You lying son of a gutter dog. What do you have to say now?

Behbehani could only whimper in pain.

Ghabel, in a fury, yanked the cable from the security officer and began lashing out at Behbehani's exposed testicles until the latter, curled up in a fetal position, passed out from the pain. Throwing the cable down in disgust Ghabel turned to the security officers.

"Take this piece of dog shit out of here. I want him off the base. I would kill the lying son of a whore, but he will be more useful to us alive than dead. The Kuwaitis should know that this is how we deal with their treachery. Perhaps they will think twice the next time they decide to fuck with us."

Chapter 12

Logan walked into the lobby of the Liberty Hotel on Charles Street. When the building first opened in the 1850s, it was known as the Charles Street Jail, where it offered accommodations for guests of a different ilk. Originally the brainchild of Reverend Louis Wright and renowned Boston architect, Gridley James Fox Bryant, the jail showcased the "Boston granite style" in vogue during the mid-nineteenth century. Looking around, Logan could see why. With its renovation into a luxury hotel in 2001, the architects had succeeded in preserving elements of the earlier design, such as its spectacular cupola and rotunda.

Nayef Al Subaie was waiting for him in the bar. Here the restoration team, in a nod to the first occupants, had left some jail cells intact, and nineteenth-century wrought iron work framed the windows.

"Thanks for the call, Logan." Nayef stood to greet him and the two men shook hands. After ordering a draft beer for Logan and a muddy martini for himself, Nayef continued. "I was pretty sure after we met the other day, that I would hear from you again. Or perhaps I should say, I hoped that I would hear from you again."

"How's that?" Taking his beer from the waitress, Logan gave Nayef a curious look.

"I could tell when we were talking about what happened to your brother, Cooper, and my nephew, that you were gnashing your teeth. Coming from that part of the world we've become numb to the senseless violence all around us. And I know from what little Millie told me, that you spent some time over there and saw some of this first hand."

"A little. I mean, violence is what I do. Or did. But it's different from this random terrorism. We were armed forces, with a military code. Sure, there was civilian collateral damage, a lot of it. But the difference, Nayef, is that I had a hard time getting to sleep at night when civilians got killed, but these Iranian bastards just high-five each other and say there goes another foreign devil on his way to hell." Logan drained his beer and signaled to the waitress to bring another round.

He folded his arms across his chest. "Let's be honest, though. Cooper and Mohammed weren't just any random civilians. They each made a decision to get into this fight, and Cooper was a uniformed soldier, so he knew what the score was. It's actually kind of bizarre that Cooper and your nephew were on opposite sides of the battle, yet they ended up getting killed essentially the same way. Sure, the circumstances were different, but it was an Iranian IED that was responsible in both cases. So what are we going to do about it?"

"Kuwait's relationship with Iran has been complicated over the years, Logan. Actually, right now our relations are better than they've been in three decades. Both Kuwait and Iran belong to OPEC and the Non-Aligned Movement. That gives us regular opportunities for political and economic cooperation. But it wasn't always so. During the Iran-Iraq War we supported Iraq, which didn't exactly make the Iranians want to be our friends."

Logan nodded, and replied, "I was aware that you maintain diplomatic relations with Iran now but I'm not clear how close they are."

"It depends who you're talking to. Some of the more conservative factions in the IRGC and Qods Force still hold a grudge against us for supporting Iraq back then. These factions are close to the Ayatollah's and represent a continued threat to Kuwait's security. Hell, the Qods Force reports directly to Iranian Supreme Leader, Ayatollah Khamenei." Nayef edged his chair closer to Logan and spoke in a low voice. "There are factions within our government that aren't so keen on rapprochement with the Iranians, and even though these people are quite powerful, they don't want to publicly antagonize them."

"But from what you said the other night ..." Logan gave Nayef a quizzical look.

"It's true that they don't want to provoke the regime or be overtly associated with any form of direct opposition to them. However, they are more than willing and able to fund an operation that will send a message to the bastards."

"What kind of resources are we talking about, Nayef?" Logan leaned forward in his chair and fixed his eyes on the Kuwaiti.

"Money, materiel support, even intelligence support. These are all available under the right circumstances. As for how much, let me just say that the people I am talking about have access to billions of dollars in assets. I venture to say that they will not quibble over any reasonable expense."

Logan set his glass down. "This whole thing about Iran's IED program has me going bat shit. There's so much evidence out there that points to Iran, but no one's been able to do anything about it. We've tried to get our European allies in the UN to support harsher sanctions against them, and the Iranians just come back and threaten to close the Strait of Hormuz, which would cut off access to Persian Gulf oil.

"It's a lot of saber-rattling and no action. What we need to do is find a way to verify Iran's involvement in this thing and then go after that." Logan heaved an exasperated sigh and sat back in his chair.

"Precisely." Nayef pulled an envelope out of his pocket. "I just got back from business meetings in New York. Yesterday, I received this from our security people in Kuwait. I think you'll find it, how shall I say, illuminating." He handed Logan the envelope and signaled to the waitress for the bill.

Logan scanned the two pages without comment and then let out a low whistle. "Is this for real? Are you telling me that this is from the guy who was in that Iranian training camp and saw your nephew get killed?"

"Yes. Unfortunately, the Iranians found out that he was reporting to our security people and almost beat him to death. When they were through they just left him on the side of the road. He was able to get out of Iran and back to Kuwait City, where he called his handler. They got him into the hospital and he's recuperating from his beating. He was able to provide this initial report." Nayef took the envelope back from Logan and put it into his jacket pocket.

"Do we know anything else about this camp near Bandar Deylam? I never heard of Bushehr Province, let alone Bandar Deylam. I have a lot of questions I'd like to ask what's his name. Behbehani?" The waitress came by with the bill and Logan handed her his glass.

"I believe that when Mr. Behbehani recovers from his unfortunate encounter, it would be useful for you to speak with him. That can easily be arranged."

"Nayef, I need to know if your people are serious about doing something. This information is huge. We now have evidence that the Iranians are training foreign fighters at this camp and developing new IED technology there. I don't see any point in taking this to the government, though. The U.S. is not going into Iran unless the Iranians actually go nuclear. And if that happens, believe me the Israelis will beat us to it.

"I'll tell you what. How about you give me a week to ten days to put a concept of operations together, and I'll come over to Kuwait and brief it to your people. This guy Behbehani should be in better shape by then and maybe I can figure out what else he saw when he was at the camp."

"I was hoping you'd suggest something like that, Logan. We seem to be thinking along the same lines." Nayef opened his bag and pulled out a manila envelope, which he handed to Logan.

"We know that you just left the Seals and Millie tells me you're planning to start your own business. We don't want this operation to impose a financial hardship on you or limit your ability to get things done. In there is a $100,000 retainer to cover your travel expenses and your initial work on this. As I told you, there is plenty more where this came from."

Logan thumbed through the packet of hundred-dollar bills and then fixed his eyes on Nayef. "Just so we're clear, Nayef, I'm not looking to make any money on this. I'm not a mercenary. But the plan I'm going to put together isn't going to be cheap. In fact, it's going to be damn expensive."

"Let me worry about the money, Logan. You just focus on putting together the best plan you can. So I'll see you in Kuwait, in about two weeks?" They shook hands and Nayef walked out of the bar.

Two weeks later, Logan stepped off his Emirates flight into pleasant mid-seventies temperatures at Kuwait International Airport. Nayef had a car waiting for him, a black Mercedes 600 that ate up the ten miles from Farwaniyah to Kuwait City in no time. Logan checked into his suite at the JW Marriott on Al Shuhada Street. Nayef had sent up a basket of fruit and an invitation to dinner later that evening at the Crowne Plaza Hotel.

When Logan walked into the Crowne Plaza at eight-thirty, Nayef and two other men that he did not recognize were in deep conversation. Nayef had reserved a private dining room so that they would have minimal distractions.

"Logan, I'd like to introduce my uncle, Ali Al Subaie, and the director of Operations for our Intelligence and Security Service, Thamir Alghanim. They are most interested in what you have to say, and each, in his own way, will be instrumental if we decide to go forward with your plan. Both speak excellent English, so there is no need for an interpreter."

Logan appraised the two men as Nayef made the introductions. Ali Al Subaie was in his early sixties and had a shock of white hair that stood in stark contrast to his desert brown complexion. He had a short goatee and a penetrating gaze that missed very little. Thamir Alghanim was in his early fifties, dark-haired and slight in stature. His handshake was limp, and he avoided direct eye contact.

"We have the option of choosing from any cuisine offered in the hotel." Nayef made an expansive gesture in the direction of the other restaurants. "However, I've taken the liberty of selecting a variety of dishes from the Lebanese restaurant. They serve authentic cuisine and it's one of our family's favorites. I don't think you'll be disappointed." The four men made small talk over tea, and after their server had brought the food, Nayef asked that they not be disturbed.

As they feasted on a specialty platter of lamb appetizers, fresh sea bass, and charcoal grilled boneless baby chicken, Logan outlined his thoughts. "This is very preliminary, and a lot will depend on what we're able to find out from your source, Behbehani, and any other intelligence that could change the picture as we now know it," he said.

"OK. I see this as a four-phased process. First is the concept of operations or planning phase, where we get the ideas out on the table and agree on our objective. Second will be our resources and acquisition phase. This is where we determine what kind of resources we are going to need to get the job done – men, weapons, equipment, intelligence, financials, etc.

"Third will be our training and rehearsal phase. This is where we go over the operational scenario until we can do it blindfolded and tweak anything that needs tweaking. Fourth, will be the execution phase, when we go in and take down the target and get out. Everybody with me so far?" Logan looked around the table and could see that he had everyone's attention.

"OK. I think our objective is two-fold. First, we want to destroy that IED facility. Our main objective should be to take it out. First cut, I'm thinking of a water landing off of a mother ship in the Gulf. We'd take a combat inflatable in and land on the coast just north of the camp. It's less than four miles in from a couple of preliminary landing points that I've identified, and we can hump that distance no problem if necessary. It's pretty desolate out there, but it would be helpful to have overhead imagery and feet on the ground to verify my thinking on this.

"There are Air Force and Navy Bases in Bushehr City, but they're almost a hundred miles from our objective, so they shouldn't come into play. Bandar Deylam seems to just have the port there. Our secondary objective, and one that I think could have longer-term impact, is to collect as much Intel as we can while we're in there to use against the Iranians later on."

"Now wait a minute," Alghanim interrupted. "We need to have an understanding from the outset. If we're to go forward with this operation, Kuwait's involvement in this has to remain completely behind the scenes."

"I don't see any reason why that would have to come out," Logan said. "I think our biggest challenge is going to be keeping this tight hold before the operation. We'll have to conceal the up-tick in activity, watch the money flow and find a discreet place to do the training and staging phase."

"As long as that is understood going in." Alghanim looked towards Ali Al Subaie.

"Thamir makes a valid point." The senior Al Subaie jabbed his finger towards Logan as he clarified his position. "It could be ruinous for Kuwait's economy if this came out. Not to mention the political fallout. Iran has nuclear ambitions and they are meddlers as well."

"All right, I understand your concerns. We'll have to cover our tracks from every angle. Often it's the money and procurement trails that come back and prove to be your undoing. We'll need to plan for that from here on out. Nayef, do you have any ideas on that score?"

Nayef called for the server to remove their dishes and ordered a platter of fresh fruit and coffee for everyone. After their server had left, Nayef turned to his uncle and had a brief exchange in Arabic. "This will not pose a problem. My uncle has a lot of experience setting up off-shore accounts. We can put something together in short order, a dummy corporation, that will have no ties to the Al Subaie family nor to Kuwait. All of the funding will flow through there."

"Good. This is probably a good place to talk about the resource side. I've taken a rough stab at what I think we are going to need to get this done." Logan passed a spreadsheet around to everyone. After they had a minute to look at it he continued. "I've based my weapons and materiel estimates on a ten-person special forces team. I can reach out to my buddies in the Seal world and put together a very experienced team. We could procure a lot of what we'll need in the U.S., but I think we want to create ambiguity about who is behind this.

"American-made weapons and materiel would be too obvious, so I'd prefer to get these items on the international arms market. Some of the big-ticket requirements like boats and a training facility need to be procured in theater. Intel support is also going to have to come from your side."

"All of this is doable." Alghanim put the spreadsheet down in front of him. "We have some people in the private sector who can handle many of these procurements, and keep the government out of it. As for a place for training, there's a villa on Failaka Island with enough room to support your team. There's an Army base there and we can facilitate your access to the base for weapons training and rehearsing the operation."

Alghanim added, "Failaka used to be a popular tourist destination, but when Iraq invaded Kuwait, they pretty much destroyed the infrastructure on the island. There's some tourism now, but mostly in the spring and summer. It's getting colder and not as many people are going there."

"That sounds perfect," Logan said. "Gentlemen, I think we have the beginnings of a plan. If you're all in agreement, I can start moving on this when I get back home."

"Logan, what's your best estimate on how soon this can happen?" Nayef handed the spreadsheet back to him.

"I know I can have ten guys signed on in, say, two weeks. We can do some of our initial training in the States to reduce our footprint in theater, so I think we could plan to be back here by the end of November. I'd like to have a month to six weeks for us to train together. I'd say that if everything goes according to plan, no glitches, we'd be ready to go eight weeks from today."

"So, we're talking mid-December?" Nayef asked.

"Now won't that be a hell of a Christmas present," Logan smiled.

Logan had a late flight the following afternoon and, as promised, Nayef arranged for him to meet Jaber Behbehani at a safe house in the Al-Shaab suburb of Kuwait City. It had been two weeks since his beating by the Qods Force thugs, and Behbehani walked gingerly into the sparsely decorated room. His handler, introduced to Logan as Simon, served as interpreter.

Logan spent four hours with Behbehani and was impressed with the young man's poise and recall. Simon had brought maps and imagery of the Bandar Deylam camp and the surrounding area, which they pored over while sipping cardamom-flavored tea. Although Behbehani had been at Bandar Deylam for less than a week, his knowledge of the area was impressive. He was able to identify each of the buildings, estimate the number of personnel assigned there, and describe the weaponry, the camp's security posture, and the daily routine.

"Ask him if he knows anything about the command structure at the camp," Logan instructed Simon.

Simon posed the question to Behbehani, who became animated, shouting and cursing in response.

"He says the camp is run by a Colonel Barzin Ghabel and the next in command is his Chief of Operations, a Major Tahmouress Samadi. Ghabel's a sadistic bastard. He's the one who beat him so badly. Samadi isn't any better, but he knows his place, and waits for Ghabel before he acts. Jaber says that right after the accident, Ghabel and Samadi came to the range and asked a lot of questions.

"When they found out that the Kuwaiti student who was killed was Al Ateeqi, Jaber noticed a change in their demeanor," Simon continued. "Immediately after that, Samadi issued an order to the rest of the Kuwaiti fighters that there be no outside communications, and Ghabel disappeared the next day. Jaber speculates that Ghabel went to Tehran to talk to his bosses. When he got back to Bandar Deylam, he already knew that Jaber had contacted me, and called him in for interrogation. That's when Ghabel tortured him."

Simon walked over to adjust the volume on the

sound-masking system, whose purpose was to keep any casual passers-by from overhearing sensitive conversations. "These bastards are really arrogant. They wanted us to know that they had discovered Jaber was working for Kuwaiti Intelligence. Ghabel could just as easily have finished the job there and disposed of Jaber's body. We never would have known what happened."

Logan glanced at his watch and realized with a start that they had been going at it for four hours. He stretched and went over to clasp Jaber's hand. "Thank you for your help. I hope you're feeling better soon." Turning to Simon, he asked if Jaber would be available for future follow-up questions.

"God willing, Mr. Alexander. God willing."

As Logan left the safe house and settled into the Mercedes for his ride to the airport, one grim thought consumed him. He couldn't wait to meet Barzin Ghabel.

Chapter 13

After transiting Dubai, Logan settled in for the twelve-hour flight to Logan International Airport. He chuckled, remembering how important he'd always felt as a young man flying in and out of the Hub. Logan Airport was the namesake of Lieutenant General Edward Lawrence Logan, who had been his great-grandfather's roommate and best friend at Harvard Law School. Mom and Dad had thought it a fitting tribute to the old soldier, who'd gone on to have a storied career in Massachusetts politics and as a judge in Boston, to name their first son after him. Interesting that he had been a warrior as well.

Logan fell asleep, and the next thing he heard was the flight attendant advising everyone to fasten seatbelts for landing. He was groggy, but by the time he had retrieved his carry-on from the overhead bin and made his way to Terminal E for customs and immigration processing, he realized that he was famished. After clearing customs he gave Millie a call.

"Hey, Mills. I just got in. I need to grab a shower so I'll feel human again, but after that do you want to get something to eat?"

"Logan! Welcome back. How was the trip? I can't wait to hear about it. Why don't you just come over to Ryan's? I got him a fondue maker from Williams Sonoma for his birthday and he's showing off his culinary skills tonight."

"I hope this involves copious amounts of wine," Logan joked. "We haven't had a home-cooked meal since I've been staying there. I don't know if he's ready for prime time. OK, seriously. I should be there in about twenty minutes."

A half-hour later Logan let himself into Ryan's Beacon Hill apartment. Time and space, he mused to himself as he walked through the tastefully decorated living room with Persian area carpets on Brazilian cherry floors. Sixteen hours ago he'd been sitting in a sparsely decorated safe house debriefing a Kuwaiti asset who had come very close to being road kill on a desert highway in Bandar Deylam. Logan followed the sound of laughter towards the kitchen but stopped short of the doorway. Millie and Zahir were laughing at something that Ryan had just said.

"Logan!" Millie ran into his arms and he swung her around in a bear hug. Looking over her head, Logan grinned at Ryan.

"Hey, chef man. I understand we're in for a real treat tonight." He released Millie and gave Ryan a high five.

"Nothing elaborate, just cheese fondue for starters. I like to mix it up with a little cheddar but mostly Gruyere, and then we'll have a beef bourguignon as the main course. I was going to do a chocolate fondue with fruit but I don't think we'll be hungry after all this."

"You're awesome. Now I know why Mills keeps you around. It's not for your good looks or your smarts. She just wants you to feed her."

Logan glanced at Zahir and caught his breath. She was strikingly beautiful, and for the first time since he had met her in Montpelier, laughter was on her lips instead of sorrow. He realized that he had been avoiding her ever since the funeral and felt bad that he had been such a boor.

"Hey, Zahir. How's it going? Any luck with the apartment search?" He moved over to stand next to her and looked down as she turned her face up to meet his gaze.

"Hi, Logan. I hope your travels went well. Yes. Initially I thought I might rent something, but the market's actually pretty good right now for condo sales and I've decided to buy a place. I've narrowed it down to an apartment on Channel Center Street in the Seaport District, and a loft on Bennington in East Boston. They're pretty close in price, but I'm leaning towards the loft." She walked over to the counter and spilled some wine from the open bottle of Syrah into her glass. "Do you want to try the Syrah?" she asked, holding out the bottle.

Logan held out a glass and after Zahir had poured his wine, they touched glasses in a silent truce.

Ryan stirred the thickening cheese fondue and soon announced that it was ready. They moved into the dining room and before long were spearing crusty chunks of baguette to dip into the bubbling cheese.

"So, Logan, tell us about your trip." Millie passed the salad bowl to Ryan, and peered at her brother.

Logan scrutinized the faces around the table, pausing for a moment before responding. "OK. What I'm going to tell you doesn't leave this room, all right?" When they nodded their understanding, he continued. "I just spent a couple of days in Kuwait, meeting with Nayef Al Subaie, his uncle, and a Minister-level guy in the Kuwaiti government." Looking towards Ryan and Zahir, he said, "Nayef is a client of Millie's that I met about three weeks ago."

"The Al Subaies do a lot of business in the U.S.," Zahir interrupted. "Last year they probably imported millions of dollars in power generating and telecommunications equipment."

Logan looked at her in surprise. "How —"

"Minor in economics." She flashed a smile. "Arabic language in a vacuum isn't worth very much. You have to grasp the history, politics, personalities and economic realities in the Middle East if you want to change what's happening there."

"Logan, I gather you weren't talking to the Al Subaies about competing with Motorola for market share," Ryan quipped as he went into the kitchen for another bottle of the Syrah.

"Come on, you guys. I want to hear what Logan has to say." Millie looked pointedly at Ryan.

"OK. Here's the thing. After what happened to Cooper I started looking into the whole issue of IEDs. I mean, I knew about how big of a problem they were from my time in

Afghanistan. I guess I just never focused on the number of guys who've been killed or maimed by them and the role the Iranians have played in putting them out there." He summarized what his research at the Boston Public Library had revealed.

"Anyway, I found out that Nayef has an axe to grind with the Iranians too. It turns out that his nephew, who was just some screwed-up kid that got caught up in a bunch of Jihad chatter, got himself killed by an IED at an Iranian IED training camp for foreign fighters. For all we know these are the guys that provided the IED that killed Cooper in Iraq."

Logan took a sip of his wine and with a glint in his eye looked around the room. "It's time somebody taught them a lesson."

"How are you going to do that?" Ryan replenished the breadbasket from the sideboard. "The U.S. has been accusing Iran of backing these IED attacks for years. Everybody has pretty much figured out that they're the ones behind it. But nobody in the Middle East wants to take them on, especially if it's a U.S. or European-led initiative."

"The other thing is nobody wants to risk getting into another war," Millie interrupted. "It's been non-stop since 9/11. That's over ten years, and I don't think the country or the military could deal with it."

"I agree. Just the other day one of their ayatollahs was on Al-Jazeera threatening to close the Strait of Hormuz if there was any military action against Iran. That would have huge implications for world oil supplies. But it wouldn't just have implications for oil consumers. The suppliers would be in trouble too because they count on those oil exports for revenue." Logan put his glass down. "They don't seem to care who they take down. They've got their political agenda and they're not backing away from it."

"You know, these aren't the most forward-leaning political leaders in the world," Zahir broke in. "Iran was on its way toward modernization under the Shah. Sure, the regime was corrupt, but there was at least some pretense of bringing Iran into the twenty-first century.

"When the ayatollahs came into power in 1979 they established a philosophy of governance known as *Velayat-e Faqih,* otherwise known as the Guardianship of the Islamic Jurists. This theocracy has one world-view and it's intolerant of anyone or anything that doesn't support that viewpoint."

"So you're saying that Iran's leaders look at everything from the point of view of these Islamic Jurists?" Millie asked.

"They are the Jurists," Zahir replied. "In Iran, Islamist ideology overrules everything. Of course, there's the president and parliament, also known as the Majilis, and an Assembly of Experts, but it's the imams who have all the power.

"The majority of Iranians practice Shia Islam. They're also known as Twelvers because they believe there were twelve divinely ordained imams who were the successors to Mohammad's son-in-law, Ali. The key thing to remember is that they practice Sharia law, which makes them infallible when they take positions on, not only social or religious issues, but political ones as well. So if you have a hard-line ayatollah taking a position on nuclear policy or closing the Strait of Hormuz, there is no possibility for a moderate voice to counter that."

"Wow, that's really screwed up," Ryan exclaimed as he and Millie started to clear the table.

"A lot of Iranians have had second thoughts since the Revolution," Zahir said. "My parents got out right around the time the Shah left. There's no way they could go back and live under that kind of repression. The imams have a group of thugs who work for them and make sure everybody stays in line. It's the Iranian Revolutionary Guard and their foreign arm, the Qods Force."

Logan looked at Zahir with newfound respect. "You really know your stuff. When I met Nayef in Kuwait, he pretty much confirmed that the Qods Force runs the training camp where his nephew was killed. The commander there is a Qods Force colonel by the name of Ghabel. Barzin Ghabel."

"Never heard of him," Zahir said.

"No reason you would have. But his boss in Teheran is a name you would recognize. General Hassan Salehi. There are factions in Kuwait that don't want to rock the boat with the Iranians. They have diplomatic relations with Iran for the first time in years, and trade is picking up. But there are other Kuwaitis who don't trust them. Nayef and the others I met with understand that they can't afford to take on the Iranians in any public way. But they still don't mind sending them a strong message, even if it's under the table."

"What kind of message?" Millie came out of the kitchen carrying a platter of steaming beef bourguignon. Ryan followed her with a big bowl of egg noodles.

"We're going to take out that Qods Force IED training facility."

Millie almost dropped the platter she was carrying. There was a moment of stunned silence and then everyone started talking at once.

"Whoa, whoa, whoa," Logan laughed. "Don't forget. This is what I did for a living."

"Yeah, but you had the U.S. government and the U.S. military to back you up. How are you going to do this on your own?" Millie challenged.

Logan outlined the scenario he had put together and the level of funding the Kuwaitis were prepared to put into the operation.

"Whoo," Ryan whistled. "That's some serious moola. Get it? You know Mullah?"

Millie rolled her eyes and punched him in the arm. "Come on. Get serious. This isn't anything to joke about."

"Look. I'm doing this. I already have a bunch of guys in mind, and as soon as I get their buy-in we'll start putting it together. I'd say within a month we're going to be ready to go. All these guys have years of experience doing special operations. We'll just have to rehearse the scenario, make sure everybody has current weapons qualifications, and work out the details for our cover for action.

"The Kuwaitis have already started procuring the non-military assets we're going to need to support this, all the military materiel, and a commercial funding mechanism so we can cover our expenses without the Iranians tracing it back to Kuwait."

"I want to go with you."

Logan looked at Zahir in surprise. "No way. You're pregnant and in no condition for what we're going to be doing."

"I'm the only other person in this room besides you with combat experience. Being pregnant is not an issue at this point in the pregnancy. I wasn't relieved of my duties in Iraq because I was pregnant. It was because Cooper and I violated the non-frat policy, and Colonel Brighton had a no-exception rule on that. I need to do this, Logan. I need to do it for Cooper. You're going to need an interpreter anyway, so why not me?"

Logan studied her. She had a point. He was going to need an interpreter, and from what Gomez had told him, she was damn good. "Let me think about it. Give me a couple of days and I'll give you a definitive answer."

Zahir nodded and held his gaze. "I'm serious, Logan. I'm going with you."

Chapter 14

Barzin Ghabel surveyed the parade ground outside his office with a grim smile. Two Office of Security enlisted men were crawling on their stomachs back and forth in front of the reviewing stand, their punishment for failing to inspect the personal belongings of the Kuwaiti foreign fighters when they first came onto the base. The incompetent fools had failed to detect the cell phones the Kuwaitis had brought with them, allowing that spy Behbehani to alert his bosses that the Al Ateeqi kid had blown himself up. Ghabel scrutinized his watch, and saw that the two soldiers had been on their bellies for nearly an hour.

"Major Samadi," he called through the open door, "could you come in here, please."

"Yes, Colonel?"

"I want those two incompetents to continue their punishment for another hour. Afterwards I want you to issue a verbal reprimand to them and advise them that they are confined to base with no personal leave for one month. I don't want to have another security lapse. We're fortunate that General Salehi didn't focus on this breach of procedures when I met with him. That would have reflected poorly on everyone here."

Major Samadi smirked. "Of course, Colonel. But if I may be so bold, the general has no room to criticize us for lax procedures. Just last month the counterintelligence division discovered that someone on his personal staff had been secretly passing sensitive military information to a Mossad agent."

"Careful, Tahmouress. Your comment borders on insubordination. I can't tolerate that level of overt disrespect. And besides," he lowered his voice, "the walls have ears."

"Yes, sir."

"Now, I'd like to go over your after-action report concerning the misfire on the range. We've been distracted dealing with the security breach and I'm concerned that we've been remiss in searching for the cause behind the incident. Was it poor training, poor procedure, sabotage, or what?"

"Sir, if we could meet in your conference room in, say one hour? The engineer who has been leading the forensics investigation is prepared to make his report."

"Fine. We'll meet at ten-thirty then."

An hour later Ghabel opened the door to his conference room and saw that the briefing team was already in place. They all stood when he entered the room.

"At ease, men." Turning to Major Samadi, he indicated that he was to proceed.

"Colonel, immediately following the failed live fire test, we initiated our investigation. First Sergeant Tehrani, as you will recall, was at the range when the IED exploded prematurely. He reviewed the range protocol, interviewed the students and other instructors there at the time of the incident, and oversaw the actions of the first responders and others at the scene to insure that the scene was preserved and the forensics team could do its job unimpeded."

Tehrani stood up and moved to the front of the room. He distributed copies of his written report to Colonel Ghabel and Major Samadi. "Sir, if you'll turn to page six of the report, you'll see a copy of the security protocol for procedures on the bombing range. These procedures are reviewed annually and approved through the command. The next page discusses training and qualifying for weapons instructors. A review of the personnel and actions taken on that day shows that everything was in order. This is documented on pages eight through twenty."

Ghabel flipped through the report and then looked up at Tehrani. "Sergeant, are you absolutely certain about your conclusions?"

"Yes, sir. As I said, we scrub our procedures annually, and I keep a roster of ratings and qualifications for all the instructors. Anytime one of them is up for requalification we either handle it here or send them to the regional command where they are better equipped. Everyone is up to date."

"Thank you, Sergeant. You may be seated." Ghabel looked around the table. "Next."

Captain Reza Amanpour moved to the front of the conference room. He was a slender though wiry man in his late twenties with a nervous cough. "Sir, the Kuwaitis were testing a new design for an explosively formed projectile IED. We started testing our new designs in Lebanon in 2007 through our friends in Hezbollah's guerilla army. After we had developed a level of confidence in those EFP IEDs, we began putting them into Iraq with the help of the paramilitaries in the Mahdi Army." Captain Amanpour paused to take a sip of water.

"The Americans have been pretty agile in developing countermeasures to our new designs, so it's always a race for us to stay just one step ahead of them. The basic components of the EFP IED have not changed over the years. We still use an activator, a fuse, a container, explosive material, and a power source. But it's been our ability to innovate with new technology in the triggering devices that has given us so many victories in battle."

He held up an early version of a triggering device in one hand and a more recent passive infrared sensor in the other. "We've been testing these infrared sensors because the Americans were affecting our success rate using electromagnetic countermeasures against all of our other devices. If the test results are positive, we plan to begin introducing a greater quantity of these into our EFP IED packages."

"How long do you think it will be until we're ready to switch over to the new design?" Ghabel impatiently drummed his fingers on the desk.

"A matter of several weeks. Of course we'll have to conduct more training because most of the IED teams don't have experience using them."

"Yes, of course. This is a top priority. General Salehi has assured me that we will get whatever we need to make it work."

"I apologize for digressing," Amanpour said. "After examining the evidence, I believe that a faulty triggering device caused the IED to detonate prematurely, and that the amount of fuel in the gas tank was responsible for the huge secondary explosion and resulting carnage."

"How can you be sure?" Ghabel leaned forward in his seat and narrowed his eyes.

"Well, we can't be 100 percent sure. The destruction was so complete that there was not much left to evaluate. There is always the possibility of human error, but given Sergeant Tehrani's report I am prepared to dismiss that. I have my men testing the sensors we have on the shelf, in particular the prototype model that was used that day."

"Thank you, Captain. Let me know if you find anything. This matter has the highest level of attention, not just here, but in Tehran as well. Oh, while I'm thinking of it, there's one procedural change I want to implement immediately. I want the fuel tanks on the target vehicles empty when they're detonated. No gasoline at all. We are all familiar with the incendiary effects of a full tank of gas exploding, but the risk would seem to outweigh any advantage. Sergeant Tehrani, you'll see to that?"

"Yes, Colonel."

"Fine. Dismissed." As the men were filing out, Colonel Ghabel signaled to Major Samadi to remain behind.

"Tahmouress, I had a call from General Salehi on the secure line just before I came in. It seems the Kuwaitis have been making some discreet inquiries. And while doing so, they let it be known that they weren't particularly happy about the way their man was treated."

Major Samadi arched one eyebrow, but remained silent.

"Apparently the general professed ignorance over the beating we gave that little prick Behbehani. He claimed there must be some misunderstanding. Then he told me an interesting story. It seems he had our man in Kuwait ask around to see what he could uncover about Behbehani. Apparently he's one tough little bastard. Lately the Kuwaitis have become concerned about the number of disaffected youth going off to become foreign fighters, so they've been using select agents like Behbehani to infiltrate these groups.

"Last year Behbehani was part of a group preparing to infiltrate into Iraq and he tipped off his handlers and the Americans, whom they were working with, and the entire team got wrapped up. Behbehani spent six months cooling his heels in a Kuwaiti prison, just to build up his bona fides."

Samadi let out a low whistle. "That is dedication above and beyond the call of duty. At least he wasn't in Guantanamo."

As they were leaving the conference room, Captain Amanpour stopped them in the hall. "Sir, we're going to conduct a live fire exercise tomorrow morning using the prototype sensor we talked about earlier. I hope the colonel will be available to observe the test."

"Yes, of course, Captain. What time should I be at the range?"

"We should be ready to go at 1100."

"Good, we'll see you then."

When Ghabel arrived home later that evening, there was a note from Azar, saying that she had been trying to reach him all day. Her father had been taken to the hospital in Shiraz and was in intensive care. The doctors suspected a heart attack, but they were still conducting tests. She was already in Shiraz at the hospital.

Ghabel's first call to Azar's cell phone did not go through. "Damn," he growled. He tried again and Azar picked up on the third ring. "I just got your message. How's your father doing?"

"Oh, Barzin, I'm so worried. Mama said that he was fine this morning when he went to work, only that he seemed a little tired. He's been putting in a lot of hours at the university."

Azar's father was a renowned scholar at the Health Policy Research Center at the University of Shiraz. He was in his early seventies but maintained an active teaching and writing schedule. "Do you need me to come to Shiraz?"

"No. For now we are all right. Mama is handling this well, and unless Papa's condition deteriorates, we should be over the critical part in a day or two. If it turns out that he needs surgery, then I may have to stay longer."

"Give your parents my love." They chatted for a few more moments and then Azar said that she had to go.

Ghabel's stomach growled and he realized that he had not eaten anything since breakfast. He decided to drive to Ali Ghapoo, his favorite kebab restaurant for a *chelo-kebab*. Within fifteen minutes he was tucking into a steaming plate of saffron-flavored basmati rice topped with skewers of minced lamb kebab. Ghabel belched in appreciation and waved to his server to bring him a cup of chai. The faint aroma of rose petals was pleasing, settling on his tongue like a salve. He realized that it was still early and decided to visit his favorite bathhouse before returning home.

After paying for his meal, Ghabel strolled to the Sheikh Bahai Bathhouse, a modest likeness of the famous, but now defunct, establishment built in Esfahan during the Safavid Dynasty. Ornate blue tiles and floor-to-ceiling columns gave way to a small reception area where worn wooden benches and Persian carpets softened the décor. He entered the *hammam* and began undressing in the outer room.

Ghabel stored his clothes in a wooden locker and put on a linen loincloth before going into the steam room next door. An attendant directed him to lie down on a cloth that he had placed on the heated marble floor, and then proceeded to give him a vigorous massage. Afterwards he washed Ghabel's hair and scrubbed him with pumice stone. He was drowsy from the heat and decided to rest there for a few minutes before going into the soaking room. It was quiet, and after the attendant had left, he briefly drifted off.

Ghabel awoke groggy from his nap and, upon hearing other customers enter the steam room, pondered the merits of heading into the soaking room. Suddenly his head was jerked back and he could feel a knife at his throat. A hoarse voice whispered in his ear.

"Don't open your mouth."

His pulse raced and he struggled to see who was behind him, but strong hands held him down. There were at least two, he determined. Suddenly they began beating him with what felt like a rubber hose. The pain was excruciating as they struck him again and again. He writhed in torment as he was repeatedly struck. He choked back a scream as a hand clamped over his mouth, stifling any sound.

He struggled in agony, the shock and terror of the attack overwhelming him. His efforts only seemed to energize his tormenters, who repeatedly whipped the hose across his flesh. It seemed an eternity before he passed out, lying in his own vomit and blood.

Moments later, although it could have been hours for all he knew, Ghabel came to. He looked around the steam room and realized that he was alone. He shuddered at his feeling of helplessness and gasped in anguish as he struggled to his feet. Ghabel stumbled to the shower and turned it on, allowing the soothing stream of water to penetrate his skin. Somewhat revived, he returned to the changing room and pulled his clothes over his tormented body. In the reception area there was only the one attendant on duty.

"Were there any other customers in the last hour?"

"No, Colonel, just you. Why do you ask?"

"I was just curious. I thought I heard voices."

The attendant scratched his beard. "Someone may have come in looking for me. There was a problem with the water supply, and I was outside in the back where our holding tanks are. I was gone for perhaps ten minutes."

Ghabel thanked him and then trudged back to his car. He sat there for a moment as he entertained the idea of checking into the hospital emergency room, but surmised that this was ill advised because it would of necessity lead to a police investigation. It would be a blot on his career. How would Azar handle it? But who would do this to him? He knew that he had made many enemies in his lifetime, but to do this? He had no idea who could hold such a grudge.

Perhaps it was just a random attack. No. It was vicious and he felt that they were attacking him personally. They knew who he was. He did not believe in coincidences.

Ghabel started the car and slowly drove to a pharmacy where he purchased painkillers, antibiotics, gauze pads and a tube of ointment. When he got home, he undressed and examined himself. The bruising was deepening and there were traces of bleeding in some places. He carefully washed those areas and applied the medications, after which he collapsed on to his bed and fell into a fitful sleep.

The following day Ghabel arrived at the base mid-morning. He had called Major Samadi to say that he planned to attend the live fire exercise at 1100 hours but would be a little late, as he had some personal matters to attend to. He met Samadi just before eleven o'clock and the two of them drove over to the testing range in Samadi's vehicle.

"Sir, is everything all right? You seem a bit distracted this morning."

Samadi is a perceptive bastard, Ghabel thought to himself. "All is well with me, Tahmouress. Azar had to travel to Shiraz yesterday because of a family medical emergency. It's her father. A possible heart attack."

"I'm sorry to hear that, sir. Please convey my best wishes for an expeditious recovery."

"Thank you, Tahmouress. I'll be sure to pass on your concern."

They pulled up to the testing range and got out of the vehicle. Downrange they could see a municipal passenger bus that had been towed out to the test site. It was about a hundred meters from where they stood. A number of First Sergeant Tehrani's men were clambering over the bus, and Ghabel could see Captain Amanpour gesturing toward them while talking to Tehrani's second-in-command. The latter walked over to the men at the bus and spoke with them; two of the men climbed under the bus and made some adjustments. Afterwards they all walked back uprange to the blockhouse where Colonel Ghabel and Major Samadi awaited them.

"Sir." Captain Amanpour came to attention. "We've prepared the target for the live fire exercise. With your permission?" He nodded to Tehrani, who ordered everyone into the observation post within the blockhouse.

"On my signal, First Sergeant. One, two, three, fire!"

First Sergeant Tehrani activated his cell phone, sending a signal to the radio-controlled explosives detonator on the bus. Nothing happened.

Colonel Ghabel turned to Captain Amanpour, raking him with an icy stare. "Is this the best you can do, Captain? There better be a good explanation for this. We have spent a fortune developing these new sensors. First we had that malfunction on the range two weeks ago, killing one of our own soldiers and a student, and now this. Can you explain it?"

"Colonel, if you please. This test was designed as a two-phased experiment. In the first, which you just observed, we planted a device and used a cell phone as the activator. However, if you will look outside of the blockhouse you will see two of my men holding another device. This is that U.S. Army Warlock system we captured on the battlefield last month. My engineers have been playing with it and we have been able to replicate its performance."

"Go on, Captain."

"As you will recall from our briefing on this piece of equipment last month, Warlock is an electronic jamming device. Essentially what we did just now was block the signal to our cell phone by overriding it with Warlock's own low-power radio frequency signal. It interrupted the handshake between our cell phone and the IED device, causing a malfunction. Now, for the second part of our test, we have also installed on the target vehicle an IED package with a passive infrared electronic sensor as the trigger."

"Is that also activated with a cell phone?"

"No, sir. The passive infrared device operates on an entirely different principle. It reacts to changes in temperature, most notably the heat emanated by a living body, and it's sensitive up to a distance of ten meters. When, for example, an enemy soldier passes in front of the target, the sensor detects a change in temperature, which in turn activates an alarm, triggering the IED. It gives us a leg up over the electromagnetic countermeasures we've been encountering. On the downside though, this device is indiscriminate and could be triggered just as easily by a woman walking by with a pail of water as an Army patrol."

Captain Amanpour gestured to one of the men outside who went over to a utility vehicle, opened the back door and reemerged with a rather large, albeit haggard looking, jube dog tethered to a leash. Meanwhile another soldier gave the dog a whiff from a sack that set the dog into a frenzy, yelping and tearing at its leash. The second soldier then carried the sack down range and placed it on the ground next to the target.

"Raw meat," Captain Amanpour explained.

The soldier disappeared beneath the bus for a moment and then came out on the other side of the bus and jogged up to the blockhouse.

"Is the sensor activated, Corporal?" Captain Amanpour asked.

"Yes, sir. The sensor is working fine and the bag of meat is five meters from the target."

"Very well. Thank you, Corporal." Amanpour then signaled to the first soldier to release the animal. The soldier did so and then moved to within the blockhouse.

The jube dog had its nose up in the air sniffing, and soon picked up the scent of the meat. It set off at a slow trot downrange as the men within the blockhouse watched in expectation. The animal was ten meters from the bag when it drew up short, sniffing the air and eying the bus.

"He probably smells the C-4 explosive," Captain Amanpour commented, "but he isn't sure what it is. It's giving him something to think about, but the smell of the meat will be too much temptation."

An instant later the dog walked up to the bag and nudged it with his nose. There was a moment of silence and then the range erupted into a fireball, with metal bus parts flying through the air, and a dust cloud rising high above the test area as the reverberations from the shockwaves began to subside. There was no sign of the jube dog.

Colonel Ghabel looked at Captain Amanpour with a new sense of appreciation. "That was quite impressive, Captain. Quite impressive. It will give the foreign devils something else to worry about. Thanks be to Allah!"

Chapter 15

Logan scanned the expectant faces in his hotel suite. When he'd contacted John Gomez two weeks ago and asked for his help in putting together a ten-person strike team, Gomez had not hesitated. They had talked at length before the rest of the team had arrived, and Logan had decided to make Gomez his de facto number two.

The assembled team had flown into Tucson from all around the country earlier in the day and was staying at the Hampton Inn Tucson Airport. Logan had registered everyone under the name of a dummy offshore company the Kuwaitis had set up. It was mid-afternoon and they were all meeting in Logan's suite as a group for the first time.

"OK, everyone listen up," he began. "First, I'd like to thank you all for coming. I know you have a lot of questions and I'll try to answer them as best I can. I know many of you, all the Seals anyway. Hoorah! First, let's do some quick introductions – name, where you're from, branch of service. I'll start us off. Logan Alexander. I'm from Montpelier, Vermont. Just got out of the Seals a few months ago." He looked to his right where Gomez was seated.

"John Gomez, Chico, California, Army Ranger."

"Francis Tyler, Mount Vernon, Ohio, Army Ranger."

"Le Brian Delray, Long Meadow, Massachusetts, Navy Seal."

"Ed 'Blackjack' Wozolski, Princeton, New Jersey, Navy Seal."

"Tony Barbiari, Louisville, Kentucky, Army Ranger."

"Kyler Jones, Beaufort, South Carolina, Army Ranger."

"Norman Stoddard, Burnt Cabins, Pennsylvania, Navy Seal."

"Bruce Wellington, Custer City, Oklahoma, Navy Seal."

"Zahir Parandeh, McLean, Virginia, civilian."

"OK, thanks. Nice to meet you all. Like I said, thanks for coming out on such short notice. All right. So what's this all about? We're here to set in motion an operation to take out an Iranian IED research facility and training camp for foreign fighters. Everybody in this room has done a tour in the Sandbox. Most of us have had multiple tours over there – Iraq, Afghanistan. We've all been affected, either personally or through someone we know, by IEDs on the battlefield. For me it got real personal a couple of months ago when my younger brother Cooper was killed in an IED attack while on patrol near Ramadi."

He looked over at Zahir, who had not visibly reacted to what he had said. He had been unenthusiastic about having Zahir on the team, but Gomez had convinced him that she was good. They had agreed not to raise her relationship with Cooper to the other team members.

Logan then walked everyone through his research on IEDs, his encounters with Nayef Al Subaie in Boston, and his two-day trip to Kuwait to meet with Nayef and Ali Al Subaie, and Thamir Alghanim. He looked around the room as he concluded with an account of his meeting with Jaber Behbehani. "Is everybody still in? If anyone's having second thoughts, now's the time to put them out there." Not a hand was raised.

"All right. Good. Did everyone have a chance to read the admin packets I gave you?" The packets contained contracts, a security memorandum, emergency contact instructions and a form for their alias passport biographic information.

"I'll need passport photos and the completed bio sheets before we head out tomorrow, so the Kuwaitis can start working on our alias passports. There are several photo shops in town, so fan out and get those done first thing in the morning. On the bio sheets I recommend you stick with your true date of birth, maybe change the year up or down one. Keep your true first name and come up with an alias surname.

"I understand the Kuwaitis procured some Canadian passport stock and that's what we're going to use. OK, that's everything I've got. We'll meet in front of the hotel at 1030 hours tomorrow morning, packed and ready to go. Don't worry about the rooms; I'll put them all on my tab."

The next morning the team was loaded and on the road by 1030 hours. Logan set a northwest course on Interstate Highway 10 towards Casa Grande. To the west, Logan could see Saguaro National Park, named after the saguaro cacti that are unique to the Sonora Desert. Logan recalled reading somewhere that saguaros sometimes lived 150 to 200 years and could reach a height of sixty feet and weight of several thousand pounds when fully hydrated.

An hour later they reached Casa Grande, founded in 1879 at the height of the Arizona mining boom. The town had originally been the terminus for the Southern Pacific Railroad, with a population of five, and today had grown to around thirty-five thousand. Logan pulled into a parking space in front of Cantina de Eva, a hole in the wall on a dusty side street. Despite its forlorn look, the Cantina had a reputation for its southwestern fare, featuring mesquite-grilled steaks, mojito-grilled chicken, grilled jalapeno poppers and homemade blue corn tortillas.

Once inside, Logan could see into the kitchen where Eva, a plump brown Mexican, had been shaping tortillas by hand, and now was shouting out orders in Spanish, and moving with surprising alacrity and grace from one workstation to the next.

"Now this is what I'm talking about." Bruce Wellington, the Navy Seal from Custer City, Oklahoma, pulled up a chair to one of the scuffed, formica-covered tables, and sniffed at the pungent air of chilies and grilled meats. "How'd you find this place, Logan?"

"I was out here, maybe five years ago. We were doing some desert training with Homeland Security, an escape and evasion course we designed especially for their agents. Anyway, Eva's was here then and I figured it was worth giving it a shot."

"It's the real deal." Gomez grabbed a seat next to Wellington. "I grew up in Chico, California and had a Mexican mama."

"Oh yeah? Where?" Francis Tyler pulled back a chair across from Gomez and sat down. "I used to go out with a girl from Chico."

"Barber. Just south of Little Chico Creek."

"Yeah, I know where that is. There used to be a big factory near there."

"Right. Diamond Match. My old man worked there for twenty years. Anyway, there wasn't like a big Latino community in Chico. Mostly it's white, with Latinos making up about fifteen percent. But my mama was all about Mexican food – chilies, tamales, enchiladas, carne asada, chimichangas. I love it all."

"Better enjoy it while you can," Logan broke in. "We're going to be roughing it for a couple of weeks."

After lunch, washed down with abundant quantities of Thunder Canyon IPA, they got back into the SUVs and followed Trekell Road to Interstate 8 west in the direction of Gila Bend. A few miles west they crossed the tiny Santa Cruz River, not much more than a trickle. As the Santa Cruz flows northwest and merges with the Santa Rosa Wash just north of Casa Grande, it picks up volume, eventually emptying into the Gila River, a tributary of the Colorado River.

About twenty miles west of Casa Grande, Gomez's vehicle lurched to the shoulder and Wellington sprinted away from the road into the desert. He circled for a moment in despair, then dropped his trousers and emptied his bowels.

Logan made a U-turn and pulled up behind Gomez's vehicle to see if everything was all right. He watched a sheepish Wellington hitch up his pants and tramp back to the Tahoe. Wellington received a boisterous ribbing from his fellow travelers as he slid across the seat. "Too many of those damn jalapeno peppers." He grimaced. "Guess I'll have to be more careful."

An hour later, just east of Gila Bend, Logan turned south on Highway 85 and drove another forty miles in the direction of Ajo. He was headed for a defunct cattle ranch that bordered the Cabeza Prieta National Wildlife Refuge. The thousand-acre property was on the market for five million dollars, and had been listed for over three years. Logan had had little difficulty convincing the realtor to lease the vacant property to him for two weeks, ostensibly to conduct an Outward Bound-type desert survival program.

Once on the property, the two SUVs turned onto a rutted cattle trail, traveled another twenty minutes and came to a stop in the shadow of Tordillo Mountain. Cattle pens, a crude cookhouse and rustic bunkhouse were the only structures for miles.

Parked in front of the bunkhouse was a dirty Hummer towing a trailer. A weather-beaten giant of a man, sporting a grimy Stetson and scuffed boots, walked over to where they had parked the SUV's and surveyed the group. Spotting Logan, he walked over and wrapped him in a bear hug.

"Aren't you a sight for sore eyes. Logan Alexander. Last time I saw you, we were getting our asses shot at in Afghanistan."

"Hey, Kevin. Great to see you, man. Yeah, that was something else. Everybody, I want you to meet Kevin Haynes. Best breacher to ever come out of Seal Team 8. When Kevin got out a couple of years ago, he came down here and set up his outfitters business and weapons dealership."

Kevin smiled. "Yeah. Things are going pretty good. Married a local girl. She runs our Internet business. Anyway, I got all the provisions you asked for in your email, Logan. There's water and food supplies for ten people for a week, and then I'll come back out and resupply you for the rest of the time. There's enough ice in those chests to keep your meat and vegetables cool for two, maybe three days and then you'll have to switch to MREs.

"There's sleeping bags and air mattresses for ten. I checked inside. They've got racks for a dozen cowhands, so you should be pretty comfortable. On the weapons side I got everything on your list: AK-47s, M-203 grenade launchers, laser scopes, night vision goggles, Simunitions, C-4, det cord, blasting caps. And then there's all that miscellaneous stuff – rope, stakes, spray paint, and tarps."

The team unloaded their provisions from the Hummer and trailer and, after Kevin had pulled away, stowed everything in the bunkhouse and cookhouse. Logan wondered how Zahir was going to handle roughing it and dealing with the lack of privacy entailed in camping out with nine guys. His question was answered when she took charge of organizing the cookhouse, and drafted two of the men to begin cleaning out the bunkhouse. There was a rudimentary outhouse and an outdoor pump beside the cookhouse. Zahir enlisted Delray and Barbiari to erect a basic shower stall using a couple of the tarps and some poles from the corral.

Logan gathered everyone together after dinner. "Everybody get enough to eat? OK, I thought I'd run through some admin issues and then talk about our training schedule. We're not too far from the Barry M. Goldwater Air Force Range and the Yuma Proving Ground. They both do a lot of training, so we'll probably hear aircraft in the area but I don't think it will impact what we're doing here. Most of you probably know that Yuma is where the Special Operations Free Fall School is located. Any of you go through there?" There was a show of hands.

"One of the reasons we're going to stay on the ranch is to maximize our training, but also to keep a low profile. We don't want to be running into any old buddies out there asking questions. Kevin's smart enough not to buy into our Outward Bound cover story, especially with all the weapons he got for us, but he's discreet and we're paying him a lot of money, so he won't say anything."

"I've worked out a rough schedule for the time we're going to be here. Our activities will break down into three core areas – conditioning, desert operational training similar to the Seals' desert training program at Camp Billy Machen, and tweaking our operational scenario for Iran. Any questions?"

"Yeah." Barbiari raised his hand. "What's your take on the Kuwaitis? I mean, I know you'll probably get into it, but from what I've heard, a lot is riding on the support they're giving us. Do they know what they're doing?"

"Good question, Barbiari, and yes, I was going to get into that a little bit more when we talk about the specific scenario. So far they've been making the right noises and have given us pretty much whatever we need in terms of material support. Let me put it this way. They're motivated to get this done. They have a lot of history with the Iranians, not all of it good. Some in their government want to curry favor with them, because they see the writing on the wall, and others don't trust them but don't want to overtly confront them. So this operation is right up their alley.

"Now, as far as specific support goes, they are bankrolling this whole thing. They'll take care of the training facility we're going to need in Kuwait, procure our weapons and ammo through a third party international arms dealer, and acquire a private motor yacht that'll be the mother ship we deploy from in the Gulf. They're also getting a Zodiac FC 420 Futura Commando boat for the last leg of the infiltration. Their Intel guys have got some people on the ground in Iran who may be able to take care of local transportation procurements there and who can keep an eye on the Base to give us an update on the security profile, manning, etc."

"I wasn't too impressed with the way they handled that one asset you told us about, Behbehani." Delray spoke up. "I mean, he called their headquarters from inside enemy territory. That was really stupid, and if that's the level of tradecraft they teach their agents, it doesn't say much about their professionalism."

"I agree that was weak. Behbehani was lucky to get out of there with just a beating. They could've just as easily killed him, and the Kuwaitis wouldn't know squat. Apparently they do have some capability on the ground though. I understand they had a couple of local thugs go after the base commander who tortured Behbehani. They got to him when he was alone and beat him up in a bathhouse."

Logan paused before continuing. "One reason I feel good about this, though, is that we're going to control what happens on the ground. We'll be calling the shots. And I think the Kuwaitis have a vested interest in keeping this close hold. They don't want the word to get out, because it would be controversial within the Kuwaiti government, and set them up for a confrontation with the Iranians. So, there are only a handful of people in Kuwait that know about the operation, the two Al Subaies and Alghanim.

"Ali Al Subaie has enough autonomy to be able to move huge sums of money around without bringing anyone else in. And Alghanim is the head of their Intel service's Operations Directorate and can task assets and get Intel updates as a matter of course without raising any eyebrows."

"We also need to make sure that we're practicing the best security on our end." Logan held up a cell phone. "This is a randomly procured cell phone, and I'm using a randomly procured, non-attributable calling card. It's not tied to me, but we have it for emergencies. Our families are used to us going on deployment, and nowadays with technology they're used to getting a phone call or doing a video chat, even from a war zone. We won't have that. We're going to be out of pocket for these two weeks, and then for the two weeks when we're over there. After this is over, we don't want anybody to be able to trace what happened back to any of us on the team, or the Kuwaitis. I don't want some Qods Force hit team going after us because we were weak on communications' security.

"All right, why don't we hit the hay? We've got a full day tomorrow and I want everyone rested up."

As Logan settled into his sleeping bag, he sensed someone next to his bunk. Turning he could just make out Zahir, who had come in from outside and had paused next to him. Coming closer she looked into his eyes and whispered, "I miss Cooper, Logan. I miss him very much. But thank you for letting me be a part of this. It means a lot to me." She moved without further sound to her bunk and climbed in.

Logan watched her as she snuggled into her sleeping bag and realized that Zahir felt the same sense of loss and despair over Cooper's death as he did. In a sense her situation was even more tragic than his. Zahir's family had abandoned her because of her illicit love, whereas his had come together to console one another. As he drifted off, he imagined Zahir's eyes, soft and loving, looking at him, but no, she was looking past him. He turned to see what she was looking at and saw Cooper's face, looking back at Zahir.

Chapter 16

Logan awoke groggy with sleep, and shivered as he stuck his nose outside of his sleeping bag. It was brisk, mid-forties, but held the promise of warming up to the mid-seventies by noon. Perfect weather. He looked over in the direction of Zahir's bunk and realized with a start that it was empty. He fumbled for his flashlight and shined the light on his watch. Almost seven o'clock. Slipping out of his sleeping bag, he pulled on his military camouflage outfit, field coat with liner and steel toe boots.

Outside, the desert sky was just beginning to lighten, a palette of colors daubed across the horizon as first light began to glow. Looking around, he could see a glimmer from the cookhouse and a plume of smoke emitting from the chimney. The aroma of alligator juniper burning in the stove was pleasant. Pushing the cookhouse door open, Logan saw Zahir working at the ancient iron stove. An enormous pot of coffee was beginning to perk and an iron griddle was just beginning to redden from the heat of the cook stove.

"You're up early."

Zahir smiled, and pushed back a wisp of hair from her face. "I've always been an early riser. Two summers in college I worked for an outdoor adventure company in northern California. We led small groups on backpacking treks in the wilderness. You got used to a different kind of daily rhythm. Up at first light, a full day of hiking and then early to bed."

"Sounds like fun. So what's for breakfast?" Logan sniffed the breakfast aromas with eager expectation.

"Blueberry pancakes and bacon. Coffee's almost ready and there's some fresh fruit if anyone wants that."

"All right, let me round everybody up."

Fifteen minutes later, over a hearty breakfast, Logan sketched out plans for the routine they would follow over the next two weeks. "OK, folks, so let's get to it. We'll start off with some basic PT to get loose. Then, while it's still cool we're going to do a ten-mile hike through the desert. We'll come back and break for lunch. Then we'll take a page out of the land warfare training manual and do some small arms and demolitions training. Later on we'll do an Intel briefing and start rehearsing the specific scenario for Iran. Any questions?"

"Yeah, Logan." Norm Stoddard raised his hand. "How current is our Intel on the objective going to be?"

"Good point, Norm. I brought overhead and some other reporting with me that was current, as of last Friday. We'll be working off of that to start with. The Kuwaitis have been passing me overhead and SIGINT reporting that they probably get from the Brits. It may even be U.S. reporting. I can't tell for sure because they've sanitized it. You can bet that MI-5 and the CIA would be pissed if they knew this stuff was getting passed to us. It violates all kinds of third party rules.

"In addition, the Kuwaitis also have some low-level assets on the ground in Iran that can report on stuff like readiness, troop strength, etc. If there are any significant changes, I've worked out an arrangement with the Kuwaitis to get that passed to us here. It'll be a lot easier when we're over there for those two weeks, and more important frankly as we get closer to D-Day. Anybody else? OK. Let's meet out front in a half hour dressed for PT."

Thirty minutes later the group met in front of the bunkhouse. Forty minutes into their workout, Kyler Jones, who was on his stomach doing push-ups, let out an anguished cry.

"Damn, something just bit me!" Grabbing his leg, he winced in pain as a seven-inch scorpion scurried away from him.

Gomez ran over to get a look at the scorpion before it disappeared into a nearby creosote bush. "You got lucky, Jones. The only scorpion in Arizona that's a real threat to humans is the Arizona bark scorpion, and that wasn't one. They can be deadly, especially with children. And by the way, scorpions don't bite. They sting. Let's get you inside so you can elevate your leg. We'll wash it out real good, and put a cool compress on it to keep the swelling down. Do you feel anything else?

"Nah, it just stings."

"It's getting kind of red and irritated, but I think you'll be all right. Logan, I think Jones needs to rest a couple of hours, at least until the swelling goes down. I'll stay here to keep an eye on him."

"All right, thanks, John. OK, people, listen up. We need to stay alert out here. This ranch hasn't been worked for a couple of years, and I doubt there've been many people out here in that time, so Mother Nature rules. There're all kinds of venomous snakes, spiders and scorpions in this area, so be alert. The rest of you grab some water and meet me out here in ten minutes."

They hiked at a moderate pace for three hours, initially following the foothills of Tordillo Mountain before striking west through a rugged boulder-strewn patch and then crossing a deep wash lined with Palo Verde trees. Long-eared jackrabbits, spooked by their movement, burst from the scrub, zigzagging at breathtaking speeds until they were out of view. At one point they spotted a lone coyote loping toward them on the far bank of the wash, but he caught their scent and paused, emitting a series of short barks before scurrying away from them.

Taking a water break, they could feel a distant roar and then the thundering shriek of engines as four F-16 Fighting Falcons streaked across the sky. "Must be from the 56th Fighter Wing at Luke Air Force Base." Logan shielded his eyes as he followed their flight. "They were talking about doing F-35 training out of the 56th, but now with the future of the F-35 up in the air, who knows where that's going to go. We had F-16s in Afghanistan when I was there. They were the 'Black Widows' out of the 388th and 419th Fighter Wings. I think they're out of Utah."

"Yeah, we had F-16s in Iraq back in 2008." Ed Wozolski shaded his eyes as he followed the F-16s flying low over the desert. "They were home based with the 421st Fighter Squadron, which I think belongs to the 388th. They're all out of Hill Air Force Base in Utah."

"Well, we sure as hell won't have any F-16s covering our asses in Iran," Logan joked.

"Can you believe that thirty-five years ago the U.S. was selling military aircraft to Iran?" asked Zahir.

"No way!" Logan looked at Zahir in disbelief.

"Yes. There was a lot of defense cooperation between the Shah and the U.S. government back then. Bell Helicopter was selling the Iranians Cobras, and a couple of troop transport models like the 214 and 214-A. They had a school co-located with the Imperial Iranian Air Force at Khatami Air Force Base in Esfahan. Bell Helicopter even subcontracted an English language program through a company called Telemedia that trained pilots and mechanics in specialized English. You know. This is a main rotor. This is a vertical stabilizer. That's a swashplate assembly."

"You're kidding me, right?"

"No, I'm serious. I know it's hard to believe given the state of U.S.-Iranian relations today. I don't think we'll ever forgive Iran for what they did to our Embassy in Tehran back in 1979 and the fact that they held our diplomats hostage for a year."

Logan looked thoughtful. "Even if we could get past all that, and that's a big if, the ayatollahs will always paint the U.S. as The Great Satan. And given our support for Israel it's unlikely they would ever really trust us." He stood up and stretched. "OK, people. Let's move out. We've got about an hour of hiking to do before we get back."

When they got back to their base camp, Logan was surprised to see a Pima County Sheriff's Department squad car parked in front of the bunkhouse. A lean Mexican-American deputy sheriff with a drooping left eyelid, whose nametag identified him as Salona, was in conversation with John Gomez.

"Hey, Logan. This here is Deputy Sheriff Angel Salona, with the Pima County Sheriff's Office. He was in the neighborhood, and stopped by to check in on us."

Salona shook Logan's hand. "Nice to meet you. We got word earlier this morning that there was some Mexicans trying to sneak across the border somewhere in the vicinity of Sonoita. So we've been checking routes that illegals have been known to use in this area in the past. Word is out amongst the Mexicans that this ranch has been vacant for a couple of years, and sometimes we catch them hiding out in here while they're in transit."

"How do you track them with all this wide open country around here?" Logan asked.

"Well, I'm sure you've heard about the virtual and physical fences that Homeland Security has been building out here for several years. We've got both. The virtual fence has sensors implanted up and down the border and in theory it will detect human movement and then send a notification to Border Security. But hell, all kinds of animals set them things off. They're not very reliable. Guess that's why the virtual program's being discontinued. I don't know about the actual physical fence. It's controversial and money is an issue. It looks like it's still going up in these parts for now though."

"Well, if we spot anybody that looks suspicious we'll contact your office. We're just going to be here for a couple of weeks, doing this desert survival course."

"Are you all military?"

"Former military. We're putting together a survival course for civilians, kind of an Outward Bound-type of experience, and we're working out the different skills we want to stress in the program."

"Well, you all look like you can take care of yourselves, although I hear that fellow over there managed to get himself stung by a scorpion already." Salona gestured towards Jones.

Jones grimaced. "Yeah, the little bastard snuck up on me when I wasn't looking. That won't happen again."

"Be careful. There's a whole lot of bad shit that can happen to you out here." Tipping his hat, Salona turned towards his car. "I'd appreciate a call if you do see anything unusual. I left my card with Gomez there. See you all later."

After Salona had pulled away, Gomez looked at Logan. "Do you think he bought our cover story about us being an Outward Bound bunch?"

"Hard to say. It's not too far-fetched. I mean, just looking at us he could tell we've got military backgrounds. He'll probably check with the realtor we're dealing with, and he'll get the same story there. We didn't mention all the automatic weapons and explosives we've got stashed in the bunkhouse, so if he'd nosed around in there it might have taken some explaining. I still think we're OK, though. I mean, Arizona's probably one of the most pro-gun rights states in the country. Let's grab some lunch and figure out what were going to do this afternoon."

After lunch they broke out the AK-47s and spent the next couple of hours sighting them to zero and practicing on a makeshift range they had paced off. Their weapons were set with a 1,000-meter battle sight of zero, meaning theoretically any shots fired up to that distance that were on target would fall within a sixteen-inch circle. To accomplish this, Gomez set up ten twenty-five-meter zero targets and the team began firing three-shot groups at them, making adjustments to their front and rear sights until a tight pattern of shots appeared on the targets.

The AK-47 has a fairly basic rear-notched, rear-tangent iron sight that can be adjusted in 100-meter increments between 100 and 1,000 meters. The front sight's a rotating sight post that is adjustable for elevation. For the former Seals and Rangers this was Weapons 101, but for Zahir, who had minimal exposure to firearms, it was mostly new. Logan spent some time working with her, and after a short time of practice she was putting her rounds into a compact pattern on the target.

Logan gathered everyone around after two hours of practice. "Let's take a break and I'll tell you what I'm thinking in terms of everybody's primary responsibilities. If we get that out of the way early on, we'll be able to train more effectively. Gomez and I went over your bio packets before our meeting in Tucson the other day, and this is a first cut, so I welcome any feedback you have.

"We're smaller than a traditional squad would be, and there are some functions that we just won't have. For instance, we won't need tactical air controllers. Mostly I see it breaking down into breachers, shooters and demolition experts, and of course Zahir as our linguist. Right now I've got Wellington, Wozolski, and Tyler as breachers; me, Gomez, Barbiari, and Jones as shooters; and Stoddard, and Delray on demolitions. Any questions so far?" Logan looked up from searching his notes.

"Yeah." Delray raised his hand. "Maybe this is just more of an observation than a question. We all cross-train, so, maybe if anyone doesn't feel as sharp as they should, or feels like they're better suited for another role, we could talk about changing roles."

Logan eyed Delray. "That's a good point, Delray. Anyone feel like they're really out of their league?" There was no show of hands. "To be honest, one of the things I first looked at when I was putting this together was current experience. Everybody in here has been out for less than a year. Some of those skills get rusty, but we've got a month to dust them off and get everyone back up to speed. We'll also have plenty of time to do some cross-training.

"We'll spend the rest of the afternoon doing stress tests. It'll probably take us an hour to lay out a point man course out this way." Logan pointed to an area of desert scrub east of the bunkhouse.

"When we're done laying it out, we'll take rotations doing instinctive fire drills. We don't have any live ammo out here, it's all Simunitions, so I'm not too worried about anyone getting hurt." He looked over in Jones' direction. "That is unless Kyler's friend brings back any of his family members."

"Aw damn, Logan. Am I going to keep hearing about that damn scorpion?" He shuffled his feet and then spat on the ground.

Everybody laughed and Logan gave Jones a playful punch on the arm. "I won't bring it up again. Truth be told, it could have happened to any one of us. By the way, how's it feeling?"

"It's a little tender, but I'm fine."

They worked until just before sunset and then tramped through the scrub back to camp. There was a sense of camaraderie, as they kicked up the desert sand. Without prompting, Barbiari began singing "The Ballad of The Green Berets." His deep baritone punctured the desert stillness. One by one the others began to chime in, even the Seals, who, at this moment, felt no sense of inter-service rivalry.

Logan looked over at Gomez and they shared a smile as they filed into camp. We are a Band of Brothers, he mused. No matter that, with the exception of Gomez and Zahir, none of us have ever served together, but we share the same experiences and a common cause. Surveying the group, he noticed Zahir looking at him with the faintest hint of a smile on her face. He smiled back. And sisters, he reflected. And sisters.

Chapter 17

"Colonel, it's General Salehi's aide de camp for you on secure line one."

Colonel Barzin Ghabel looked up from the file he was reading and acknowledged his orderly with a wave of his cigarette. "Thank you, Sergeant Yavani." Picking up the handset from the secure phone on his desk, Ghabel punched in his personal code and waited for General Salehi's aide, Captain Saatchi, to come on the line.

"Colonel, one moment please and I will transfer you to General Salehi."

"Thank you, Captain. How are things in Tehran?"

"Everything is fine. Thank you for asking, sir. One moment please."

Ghabel reached into his desk drawer and withdrew a pad of paper and a pen to take notes. Waiting for the transfer to the secure phone on General Salehi's desk, Ghabel stubbed out his cigarette. He wondered what was on the general's mind and why it merited a personal phone call.

"Hello, Colonel Ghabel. Salehi here. How have you been, Colonel? It's been what, two, three weeks since you visited us in Tehran?"

"Yes, sir. I believe it's been closer to three weeks."

"I just received your final report on the training incident from last month, and the analysis from your engineers on the IED component that caused the misfire."

"Yes, sir."

"Very thorough. Your men are to be commended. I was most interested in the work your team's doing on passive infrared sensors. According to the report, you've had some favorable results in the tests that you've conducted since then. Have you ironed out the problems that led to the mishap on the range?"

"Yes, we have, General. My chief engineer, Captain Amanpour, now feels that we should transition completely into passive infrared sensor technology. The Americans have become fairly adept at devising electromagnetic countermeasures to the devices currently in our inventory. As a result, our successes on the battlefield are less impressive than they once were." Ghabel tapped his fingers on the desk.

"I agree with Captain Amanpour's assessment, Colonel, and this is one of the reasons why I'm calling you. If you've been reading international press reports and our own intelligence reporting over the past several weeks, you will have noticed that the rhetoric spewing out of Washington, the international community, and Israel with regards to our nuclear program has become rather antagonistic. The U.S. Secretary of Defense has even remarked publicly that all options are on the table in dealing with Iran, but at the same time he's felt obliged to signal a warning to Israel not to do anything rash.

"We don't have any evidence, but I'm convinced either the U.S. or Israel is behind the recent murder of one of our top nuclear scientists when he was on his way home from the lab. We're likely to see more of this type of covert action in the near future rather than an out-and-out military attack. It would be smart on their part because they would have plausible deniability. And besides, the American people have little stomach for another war in the Middle East after a decade in Afghanistan and Iraq."

"Yes, General. I completely agree. They are unlikely to back off though, despite our leaders having made the case that our defense doctrine is based solely on deterrence. We have no nuclear weapons' ambitions. Still, the Americans and Israelis continue to harp on this with the international community. At the end of the day we will most certainly endure increased threats and sanctions."

Ghabel could feel the bile rise in his throat as he recalled the smug expression on the Israeli prime minister's face at his latest televised press conference.

"Exactly. In this regard, you'll soon see an order directing all base commanders to increase their readiness levels. We'll be initiating a series of military exercises, primarily in the Tehran region, but elsewhere as well, in the next ten days. The heightened readiness of our combat and operational units, along with our intelligence cadre will, we hope, convey the message that we won't be intimidated by rash statements from our adversaries."

"Sir, of course we'll do our part."

"What I want from you, Colonel, is for you to continue doing exactly what you're doing now."

"Sir? I'm afraid I don't understand." Ghabel stopped writing and sat back in his chair.

"I don't want your men distracted from their primary purpose by these exercises. Your principal mission is to expedite the development of new and improved IED components, step up the training of foreign fighters on these new technologies and facilitate the deployment of these weapons to the battlefield."

"Yes, sir. Of course we're at your command. My men are highly motivated to get the new triggering devices into the hands of the foreign fighters. I don't wish to overstep my bounds, sir, but it occurs to me that with the American military now out of Iraq, we should reinvigorate our program in Afghanistan."

"Well, there is a silver lining with the departure of the Americans from Iraq, Barzin; we will no longer have a massive U.S. military presence on our border. Initially their withdrawal will leave a void, so why not exploit the opportunity that presents? As you may well know, Ayatollah Khamenei has maintained a regular dialog with Iraq's prime minister. We know the Sunnis in Iraq are agitating for greater representation in the central government and, given the chance, would run the current prime minister out of office. Perhaps some mischief on our part in support of our Shiite brothers would calm these troubled waters."

"What kind of mischief did the general have in mind, sir?"

"A well timed attack against Sunnis during Ramadan or perhaps an unfortunate accident involving a Sunni political or religious figure. I believe these ideas merit discussion with our political leadership. Of course, going back to your original point, we should not ignore Afghanistan. Indeed, I have concluded that we can redirect additional resources to that effort, to inflict greater damage on the Americans and their coalition partners without materially diminishing our efforts in Iraq. If this has no other effect than to hasten their early retreat from Afghanistan, it will be worth the undertaking. Give me some recommendations and we will reevaluate all the thousand and one things we have going on there."

"Yes, of course. When would you like them?"

"Within a week would be fine, Colonel. So we'll leave it at that. I look forward to receiving your proposals."

After hanging up, Ghabel looked at his watch and decided to call it a day. Azar had been gone for two weeks, because her father had needed surgery and her mother was having difficulty grappling with the increased demands at home. Azar was due home this evening, and he was anxious to see her. He said goodbye to Sergeant Yavani and walked out to where his black BMW 318 was parked. The car had cost him the equivalent of $40,000 and, with inflation running at twenty-five percent, had not been inexpensive. Still, it was one of the few luxuries that he permitted himself.

"Colonel!"

Ghabel glanced back in the direction of the Administrative Building, and saw Major Samadi hurrying towards him. "Tahmouress. What's going on? I'm leaving a bit early today because Azar is due back from Shiraz."

"I won't keep you long, sir. I just wanted to run something by you. We have a group of Al Qaeda foreign fighters coming in for training in December. It's the same group that botched the IED attack against the American platoon in Ramadi a couple of months ago. You know about the Al-Qaeda operatives that have been more or less on ice here for some time. We just received a communication from

Headquarters that the government is planning to release most of them from house arrest sometime around the end of November. I know that not all of them are leadership cadre. In fact, there are a couple of bombers that I've had my eyes on.

"Perhaps we can look into rehabilitating some of these fighters by reinserting them into the foreign fighter networks that come through our training program. I've seen their profiles. Several of them are actual combat veterans with impressive resumes."

"Take a look into it, Tahmouress. I would be willing to wager that they're eager to get back into the fight. It's not as though they've been mistreated in captivity here. If the Americans had captured them they would've been detained, perhaps sent to Guantanamo and water-boarded. Then they would be dying for revenge. No matter. These Al Qaeda fighters are relentless. They're consumed with killing Americans. It's a good idea to get them back into circulation."

"I'll get right on it then, Colonel. Please give my regards to your wife. I trust that her father is recovering from his surgery?"

"Yes, thank you for asking. His biggest problem is just slowing down long enough to get the rest he needs. He was so active before the surgery, and now the doctors have ordered two months of very light activity so he can fully recover. He's been moping around the house since he was released from the hospital, driving my mother-in-law crazy. I'll see you tomorrow."

Ghabel slipped into the BMW, and smiled with satisfaction as it roared to life. He headed west away from the base and then turned south on the road towards Bandar Deylam. The sun was just setting and he had to be extra cautious because of the number of workmen bicycling back into town.

Fifteen minutes later Ghabel pulled up in front of his apartment building. Azar would have stopped at the bazaar in Bushehr before returning to Bandar Deylam. With a population of just over 20,000, shopping here was limited. Besides, he had not been cooking for himself since she had been away, and the refrigerator was nearly empty. Unlocking the door to his apartment, the fragrant aroma of a simmering stew greeted him.

"Barzin, I'm in the kitchen."

Azar's voice floated towards him, and Ghabel felt a rush of emotion to have her back home. He walked into the kitchen where he saw her standing at the counter cutting into a pomegranate. As she turned towards him he was startled by the change in her appearance. "You cut your hair."

"Yes. I was getting bored with it and decided to try something different. Do you like it?"

Ghabel cocked his head to one side and studied his wife. " Of course, Azar. You know that I love the way you look. But you should have asked me first." He walked up to her and they embraced for a moment. Then he released her. "I missed you these past two weeks. How are your parents? I imagine they were sad to see you leave."

Azar turned back to the pomegranate she was cutting and sighed. "They'll be fine now, I think. Papa's impossible of course. He's normally so even tempered, but I think this issue with his heart has really scared him. And now, he can't do anything except sit around the house. He's not even supposed to go outside for several weeks. Mama is trying her best to please him, but I think she's at her wit's end."

Ghabel lifted the lid on the simmering pot, bent over and inhaled deeply. "Ah, *fesenjan*?"

"Yes, with duck. I thought you would like it, since I imagine you haven't been eating very well these past two weeks. It's almost finished cooking. We're having saffron rice and Barbari bread to go with it. I'm glad you had yoghurt in the refrigerator. That's the one thing I forgot to pick up. Shall we eat on the carpet in the living room or would you prefer to sit at the table?"

"Let's eat on the carpet. Let me get out of my uniform and I'll be right back." Ghabel went into the bedroom and took off his uniform. Thankfully the bruises from the assault two weeks ago had faded, and because he had been diligent about applying the antiseptic cream, he was almost completely healed. There had been no lingering effects from the attack, although twice he had awakened in a cold sweat from a nightmare about that night. Returning to the living room, he saw that Azar had already cleared a space, and was bringing the food out.

After they had eaten their fill, Ghabel looked into Azar's eyes, knowing that she would understand that he wanted her. "Shall we leave this for later?" he asked.

He took her hand and led her into the bedroom, where they disrobed and climbed into bed. Ghabel ran his hands over Azar's body, relishing every familiar curve. The longing he felt for her was acute, their two-week separation intensifying his desire. He rolled her over on top, and massaging her buttocks, pulled her close. Taking a taut nipple between his teeth he teased it with his tongue as she moaned in pleasure. Pulling back, she straddled him and leaning forward, teased him by brushing her breasts across his face. Arching back she grasped his penis from behind in her hand and began to deliberately massage it. Finding no response, she slid down and took him in her mouth, as Ghabel let out an involuntary gasp. When after a few moments of this, he remained limp, Azar slid up next to him, continuing to gently stroke his unresponsive member.

"It's all right darling." She looked into his eyes. "We can try again later. Perhaps it was too soon after eating."

Ghabel grunted and looked away in embarrassment. He was certain of one thing. His failure to achieve an erection had nothing to do with when they'd finished dinner. He suspected though that it had everything to do with what had happened to him that night in the bathhouse. He kissed Azar and turned onto his side, staring into the darkness. If he ever found the bastards that had done that to him, he would make them wish that they had never seen the light of day. He scowled into the dark as he let his mind entertain the horrors he would visit on them. Just wait.

Chapter 18

Logan studied the team gathered in the bunkhouse. They had just finished packing their gear and stowing it in the two Tahoes. Now they were sprawled around the room, wiping down their weapons and ribbing each other as they waited for Kevin Haynes to come by to pick up his equipment.

Two weeks in the Sonora Desert had gone much quicker than he had imagined. Jones' encounter with the scorpion had turned out to be the most serious health scare they'd confronted, and except for sore muscles and a couple of cases of sunburn, everyone had come out of the two-week exercise in pretty good shape.

"OK, everybody listen up." Logan waited for the chatter to subside before continuing. "I just want to say that I'm pleased with the way things went over the last two weeks. You all worked hard, and I feel like we're right about where we need to be. The mock-up we put together of the target objective wasn't the best substitute for the real thing, but it gave us a pretty accurate idea of the target layout and the spatial relationship between the various buildings on the base."

The team had used imagery of the base to calibrate the size of the buildings and their spatial distance from one to another. Unfortunately, their mock-up was one dimensional, laid out with spray paint and rope, so that the breachers – Wellington, Wozolski and Tyler – had had to simulate bursting through the doors and taking out imaginary bad guys inside. They'd practiced their approach to the base and drilled the scenario several times during daylight hours and for the last four days had drilled it at the same time they expected to make the actual assault, in the early hours before dawn.

"Now, one of the areas I am concerned about is the whole maritime piece, starting with our approach from Failaka Island to the Iranian coast. Obviously we haven't been able to look at that from here, and we're not going to be able to do anything about it once we're in Kuwait because it'll raise our profile. So I've made arrangements for us to spend a couple of days in San Diego to work on our maritime skills before we break off."

The Seals in the group perked up when Logan started talking maritime operations. "So what's going on in San Diego, Logan?" asked Blackjack Wozolski.

"I've got an old Seal buddy there who's working in the boat chartering industry. We're going to charter a sixty-five-foot bare-boat motor yacht from him and he's going to get his hands on an inflatable Zodiac like the one we'll be using for our insertion. That way we'll have a chance to practice inflating it on board the motor yacht, getting it into the water, loading up and casting off. We'll also practice the recovery operation."

"Do we have any Intel on likely threats we'll encounter when we're on the water over there?" Le Brian Delray fixed his gaze on Logan, gnawing on a fingernail.

"We all know that the Gulf has been getting a lot of attention lately. It's definitely heating up. Much of that has to do with the importance of Gulf oil to the Iranians, and the rest of the world for that matter. So it makes sense that they've put quite a few naval assets in there to protect their interests. They've got everything from missile patrol boats to a hodgepodge of civilian craft patrolling the Gulf. Much of this activity is centered in the Strait of Hormuz, which is way south of where we're going to be operating.

"There's a lot of tanker traffic through the Strait and it comes pretty close to the Iranian coast. Those ships that navigate in the Strait follow a traffic separation scheme that's set up with inbound and outbound sea-lanes separated by a two-mile buffer zone between them. We won't be near any of that mess. The closest hot spot for us will be around Kharg Island, almost a hundred nautical miles south of our target objective. Kharg Island is about sixteen miles off the coast of Iran, not far from Bushehr City. Our insertion point is going to be north of Bandar Deylam, a port city about ninety nautical miles north of Bushehr City."

"Bushehr City's the capital of Bushehr Province," Zahir chimed in. "The reason there's so much security around Bushehr City is that Kharg Island's the main sea port for exporting Iranian crude oil. There's also a nuclear power plant about seventeen miles southeast of Bushehr City. Iran has a significant military presence in that area as well. The Southern Area Command's Bushehr Air Force Base is co-located with Bushehr Airport and the Iranian Navy's Bushehr Navy Base is a technical supply center in Bushehr on the Persian Gulf. They also have a large storage facility and an R&D facility at the navy base."

Logan looked at Zahir with newfound respect. "And how —"

"A graduate course in Near East Strategic Leadership," she replied, anticipating his question. "I did a paper on how nations project power, and for part of that I had to analyze what Iran's military capabilities were."

"Thanks. We may want to pick your brain some more about that later. OK, so what I'm thinking right now is that we're going to come in under the radar north of Bandar Deylam Port. We know there's regular maritime traffic between Iran and Kuwait in this area; a weekly commercial ferry service between Kuwait and Bandar Deylam, and some fat cat Kuwaitis who take their private yachts over there from Kuwait City on business. Bandar Deylam's not very big, maybe 20,000 people, but where the base is, north of the port, it gets desolate pretty quick.

"Anyway, our approach on a Kuwaiti vessel will be under the guise of either a commercial ferry, a fishing boat or a private yacht. We'll unload our Zodiac a couple of nautical miles offshore. From imagery I've looked at there are some coastal caves just north of the base where we should be able to cache the inflatable until we complete the mission."

The sound of honking interrupted Logan's response to

Delray's question. He looked through the grimy bunkhouse window, and could see Kevin Haynes' Hummer pulling up outside. "All right, let's get all of Kevin's gear loaded up. We'll have plenty of time to go over the maritime scenario later. Once we're done with Kevin we're going to take the Tahoes up to Yuma and overnight there. It's only three hours from Yuma to San Diego, so we'll get an early start tomorrow and be in San Diego late morning. My buddy's going to meet us around noon and we can get right to work."

Logan had a surprise waiting for everyone when they reached Gila Bend forty-five minutes later. It was ten-thirty and the morning sun had warmed the air to a pleasant seventy-seven degrees. Logan pulled into a dusty parking lot, where a sun-bleached sign proclaimed that they had arrived at the Gila River Rafting Company. From Gila Bend the river flows southwest until it merges with the Colorado River, at Yuma. Because of widespread irrigation and water diversions for human consumption, the Gila is often no more than a trickle from Gila Bend to Yuma. November had been an unusually wet month, and the rapids, though only category one and two, were flowing freely westward.

A freckled redhead with plaited pigtails, wearing ragged cutoffs and a taut T-shirt depicting a bicycle with the caption "Put some fun between your legs," strolled over to where they were all standing. "Hi! Are you all the Alexander group? I'm Jessie Collins."

"Hi Jessie. I'm Logan Alexander. We spoke on the phone a couple of weeks ago. Looks like we've got some water to play in."

"For a change. It's pretty parched along this stretch of the Gila. The river's fed from the Salt River in western New Mexico. We normally only get something like seven inches of rainfall a year around here, so for any given year a lot depends not just on how much rain we get, but how much snowfall there is in the mountains of New Mexico. Well, let's get you all set up."

Thirty minutes later the team was lazily floating down the Gila River's brown expanse in large truck-sized inner tubes.

Jessie had set up a separate inner tube for them equipped with a full cooler of iced beer and sandwiches. As they floated past strands of cottonwood trees, they soaked their aching muscles in the slow moving rippling current. Six miles and three hours later, refreshed and none the worse for the trip, they reached their take-out spot at Gila Flats. Logan had arranged to have the two Tahoes moved ahead so they wouldn't have to back-track to pick them up. They got into clean clothes and continued on their way to Yuma.

Gomez was first to spot the flotilla of hot air balloons rising into the sky and crossing the Colorado River as they approached Yuma. Dozens of fantastic shapes, every color of the rainbow, seemed to touch the clouds, their silent ascent interrupted by hissing bursts of burning propane as the pilots caught the faint breeze and rose above them. Gomez and Logan pulled over and everyone piled out to watch the aerial spectacle. They stood there in silent appreciation until the last balloon glided out of view. Moments later they got back on the road. They reached the Best Western Inn and Suites on South Castle Dome Avenue at five o'clock.

Logan's cell phone vibrated, and he noticed that he had a couple of missed phone calls and a voice message from Nayef Al Subaie. "Logan, I hope your trip to the desert was beneficial. I'm going to be in Boston next week, and was hoping that we could get together briefly to discuss travel arrangements before you take off. Everything is on track here. Talk to you soon."

"Any problems?" Gomez paused from pulling bags out of the Tahoe.

"No. That was a message from Nayef. We had a pre-arranged signal for when the alias passports are ready. Sounds like they're good to go."

"Any thoughts on how we're going to use them?"

"Well, they're Canadian docs, so we definitely don't want to fly out of Canada on them, and Homeland Security is a tough nut to crack so we don't want to try flying out of the U.S. on something fake. I'm thinking we fly into Europe, probably London, on our U.S. passports. The Kuwaitis can pass us the Canadian passports in London and we'll stash our U.S. passports and all our other true name documentation in public lockers there. Then, to break up the group's profile, we'll split up and transit Europe from different countries. We'll meet up in Kuwait City."

"Don't the Europeans have a deal where you don't really need a visa if you're using ground transportation to travel between countries?"

"Yeah, they've got this Schengen Visa program. I think something like twenty-five countries are members. We won't draw attention to ourselves in Europe by applying for visas and running the risk that some hotshot immigration officer's going to question us. It'll be easier to keep a low profile this way. We'll play it low key in London. Fly in and out separately and meet one on one to distribute the passports rather than meet as a group."

When they had finished checking in, the survivors of the Gila River decided they were too tired to explore the neighborhood. A simple dinner at a nearby burgers and beer joint hit the spot, and after walking back to the Best Western, they called it an early night. Logan tumbled into his king-size bed, savoring the crisp clean sheets and firm mattress. He was no stranger to roughing it; he'd gone months in the field without a decent night's sleep. Yet tired as he felt, soothing sleep evaded him.

Tossing back and forth in a restless dream-like stupor, a face he didn't recognize leered out at him. He awoke with a start and realized that he had been staring into the face of Qods Force Colonel Barzin Ghabel.

The next morning, after depleting the breakfast buffet, the team set out for San Diego. Logan didn't mention his eerie dream to the other team members. They picked up Highway 8 West and soon afterward were skirting the northern border of Mexicali, the capital of Baja California. They could see an early winter crop of asparagus and scallions in the fields, produce of the fertile Imperial Basin. Mexican *campesinos* using long flat spatula-shaped knives cut the asparagus in nine-inch lengths and gathered it in rows for so-called burros, other campesinos, to haul to a central collection point. There the asparagus was loaded onto flatbed trucks and transported to a nearby processing center.

Leaving the Imperial Basin behind, the two Tahoes sped through the Anza-Borrego Desert before reaching the steep foothills of the Laguna Mountains. The twisting highway climbed to 6,000 feet, as desert gave way to a forest of Jeffrey pine trees. Logan opened his window and inhaled the strong butterscotch odor emitted by the pines.

An hour later they pulled up to Davis Mission Bay Marina in San Diego. The marina was located in Quivira Basin, within a stone's throw of the Pacific. Just to the south loomed Coronado Naval Base and San Diego Naval Station.

Logan's buddy, Hal Conroy, greeted them on the dock and led them over to a slip where the Sea Knight, a sixty-five-foot Pacific Mariner Flybridge motor yacht was moored.

"Come on board and I'll show you around," Conroy said. "I got everything on your list, Logan. Food supplies for ten, wet weather gear, coastal charts, and the Zodiac. I was able to get my hands on a Futura Commando F470. It'll hold up to ten people, is equipped with a 55-horsepower engine, and can be inflated in just two minutes using a scuba tank."

"That stows into a pretty tight package." Logan ran his hand along one side of the Futura Commando, which Zodiac classifies as a combat rubber raiding craft, or CRRC.

"Yeah, it's like two-feet-six-inches by four-feet-eleven, stored. Zodiac developed a new deck system for this boat. It's a high-pressure air deck that did away with the need for a thrust board. Their modifications reduced the weight by sixty-some pounds over their earlier model."

"Nice."

Hal led them around the Sea Knight. "This baby will cruise at twenty knots. It's got two MTU-60 825-hp engines, a couple of generators and plenty of water storage capacity. The way it's configured, it'll easily accommodate all ten of you, but you'll have to double up or hot rack it when it comes to sleeping." Below decks Hal pointed out the staterooms and the lower helm. Above decks he showed them around the cockpit, galley and saloon.

"Perfect, Hal. This is going to work out just great." Logan ducked his head as they returned to the cockpit. Hal spent another thirty minutes with the team going over the instrumentation in the cockpit and then they were done.

Stepping back onto the dock, Hal turned back to the group. "We get most of our annual precipitation between November and March. The forecast for the next couple of days looks pretty good though. It's going to be mild, highs in the low seventies and lows around fifty-five. The water temperature's about sixty degrees, so it might be a little cool if you decide to go swimming. If you run into any problems, you can get me on marine radio VHF channel 09, or try my cell phone." Waving goodbye, Hal walked back up the dock towards the marina offices.

"All right, people, let's get going. Stoddard's got the most time in boats and is probably the best qualified to pilot the Sea Knight, so he's got the conn. Let's plot a course that'll take us west and then north; we don't want to attract any attention from our buddies at Coronado."

As Stoddard maneuvered the Sea Knight out of its slip, he eased by magnificent motor and sailing yachts moored in and around the Quivira Basin. Once clear of the Basin, Stoddard set a course due west, heading out to sea.

"Will you look at that?" Logan gestured past the Sea Knight's port bow to an aircraft carrier churning toward the open seas, slicing through the waves as it left the confines of San Diego harbor in its wake. Grabbing a pair of binoculars, Logan focused on the ship. "It's a Nimitz Class. Wait a minute." He adjusted the focus wheel. "It's The Gold Eagle, the USS Carl Vinson."

"I was on the Vinson when we buried Osama Bin Laden at sea," said Wellington. "That was something else. You want to talk about a hallelujah moment."

"Our brothers on Seal Team 6 did something special when they put that bastard down. It's just too bad it took us so long to find him. Damn Pakistanis were hiding him all along. Don't mess with my man, though. We'll get your ass eventually. Hoorah!" Delray did a little war dance on the deck and then collapsed in laughter.

Over the next two days and nights the team practiced inflating the F470 and launching it from the Sea Knight. At 265 pounds fully inflated, it wasn't exactly light, but proved manageable, even in the tight confines of the Sea Knight's aft deck. They devised a system for inflating the Zodiac while allowing it to feed over the stern and into the water. After practicing dozens of times they could inflate the boat, mount the engine, load up, and be underway in seven minutes. The F470 is built to be super-buoyant, making it reliable in high seas.

Zahir hung right in there with the rest of the guys through all of it. She was nauseated on their first day out and became seasick in a bad swell, but after that she seemed to find her sea legs. Logan found himself admiring her for her pluck.

On their second night out, the team did three practice runs into shore. They picked a spot two miles west of Blacks Beach, just south of Torrey Pines and ran the Zodiac in full throttle. The Seals showed the Rangers how to straddle the Zodiac's gunwale in order to reduce their silhouette on the water. Fully loaded with nine people, it took them ten minutes to get to shore.

"I think we're in good shape people." Logan was helping Gomez and Wellington deflate the Zodiac and get it stowed. "One thing I've been thinking about, and the past two days has solidified my thinking on this, is that one of us is going to have to stay with the mother ship when we infiltrate the base. There's too much at stake getting us launched properly, and more importantly being there for the recovery operation once we're done. I want the confidence that my guy is going to be there and has our back." He didn't get any arguments from anyone, but Logan could tell from the looks in their eyes, that nobody wanted to be the one riding this operation out on the mother ship.

At daybreak they pointed the prow towards Quivira Basin. They would be splitting up for a few days of R&R

and then would each fly separately into London, where they would meet per pre-arranged plan on December 2. Logan surveyed the team as Stoddard nosed the Sea Knight into its slip. They were coming together as a team. He was confident they would be successful. And every day the image of Barzin Ghabel was becoming just a little bit clearer in his mind.

Chapter 19

Nayef Al Subaie lit his Cohiba Siglo VI, drawing on it as he formulated a response to Logan's question. The two men were reclining in deep leather armchairs, the type found in turn of the century private men's clubs, at an upscale cigar bar in Boston's north end.

It had been two days since Logan had returned from his trip out west. He had just finished providing Nayef with details of the team's activities over the past two weeks and had asked him how preparations for their arrival in Kuwait on December 5th were going.

"Everything's on track for your arrival on the 5th. Your plan to have everyone fly into London on U.S. passports and then travel into Kuwait separately on alias passports was a good idea. Thamir feels that it will enhance operational security by lowering the team's profile before the operation.

"Also, after it's all over, it will be much more difficult for the Iranians to go back and do any kind of meaningful damage assessment. They won't have anything to go on. You have to understand that anything that enhances operational security and deniability makes Thamir's job a lot easier. By the way, I had a meeting with Millie earlier today on a business matter and she told me that she was recusing herself from any matters involving our firm until this is all over."

"Smart on her part. It wouldn't be good for Huber, Steele and O'Reilly if our operation were to become public knowledge and one of their associates turns out to be linked to both of us. I'll bet her partners would be more than a little concerned if they knew about this."

"That's one reason we've taken the precautions we have." Nayef signaled their waiter for the bill and lowered his voice. "Thamir tells me that our intelligence sources are reporting an up-tick in Iranian military units' readiness this week. From SIGINT and IMINT, he's seen more Iranian warships patrolling in and around the Strait of Hormuz and north to the area around Kharg Island. Analytical reporting that we get from the U.S. indicates that it's likely a response to increased international criticism of their nuclear program, especially tough language from the Israeli and U.S. governments."

"Was there anything in those reports on Bandar Deylam?" Logan sat up straight and drummed his fingers on the coffee table.

"No, nothing was reported. But I don't find that so unusual. The Iranians must feel that the base is an unknown quantity to the outside world. Of course, they should know that the more foreign fighters they train there, the greater the possibility is that someone will be captured and reveal details of the base to his captors."

"If anything else comes up let me know. I'll be here one more day and then I'm off for London. I've got contact instructions for your man in London. You said he's already got the passports there?"

"Yes. I saw them before we had them couriered over. They did a really good job. Oh, that reminds me. Thamir asked me to mention that everyone should sign their passports as soon as they get them. If you will be distributing them, you might want to suggest that they practice signing their alias several times before signing the actual document. There will also be some pocket litter to go with each passport to bolster your alias identities."

"Thanks for the reminder. It's the little things that can trip you up. Can you imagine that you forget to sign your passport, and when the immigration officer calls you on it you freeze because you forgot how to sign the name? Nightmare! Oh, Nayef, before I forget. Please tell your uncle that the offshore banking arrangements he put together are working like a charm. I don't know how he got that set up so fast, but all of our charges have gone through without a hitch.

I'm keeping good accountings of our expenses, and we can go over that whenever he wants."

Both men stood, and shook hands. Nayef planned to fly down to New York the next day for business meetings and then back to Kuwait the following day.

"Safe travels, Logan. I look forward to seeing you in Kuwait City on the 5th."

"Likewise. See you then."

Logan zipped up his down jacket and headed in the direction of Stillman Street. He was on his way over to Millie's to have dinner along with Ryan and Zahir. He recalled that there was a good wine store in the next block and decided to pick up a couple of bottles of Cotes du Rhone to go with their meal. Behind the cashier a TV was playing a story about another high school shooting, this time in Indiana. Three students had been killed in the high school cafeteria by one of their classmates, who, by all accounts, had a troubled family history and had been a victim of bullying. Logan stared at the images of grief-stricken parents, students and teachers. Their anguished faces brought back memories of Cooper's funeral and the emotion of that day.

Logan let himself into Millie's condo and could hear voices coming from the living room. Millie, Ryan and Zahir were gathered by an expanse of glass looking out over the Zakim Bridge, whose purple lights on triangular cable spans conjured up the image of shimmering petticoats against the night sky.

"Logan!" Millie caught sight of him and rushed over to envelope her brother in a bear hug, burying her face in his chest. She pulled back and studied his features. "Zahir was just telling us that you had a good two weeks out west."

"Yeah. It was a good trip. It gave everyone a chance to show off their stuff, and to get back up to speed in some areas that may have become a little rusty. The team really came together. We're all heading out tomorrow for phase two, another couple of weeks working out in Kuwait, before we go into Iran."

Logan walked over and clasped Ryan's outstretched hand, then turned to Zahir and gave her a hug. He noticed Millie's raised eyebrow, and realized that she was surprised by his show of affection. When they had left Boston two weeks ago, he had barely been civil to Zahir, but their time together in Arizona and California had changed that. They had bonded in a way that he never would have anticipated after their rocky first meeting at Cooper's interment at St. Augustine's Cemetery. He had come to trust her judgment and admire her intelligence and spunk.

"Dinner's almost ready." Millie had prepared one of their mother's favorite winter recipes, baked gnocchi served with chard and white beans. "Zahir, would you mind lighting the candles in the dining room, and Ryan, could you slice that loaf of Italian bread you brought?"

Logan watched Millie bustling about getting everyone organized, and realized how much like their mother she was. Going into the kitchen, he rummaged through a drawer looking for a corkscrew.

"Zahir, tell Ryan and Logan your good news." Millie moved around the dining room table pouring water into glasses.

Zahir's face brightened. "It's been a busy couple of days since I got back. Let's see. Where to start? I put an offer on that loft on Bennington Street that I was looking at and it was accepted. Boston University has firmed up their offer of a teaching position beginning in January." She paused and looked shyly around the table. "And finally, I went for a pre-natal exam at the university hospital, and everything looks normal."

Everyone started talking at once. "How'd you get all of that done in two days?" Logan shook his head in admiration.

"So did Boston University cover your medical expenses?" Ryan asked.

"No, I won't be eligible for their plan until sometime in the spring. The good news though is that I was able to retain my DOD medical benefits for six months so there won't be a lapse in coverage."

"I'm so happy for you, Zahir. Everything seems to be working out. We should have a house-warming for you when you move into your apartment." Millie came around to Zahir's side of the table and gave her a hug.

Zahir bowed her head and whispered, "I'm just so grateful for the kindness you've all shown me. After Cooper —" Her voice cracked, but she regained her composure. "After Cooper died and my family disowned me I didn't know where to turn. But now I can see a future for myself."

She turned to Logan. "Logan, you don't know how much it means to me to be going to Iran with you. Thank you for giving me this opportunity."

The friends talked for another hour before Logan decided to call it a night. He and Zahir would be flying separately to London the following evening, after which he would travel to Paris and Zahir would transit through Brussels. They were at a crucial point in the operation and any security gaffes now could undermine everything they had done to date and jeopardize their planning going forward.

"Be careful, big brother." Millie gave Logan a fierce hug. "I know this is what you do, and you're good at it, but it's still dangerous. I love you."

Logan hugged her back. "I love you too, Mills. See you in a couple of weeks."

Turning to Zahir, Logan gave her a farewell hug. He was surprised when her soft lips brushed his cheek. Looking into her green eyes he felt a slight stirring, but dismissed it as the wine talking. "See you in London, Zahir. Have a safe trip."

Ryan and Logan drove back to Ryan's Beacon Hill apartment. "Thanks for putting me up, Ryan. When I get back from this trip, I'm going to find some permanent digs."

"Don't worry about it. You've got a lot on your plate right now. Just take care of this business and don't even give apartment hunting a second thought. I may be gone when you get up in the morning. I'm having breakfast with the

D.A. I think it's his way of reaching out to the younger attorneys. I'll see you when you get back. Good luck over there."

Chapter 20

Logan was relieved that his flight out of Logan International the next evening was only forty-five minutes late. De-icing crews had serviced their Boeing 777 aircraft twice in that time, and they were stacked up behind eight other planes waiting to take off. Once he had settled into his business class seat, Logan ordered a double shot single malt scotch, neat, which he figured would take the edge off of his emotions. He savored the peaty taste of the fifteen-year-old whisky and bantered with the flight attendant. Once they were airborne he reclined his seat, and in a matter of minutes had dozed off.

He was surprised to awake to the sound of the captain announcing Delta Flight 0270's imminent arrival at London's Heathrow Airport. Twenty minutes later they were rolling up to their gate. Logan retrieved his carry-on and suitcase, and after clearing customs and immigration without incident, found his way to the Heathrow Express kiosk, where he purchased a one-way express ticket to Waterloo Station. He paid in cash, to avoid the paper trail of credit cards.

Logan had a reservation in his alias name, Logan Campbell, at a hotel in London's West End, less than a mile from Paddington Station. But before checking in he needed to meet Nayef's contact at eleven-thirty near the renowned Waterloo Clock, a four-faced timepiece on the main concourse at Waterloo Station. They had made contingency plans to meet then, and if for some reason one of them didn't show up, to keep trying every two hours thereafter.

Logan also had a cell phone number he could call, but he preferred to stay off the phone. He recognized the Kuwaiti from Nayef's description, a stout Arab, thirty-something with thinning black hair and a goatee, standing at the appointed location. They chatted for no more that two minutes and the Kuwaiti passed Logan a sealed manila envelope containing ten sets of alias documents.

After bidding him goodbye, Logan found a men's room near the Waterloo Bridge entrance to the station. He deposited thirty pence in the turnstile and located an empty stall. After shifting his bags around so that he could close the door, Logan opened the manila envelope and thumbed through the alias documents until he found his own. He withdrew the passport, and examined it briefly to check for accuracy. The deep blue cover depicted the Royal Arms of Canada in the center of the page. Above the insignia was the word "Canada" and below it the word "Passport" in both English and French.

After making certain to sign his Logan Campbell alias, he placed the passport in his coat pocket. He deposited his own passport, his true name credit cards and all other identifying documentation into a separate envelope, sealed it, and locked it in a bag that he had brought to check at the luggage consignment facility. When that was done, he took a taxi from Waterloo Station to the St. Pancras International Train Station and purchased a ticket for the eight a.m. Eurostar to Paris on December 4th.

"Passport please." The ticket clerk gave his Canadian passport a perfunctory glance and returned it to him.

Logan realized, as he took it back from her, that he had been holding his breath, and hoped his nervousness didn't show. Apparently he passed muster because the next thing he heard was:

"Have a nice trip, Mr. Campbell. I hope you enjoy your stay in Paris."

Logan caught a taxi in front of the station and fifteen minutes later pulled up to his West End hotel. Check-in was routine, and in a matter of minutes he had settled into his suite. He looked at his watch and saw that it was two-thirty. There was about a half hour until John Gomez was due to meet him in his room. A few minutes before three, there was a knock on the door.

"Hey, bro, good to see you." Gomez entered Logan's room and wrapped him in a big hug. "It was a long haul, man. I was in Chico visiting my parents and had to get down to San Francisco. That was no big deal, but it was like ten hours from San Francisco to here. Man, I'm beat."

"Yeah, West Coast to Europe definitely sucks. My flight wasn't too bad. Six hours and some change. I had a double scotch when I boarded, and I was out for the count." Logan filled Gomez in on his meeting with their Kuwaiti contact. "The Kuwaitis did a great job on these passports. I've already used mine three times, and not even a blink from the Brits."

Logan divvied up the passports, with Gomez taking four plus his own, and Logan keeping four.

"All right, I've got Tyler, Barbiari, Wellington and Wozolski." Gomez examined his own passport, signed it and placed them all into a backpack. He stuck his true name passport in his jacket pocket.

"Right, and I've got Delray, Jones, Stoddard and Zahir. We've got staggered times for them to come to our rooms beginning at four o'clock and then on the hour after that. You better get going because you still have to check in to your hotel."

"Yeah, I'm about twenty minutes on the tube from here. I should be all right. I just have to unload my own passport first. Any trouble finding a public locker?"

"No, they're in all the train stations."

"OK. I'll see you in Kuwait."

Less than a minute after Gomez had left, Logan heard the screeching of brakes and a crash. Looking out his window onto Regent Street he was horrified to see the mangled body of John Gomez lying on the ground. A double-decker bus had come to a stop in the middle of the street at a sharp angle away from the curb. Logan raced down to the street, his heart pounding.

A crowd was already beginning to gather, but a quick look told Logan all he needed to know. Gomez was dead. Logan scanned the crowd and spotted Gomez's backpack, lying on the ground, twenty feet from the body. If he could just get to it before anyone focused on it, maybe he could salvage something from this horrible turn of events. Easing over to where the backpack lay, Logan picked it up and began walking away from the crowd.

"Hey you!" a voice shouted.

Logan didn't turn around, but kept moving away from the scene. He heard footsteps following him, and broke into a jog and then a run. He took evasive turns down several side streets and kept moving until the sound of his pursuer had faded in the distance. His heart was beating and his armpits were sweaty. On a side street he removed the remaining alias documents from the backpack, placed them inside his coat, and stuffed the empty backpack into a dumpster.

Then he flagged down a passing taxi and had the driver take a circuitous route away from the area. When he was some distance away from the hotel, he changed taxis and drove for several minutes before he changed again. When he was certain that he wasn't being followed, he told his driver to drop him off on Marylebone Road, a block from the rear entrance to his hotel.

As Logan came into the lobby area, the concierge noticed him. "You missed a bit of excitement out here a short while back."

"What happened?"

"Poor bloke was run over in front of the hotel. A Yankee. An eyewitness says he came out of the hotel and walked straight into a double-decker bus. Happens all the time. Yanks forget to look to the right before they cross. And then, to add insult to injury some bloody twit stole the bloke's hold-all. Bob's your uncle. Poor bloke comes over for a bit of a holiday, and gets himself killed and robbed to boot."

"That's terrible."

"First you heard of it?

"Yes. I was out for a walk over in Kensington Garden and just returned."

"The police will be going over to Grosvenor Square. That's where the American Embassy is. It seems the poor bloke just got here today."

"How do you know that?" Logan wondered what else the concierge might have learned.

"I'd just finished escorting a VIP to his suite, and went down to the street about the time the police arrived. They found the poor bloke's passport in his pocket, and I heard the officer say that he had just processed through immigration this morning."

"We drive on the same side in Canada as the Americans. I'm going to be really careful to look both ways before I cross." Logan returned to his room and looked at his watch. It was a quarter to five. His mind raced. It was too late to do anything about Gomez. Once American Citizen Services at the Embassy came into play they would be able to track down Gomez's family in Chico and make the appropriate arrangements. He'd contact the family after this was all over, so they wouldn't be left wondering what the hell John was doing in London.

Logan went through a mental checklist of what he and Gomez had covered in their meeting. Gomez didn't have anything incriminating on his person. If the police had retrieved his backpack it would be all over. But they hadn't, and the team still had a chance to move forward with the operation. They had a contingency plan for missed meetings. Since Gomez would not be at the prearranged hotel to meet Tyler at five o'clock, Tyler would cycle forward to nine o'clock for the alternate and Barbiari would show up at six as scheduled.

Stoddard was due to meet him in his room in fifteen minutes. Logan decided that he would send Stoddard over to the other hotel to fill in for Gomez as best he could. It wasn't ideal, but he would have to catch Tyler, Barbiari, Wellington and Wozolski on the street before they entered the hotel, since he wouldn't have a room there.

There was a knock on the door. Stoddard had flown in from the East Coast and he looked pretty fresh. Logan filled him in on the events of the past couple of hours. "So I'm going to need you to get over to Gomez's hotel and stake out a spot where you can observe the others coming through. Just give them their alias docs, remind them to sign the passports and make sure they unload all their true name documentation first thing before checking into their hotels."

"Man, that's a bummer about Gomez. Shit. He makes it through two tours in Iraq only to get creamed by a bus in London. That's just not right." Stoddard shook his head and sighed. "So we're still a go?"

"No question losing Gomez hurts. Like you said, two combat tours in Iraq. He definitely knew his stuff. But I built in some redundancy when I put the team together. I'll probably pull off one of the breachers and move him over to shooter to replace Gomez. We'll be OK." Logan spoke with more conviction than he actually felt at the moment. But now was not the time for self-doubt.

After Stoddard left, the others came through as scheduled. To a person they were devastated upon hearing about Gomez. Zahir, who was last to come through, took it the hardest. She and Gomez were friends and had served together in Iraq. He had been out on patrol with her the morning that Cooper had been killed. She began to sob. "Why John? It's so senseless. He was only twenty-seven."

Logan sat down next to her and held her as her emotions poured forth. He didn't say anything, knowing words could not ease the pain she was feeling. She wept until exhausted, falling asleep at last on his shoulder. Logan carried her into the bedroom, removed her shoes and settled her into the bed. He stood there looking at her for a moment and then bent down to kiss her on the cheek.

After he had made up the rollaway bed in the other room, he climbed in, hands clasped behind his head, and thought about the day. They had been dealt a blow with Gomez's death. That was for sure. It had been a close call, but then life had been a series of close calls. In two days they'd be in Kuwait. And then the countdown would really begin.

Chapter 21

"I like your idea of working more closely with the Taliban, Tahmouress." Colonel Barzin Ghabel and Major Tahmouress Samadi were sitting in Ghabel's conference room going over the first draft of a proposal to bolster the Qods Force role in Afghanistan that Samadi had put together.

"Of course, you know that Tehran has been behind the coalition government in Kabul from the beginning. Hamid Karzai would never have been able to form his government if we hadn't put political pressure on our allies in the Northern Alliance, the Shias and the Tajiks, to support it."

"Yes, I know. I also know that our support for Afghanistan's central government hasn't been only political. We've pledged hundreds of millions of dollars in aid to Afghanistan. Iran may in fact be one of the biggest, if not the biggest, aid donor." Samadi crushed his cigarette in an ashtray. "That's why I'm a little apprehensive that Tehran will find our idea to support the Taliban out of synch with current policy."

Ghabel stroked his chin. "It does have all the evidence of being contradictory, Tahmouress, but let me tell you why it will work. If you go back ten years, you will find, as inconceivable as it seems, that U.S. and Iranian policy goals for Afghanistan were not dissimilar. The U.S. was pushing for a strong central government in Afghanistan from the beginning, as were we. But since then the U.S has taken a very belligerent attitude towards Iran. They continue to harp on our nuclear program, and have imposed so many sanctions that they have our balls in a vise." Ghabel grimaced at the image.

"A few years ago, at the urging of the Supreme Leader, the

Revolutionary Guard Corps began funneling money to the Taliban specifically to enhance their capabilities against the Americans and NATO forces. As you know there's a NATO base in Herat, and our military advisors have been instrumental in Taliban successes against those forces. There are a handful of IRGC military advisors working throughout western Afghanistan."

"I didn't know we had military advisors working with the Taliban inside Afghanistan."

"Obviously it's a sensitive subject, so it's been kept closehold. General Salehi himself told me about it." Ghabel called out to his orderly in the adjoining office.

"Yes, Colonel?"

"Sergeant Yavani, type these recommendations into a final proposal under my signature. The message should be directed to General Salehi, Eyes Only. Classification is Top Secret. I would like to have it for my final review as soon as possible."

Sergeant Yavani took the document and gave it a cursory exam. "I should have it ready for you in an hour or so, sir."

"Thank you, Sergeant."

Ghabel looked at his watch and turned back to Major Samadi. "So you and I are going to meet one of the Al Qaeda operatives that's been released from house arrest in Borazjan this afternoon. Is that right?"

"Yes, Colonel. I've done some background checks on him. His name is Mustafa Al Adel. He was originally trained by that Saudi bomber Ibrahim Al Asiri several years ago. He had a few big successes early on but then had to lay low because the CIA had put a bounty on his head."

"What were these so-called big successes?"

"The first thing I found had to do with his involvement in a 2007 attack in Pakistan against the French Embassy. This was a car bomb attack, sixteen people killed and many more injured. Then in 2009 he actually trained the Jordanian double agent who went into Forward Operating Base Chapman in Khost, Afghanistan, killing seven CIA officers."

"No wonder the CIA was after him."

"After that, Al Qaeda decided it would be wise to move

him out of Afghanistan and insert him into Iraq. He was instrumental in a series of November 2010 bombing attacks in Baghdad that resulted in over 100 deaths."

"Impressive resume. So how did he end up here under house arrest?"

"Al Qaeda got word that the CIA had an informant in Baghdad who was about to finger Al Adel. They moved quickly to get him out of the country. A few days later he showed up here and was placed under house arrest. He was just released two days ago."

Ghabel rubbed his eyes. "OK, so where are we going to meet this guy?"

"There's a tea house on Bimarestan Street that should be quiet in the afternoon. I told Al Adel to be there at three. Perhaps we can leave as soon as Sergeant Yavani has finished typing the Afghanistan proposal and you've had a chance to review it."

"That's fine. I'll drive." Ghabel preferred to drive because it was about eighty miles to Borazjan, and if they went in Major Samadi's 2006 diesel Samand it would take forever.

Ghabel and Samadi departed the base at one-thirty. About twenty miles south of Bandar Deylam, the highway jogs west where it parallels the coast to Bandar Ganaveh, then veers back inland to Borazjan. Along the coast they could see ships plying the Gulf, but once they turned inland towards Borazjan the scenery changed dramatically. Farms surround Borazjan and in the spring and summer wheat fields and date palms flourish. Families living on small farms cultivate melons and sesame seeds there as well. But today the fields were barren.

South of the city the fields give way to an expanse of desert salt flats extending all the way to Bushehr City, fifty miles southwest. In its earliest days Borazjan was situated on the Persian Gulf, but the Gulf waters had receded over the centuries and the coastline is now at Bushehr City.

Just before three, Ghabel pulled up before the *chaikhaneh,* a Persian tea house, on Bimarestan Street. Going inside he and Major Samadi found Al Adel seated with a view to the entrance on a low-rise platform covered with a luxurious brick red Baluch tribal carpet and cushions. In the middle of the room an immense brass samovar heated water for the chai. There were few other patrons at that hour, and after ordering chai and a water pipe, the three men settled back against the cushions.

Ghabel studied Al Adel. The Al Qaeda bomber looked none the worse for his house arrest ordeal. He was of slight build with brown eyes and short black hair, and wore a neatly trimmed beard. As Ghabel understood it, the Al Qaeda detainees had enjoyed a comparatively carefree house arrest. They'd been given sufficient funds to purchase life's necessities, had access to decent medical care, and had been given ample reading material and videos to help them wile away their days. They had not been permitted to have Internet or cell phone access out of concern that the Americans, who would then have had one more excuse to attack Iran, could track their communications.

"So, Mr. Al Adel, Major Samadi has informed me of his conversation with you and that you might be interested in helping us out."

Al Adel had placed a piece of rock sugar between his teeth and was sipping the deep reddish-brown tea through it. He placed the glass teacup back on its saucer, taking his time before answering Ghabel.

"It may be possible. Much has happened with Al Qaeda since I was forced to leave Iraq a year ago. Osama Bin Laden and many others in leadership roles have been martyred by the Americans. It's probably only a matter of time before Al Zawahiri meets a similar fate. Al Qaeda has always been a dispersed movement, but the key central role that Bin Laden played guaranteed an unwavering strategic direction for Jihad. Now the brothers on the Arabian Peninsula, the Maghreb, Iraq and Africa are all on their own. Of course, they know what the Emir's vision was – to establish an Islamic worldwide Caliphate. To do so we must do away with man-made laws and establish Sharia law throughout the world."

"Well, we've seen a breakdown in discipline amongst

the Al Qaeda in Iraq operatives. I'm not saying it's because they've lost sight of Bin Laden's vision, but it used to be that we could rely on them to carry out IED attacks without having to hold their hands throughout the operation." Ghabel poured more tea into Al Adel's cup. "We would give them targeting packages and assembled IEDs. For their part they would put together the actual operational plan and have their men execute it."

"A couple of months ago we missed an opportunity in Ramadi," Major Samadi interrupted. "We were positioned to take out a whole American Special Forces platoon, and the triggerman on the IED team completely misjudged the timing of the detonation. All we got was the platoon leader."

"You know many of these Al Qaeda fighters are poorly educated. Most of them are foreign fighters with family or tribal connections. That's where their loyalties lie. They're not sitting around at night talking about the strategic direction of Al Qaeda. How is it that you envision me helping you, Colonel?" Al Adel placed a square of flavored tobacco in the water pipe and signaled their waiter to bring over a disk of the quick starting hookah charcoal.

"We have a base near Bandar Deylam where we conduct research and development on new IED technologies. We also have capacity there to train foreign fighter groups. Typically we'll bring a group in and spend a week or so with them, familiarizing them with new equipment, going over tactics, and rehearsing their operation," Ghabel said.

"In a couple of weeks we'll be bringing in that group of Al Qaeda foreign fighters that Major Samadi just spoke about for some remedial training. We thought you could spend some time with us. Take a look at what we're doing and work with our instructors and the Al Qaeda foreign fighter trainees. What do you think?"

"I'm a bit rusty, as you know, Colonel. It's been a year since I've done any explosives work." Al Adel paused before continuing. "When I was in Afghanistan, I had the pleasure of meeting one of your colleagues. He was a Qods Force major who was there in an advisory capacity. Major Chavoshian."

"I don't recognize the name." Ghabel looked at Major Samadi, who shook his head in the negative.

"No matter. Anyway, my point is that I was very impressed with his professionalism, and he was actually helpful to me with something that I was working on."

"You mean the CIA operation?"

"Oh, you know about that?"

"We have our sources." Colonel Ghabel smiled. "So I take it that is a yes?"

Smiling, Al Adel nodded in the affirmative. "Yes, Colonel. I look forward to working with you."

"Good. Stay in touch with Major Samadi. If you could plan to travel to Bandar Deylam within the next week, we'll get you oriented and ready to work with that group of foreign fighters. Housing on the base is tight. It's really just temporary student housing, so Major Samadi will help you get set up off base. Let's just see how it goes. If both sides are happy with the arrangement, we'll talk about something more permanent. All right?"

"It's perfect, Colonel. Thank you."

The men shook hands and said goodbye. After leaving the teahouse, Ghabel continued driving up Borazjan's main street past the large modern hospital, in the direction of Borazjan Koroush Castle. Like many of Iran's historic building sites, the castle no longer served as a tribute to Iran's glorious past; for the past several decades it had functioned as a prison.

"Look at that, Tahmouress." Ghabel gestured in the direction of the castle. "No lesser man than Cyrus the Great walked this land and directed that a castle be built here. It disturbs me that in our haste to build a new Islamic Republic, we sometimes lose sight of our past." Realizing that he sounded a bit maudlin, Ghabel changed the subject. "So, what was your impression of our young Al Qaeda bomber?"

"I thought he was a bit intense. We won't know how he'll do for sure until we see him in action. But with his resume I don't think we have too much to be worried about."

On the way out of Borazjan they passed by a lofty grain silo, built by the Russians in the early 1970s, and reputed to be the largest grain silo in southern Iran. There, grain produced on the privately owned farms that dot the countryside around Borazjan is transported for storage. Other farmers grind their grain at the Al Zahra or Borazjan flour mills in town.

Thirty minutes outside of Borazjan, Ghabel's cell phone vibrated. He noted from the caller ID displayed on the screen that it was his wife. "Hello, Azar. How are you?" From the choked sobs on the other end, he knew that something was wrong. "What is it, darling?" He gave Major Samadi an anxious look.

"Barzin, I just spoke with Mama. Papa had another heart attack at home this afternoon and died just before they got him to the hospital."

"Oh, Azar, I'm so sorry. But what happened? I thought he was recovering nicely. The doctors said that his prognosis was very good."

"I know. All he was supposed to do was rest at home. I think he was also taking some blood thinner medication. Mama said that he complained this morning of feeling very tired, and that he had a dull ache in his left arm. He didn't want her to call the doctor right away, but when the pain started to move from his arm to his chest he became worried. By then it was too late."

"How is your mother handling this?"

"She seemed very calm on the phone. The ambulance driver would not let her ride with them, so she had to drive to the hospital. By the time she got there he was already dead."

"I'll be home in an hour. When do you want to go to Shiraz?"

"As soon as possible."

"All right. Can you check to see how soon we can get a flight out of Bushehr City? It's over five hundred miles to Shiraz so driving is out of the question. Plus we need to get there as soon as possible."

After he had finished speaking with Azar, Ghabel looked at Major Samadi. "You heard all of that, Tahmouress. Azar's father passed away this afternoon. I have to go to Shiraz for a couple of days. You'll be in charge during my absence. If you could send a message to Tehran when we get back, and let them know what's happening, I would appreciate it."

"Yes, of course, Colonel. My condolences to your family."

"Thank you, Tahmouress. He was only in his seventies. As an academic, he didn't have a difficult life, but I think he pushed himself too hard with his teaching load, writing and research." They drove the rest of the way in silence.

After dropping Major Samadi off at the base, Ghabel returned home and found that Azar had already packed a bag for him. He held her tightly for a moment, stroking her hair as she cried. Once she had settled down he released her and carried their bags out to the car.

"'I got reservations on a flight out of Bushehr City at eight o'clock. That puts us into Shiraz around nine-thirty."

Their flight departed on time, despite severe weather thirty minutes outside of Shiraz. There was one nail-biting moment when the aircraft seemed to drop interminably as it was buffeted by powerful winds. Ghabel could feel the anxiety in Azar's body as she clenched his arm and gaped around the cabin. A few moments later they cleared the storm and for the rest of the flight enjoyed a smooth ride.

After retrieving their bags in the baggage claim area, Azar and Ghabel hailed a taxi to take them to her parents' apartment. The apartment was within walking distance of Shiraz University, and when they arrived it was past ten-thirty. Azar's mother was waiting for them and when she saw her daughter, she burst into tears. Azar comforted her, and when her tears had subsided she led them into the dining room where her husband's corpse lay in repose on the dining room table. All of the lights were on and lighted candles had been placed around the body. A Koran lay on his chest.

"Oh, Papa." Azar began to wail and threw herself to the

ground at her father's feet. Her tortured cries wracked her body, and as her mother hastened over to comfort her, she too began to wail.

Sniffling and dabbing at her eyes, Azar's mother composed herself. "It was too late in the day for his body to be moved to the cemetery, so they brought him back here. I have arranged for the body washer to come tomorrow morning to take him there. Barzin –"

Anticipating her question, Ghabel replied. "Of course, Mama, I will accompany him to assure that the washing is performed according to custom." The three of them kept vigil during the night as is customary to prevent evil spirits from attacking the body.

The next morning Ghabel accompanied the body washer to Hafez Cemetery. His father-in-law's corpse was placed on a tile table where three different washes consisting of a cleansing solution, camphor, and fresh water were performed. According to traditional practices, each wash was supposed to be performed several times, but in modern times this had given way to just three washes altogether.

As the body washer dried the corpse he placed cotton balls in all of its orifices while chanting traditional prayers. "Allah, this was a pious man, yet despite his devotion he surely offended you during his lifetime. Please forgive him for these sins that he knowingly or unknowingly committed."

Ghabel then helped the body washer place the corpse on the *kafan*, a large white cotton cloth. Before shrouding the entire corpse, the washer took strips of cotton and wrapped them around the eyes and the genitals.

"How do we fold the kafan around the body?" Ghabel asked, holding one end.

"We just wrap it around him like so." The washer demonstrated how to fold the kafan so that it covered the entire corpse. "Now, we'll use these pieces of rope to secure the kafan at the head and feet."

When they had finished, the two of them lifted the corpse off of the table and carried it over to a simple wood coffin lying on the floor. Rather than place it directly into the coffin, the men repeatedly picked the body up and set it back down on the ground while chanting verses from the Koran and shouting, "Allah is great!" The fourth time, they placed the body inside the coffin. Ghabel remembered that this ancient ritual was supposed to symbolize the reluctance of the deceased to leave this life.

Azar and her mother arrived at eleven o'clock for the interment. There would be a memorial service in three days, but today it was a small group in attendance – just the three of them, and Azar's uncles and their families. It was freezing outside, and the gravedigger worked hard to break through the hard soil. He dropped down into the hole he had excavated as Ghabel and one of the uncles repeated the ritual raising and lowering of the corpse. On the fourth raising, they removed the body from the coffin and handed it down to the gravedigger below.

The gravedigger eased the body over onto its right side, facing Mecca and placed a brick under the head to support it. He then pulled back part of the kafan covering the face. At sight of her father's face Azar broke down, and she and her mother sobbed in each other's arms.

Once the gravedigger was satisfied with the position of the body, he clambered out of the grave and family members sprinkled rose water onto the body and took turns tossing frozen clumps of earth into the burial pit. The frigid air had everyone shivering. After the gravedigger finished filling the grave, and prayers were read by the professional prayer reader Ghabel had hired, they turned and walked slowly back to their cars.

"Azar, I will stay for the memorial service, but I must return to Bandar Deylam after that. You should stay as long as your mother needs you."

"I want to be here for the Hafteh and Cheleh commemorations, so it will be over a month. I'll see how she is doing after that. Perhaps she will want to come and stay with us for awhile."

On the day of the memorial service, friends, students,

colleagues and relatives gathered at a university reception hall. Azar's father was a popular and respected professor, and the room was filled to overflowing. On a table in the middle of the hall was a framed photo of Azar's father in his youth. Two large vases of sympathy flowers – blue hydrangeas, lilies and crème roses – stood on either side. Men and women took their seats on opposite sides of the hall as a well-known mullah, a friend from the professor's college days, offered prayers and a homily. At the conclusion of these rites, simple refreshments in the form of tea, halva, apricots, dates and sunflower seeds were offered to the guests.

It was late afternoon by the time Ghabel, Azar and her mother returned home. The apartment felt strangely empty and Azar appeared despondent as she wandered about picking up her father's books and putting them back down. Ghabel watched her in silence, knowing that she was grappling with her loss. She saw him looking at her, heaved a sigh and shook her head.

"I always knew this day would come, but I'm still too shocked for words." She sat down next to him and put her head on his shoulder. She hadn't slept for two days, and in a moment was dozing there. Ghabel stroked her hair and whispered in her ear.

"Everything will be fine, my fire maiden. Everything will be fine."

Chapter 22

Logan made note of the time as he exited Covent Garden Station. It was five o'clock and he was running late for his meeting with Norm Stoddard in London's west end. He had gauged how long it would take on the underground from his hotel to Covent Garden, but hadn't anticipated the delay of a bomb scare when a passenger mistakenly left a package on the train two stops before Covent Garden Station. Logan looked up and saw the address he was searching for – 33 Rose Street.

Squinting in the dim light he could just make out the sign for the Lamb and Flag on the well tended Tudor building, reputed to be the oldest pub in London. Rumor had it that their operating license dated all the way back to 1623 when King James I sat on the throne.

Stoddard was already seated in one of the comfortable looking wooden booths cushioned with dark leather seatbacks.

"Sorry I'm late, man. I got held up because of a bomb scare in the underground." Logan took in the wood-paneled room with bare pine floorboards. It had a charming country English look. A fireplace in the back bar area was blazing.

"No problem, Logan. I went ahead and got started without you." Stoddard was nursing a pint of Guinness. "You wouldn't believe what I just found out about this beer. See that guy over there?" Stoddard gestured towards a ruddy-cheeked bartender who appeared to be in his early thirties. "Well, he's actually a Guinness draft technician. His job is to go around to all of these pubs and teach the bartenders how to pour Guinness."

Logan looked at the technician more closely, and could just make out his nametag, Patrick O'Callaghan. "Hell of a job Patrick's got."

"So when I ordered this Guinness, he came over and told me what he's doing. The big thing they worry about is over-carbonization, he tells me. They have to keep the gas pressure on their tanks exactly right and make sure they have the right proportion of nitrogen to carbon dioxide. If there's less than seventy-five percent nitrogen, the mixture ends up being over-carbonated. But that's only part of it. He showed me how he does a two-part pour, letting the head settle on the first part before filling up the rest of the glass."

"Damn. Who would have thought so much goes into pouring a glass of beer?" Logan signaled to O'Callaghan to bring him a Guinness too.

"Not just any beer. Guinness. Did you know they've been in business since 1759?"

"No, but I read somewhere that this pub is the oldest one in England, so that means for almost 140 years, people coming here weren't drinking Guinness."

Stoddard did the math in his head and emitted a low whistle. "Are you telling me this place has been here almost 400 years?"

"Yep. 1623."

"Wow."

Logan set his beer down and studied Stoddard for a moment before speaking. "So, Norm, how'd it go yesterday?"

"Mission accomplished. Everyone's all set. I found a coffee shop with a view to the hotel entrance and was able to intercept three of the guys before they went into the hotel. But I initially missed Tyler because he was early and I had gotten up to go to the bathroom. I saw him coming out of the hotel just as I got back to my seat."

"He must have been freaking out, because he'd already been there at five and Gomez wasn't there."

"He was all right. He knew something was up but he figured he'd just stick with the plan. Everybody was bummed about Gomez, though."

"Yeah. You don't know how hard it was for me to leave him out there on the street like that. But I knew that he had his true name passport in his pocket and that once the Embassy got involved, they'd be able to contact his family and take care of everything. We got lucky that I got down there right after it happened and was able to grab his backpack with all those alias documents."

"Yeah, we would have been hosed for sure."

"When are you heading out?"

Stoddard glanced at his watch. "I'm catching a seven o'clock train out of London tonight for Paris, connecting with an overnight train, the Francisco de Goya, to Madrid. Then tomorrow I've got a flight out of Madrid-Barajas Airport for Kuwait City late in the morning."

Logan looked at his watch. "You better get going. It's almost six now. Don't worry about this. I'll get the bill. And, Norm," Logan rose from his seat and gave Stoddard a man hug. "Thanks again for stepping up yesterday."

"Anytime. See you in Kuwait."

Logan ordered another pint of Guinness and sat back in his seat. It had been a strange couple of days. They had really dodged a bullet with the whole Gomez business. As bad as that was though, it looked like they were going to be all right.

His mind wandered back to Zahir. She had awakened early in the morning and had been embarrassed by her breakdown the night before plus the fact that she was sleeping in his bed.

"It's all right," he'd said. "You and Gomez went back a ways. Being in Iraq together and all that happened with Cooper. There's a lot of emotion in all that."

They'd walked over to Radnor Mews and found a small café serving a full English breakfast. Zahir was not that hungry, and had limited herself to coffee and a muffin. Logan had been famished but looked askance at the eggs, sausage, baked beans and black pudding their waiter had brought him. The food was tasty though, and they had lingered over their coffee, sharing memories of Cooper, until Zahir had to catch her train to Brussels. She had to make a stop at Marble Arch underground station on the way to stash her true name passport and identifying documents.

He had felt that same slight stirring in his loins when Zahir kissed him goodbye. He had filed it away to go back over later. There was too much at stake right now, and he didn't need any distractions.

Logan paid his bill and stepped out of the Lamb and Flag. He pulled his jacket collar up around his neck to ward off the cold and walked back to the Covent Garden underground, where he caught the next train to Paddington Station. When he got back to his hotel, he noticed the concierge that he had spoken with the day before conversing with a rugged looking middle-aged male who gave Logan an appraising look as he walked by.

"Mr. Campbell!"

Logan almost walked past them but with a start realized that the concierge was addressing him. He turned towards the two men and gave the concierge a questioning look. "Yes?"

"This is Inspector Drysdale from Scotland Yard. He's investigating the death of that American yesterday and has been interviewing guests who may have noticed anything out of the ordinary."

"Nice to meet you, Inspector. Logan Campbell. I'm afraid I won't be of much help. I was out for a walk in Kensington Garden when the accident happened and returned after all the excitement was over. Is there something wrong? From what the concierge told me yesterday, I thought the poor guy was hit by a double-decker bus."

"Yes, that's right." Inspector Drysdale paused a moment to relight his pipe and then continued. "We know from hotel video surveillance coverage that the American came into the hotel lobby just before three o'clock and took a lift to one of the upper floors. Which one we're not certain. Unfortunately there is an hour-and-a-half gap in coverage between three-thirty and five because of scheduled maintenance of the video surveillance equipment. When the coverage resumes it does not show the victim coming back down to the lobby.

"We know the precise time of the accident – four-ten p.m. – therefore I assume he left the lobby sometime between four and four-ten. The truly odd thing though is that a by-stander on the street reported that after the poor bloke was struck, someone grabbed the poor fellow's hold-all and made off with it."

"No!"

"It's a fact. I suspect it's a case of pure thievery and nothing else, but one never knows. The odd thing, Mr. Campbell, is that the description that the eyewitness gave of the thief bears a remarkable resemblance to yourself."

"What? That's preposterous. I wasn't anywhere near here." Logan's thoughts zoomed ahead as he contemplated the inspector's words. He wondered if the inspector was baiting him. If it was true that the video system was down when Gomez had departed the hotel, then it was unlikely that they would have caught him hurrying through the lobby right after the accident.

"Well, then. You wouldn't mind if we had a wee look in your room, just to put this to rest?"

"No, not all." Logan figured the risk of having the inspector search his room was minimal. Refusing would only heighten his suspicions. Besides, there was no evidence in the room linking him to Gomez.

Inspector Drysdale spent perhaps twenty minutes going through Logan's room. The only tense moment occurred when he drew back the curtains on the window overlooking Regent Street. He called Logan over to the window and pointed down below. "That's where it happened. If you'd been in your room you might have seen the whole thing."

"I'm glad I wasn't here to see it. It must have been awful. Those double-decker buses are huge. I can't imagine that anyone would survive being struck by one."

"Well, thank you, Mr. Campbell, for your cooperation. Will you be around for a few days if I have any follow-up questions?"

"No, I'm sorry, Inspector, but I'm off to Paris tomorrow. I'm afraid that I wasn't very much help."

After Inspector Drysdale had left, Logan heaved a sigh of relief. That had been a close call. He ran through a mental checklist of all the things that could have gone wrong. The Canadian docs could have been discovered to be fraudulent. His cover story could have had gaps in it. The hotel's video surveillance could have caught him exiting the hotel right after Gomez was killed. He could have missed recovering the backpack and it could have fallen into the hands of the police. The eyewitness could have been more accurate in describing him to the police.

Logan was drained from all the tension. He had noticed a fish and chips restaurant next to the hotel and called the concierge to see if they delivered. Twenty minutes later he was tucking into crunchy fillets of haddock dipped in beer batter and chunky hand-cut fries. He decided to watch TV while he was eating. There wasn't much playing, except a rerun of a Monty Python and the Flying Circus episode. Logan found himself laughing at the bizarre skit. British humor was beyond him. It was at once mocking, irreverent and campy.

Later the ten o'clock news ran a story about the accident on Regent Street. There was footage of the street in front of the hotel and the double-decker bus that had pasted Gomez to the pavement. Logan found himself gazing at John Gomez's passport photo on the screen as the reporter described the young American tourist from Chico, California. Logan shut the TV off and climbed into bed.

He tried to put thoughts of Gomez out of his mind. It was ten-thirty and he had to get to St. Pancras Station early the next morning to catch his eight a.m. train to Paris. As he started to nod off, an image drifted into his consciousness. It was a bit blurry but as he concentrated it slowly came into focus. It was Gomez, Cooper, and Zahir, walking on patrol in Iraq. Zahir was slightly ahead of the two men. She was looking back over her shoulder at the two of them, lips parted and eyes dancing with laughter.

Logan was restless and anxious to be on his way to Kuwait City. He had built additional time into his travel itinerary in the event he needed to stay in London longer than anticipated. With everyone accounted for, it hadn't made sense to stay around, particularly with Inspector Drysdale's interest in Logan Campbell.

The next morning Logan arrived at St. Pancras International Train Station at seven o'clock and entered the station from the Euston Road entrance. He negotiated the security and immigration lines before locating the Eurostar platform on the upper concourse. At seven-forty the announcer called his train number and he walked down the platform searching for car four. He was in seat 16, a solo seat in standard premier class, with a pull-down table. A few minutes after he had settled in, a waiter came by to take his breakfast order. A moment later the conductor announced their departure. The car doors hissed as they closed and the train began to pick up speed. The 307-mile journey was scheduled to take just two hours and fifteen minutes.

Logan marveled at the train's speed as he took a careful sip from the steaming cup of coffee the waiter had just brought him. At top speeds they would be traveling 186 miles per hour. After leaving the station, the train turned east and south, entering a long tunnel that traversed most of east London. Emerging from the tunnel they raced past decrepit housing and tired looking warehouses, a blot on the urban landscape.

At Dartford Crossing they plunged into a tunnel beneath the Thames River, emerging a short time later into the lush green fields of County Kent. Logan took in the pastoral scenery as they approached the Medway Viaduct. Logan dozed briefly, awakening as they sped out of the Channel Tunnel into the French fishing port of Calais. They soon left Calais behind and the terrain gave way to farmland. Here and there he saw village crowded around ancient stone churches punctuated with needle-like spires.

Logan could feel the train decelerating and, looking at his watch, noted that it was ten o'clock. At precisely ten-fifteen they pulled into Paris's Gare du Nord. It was December 4.

Logan found the subway entrance and boarded line 5 in the direction of the 13th Arrondissement. His destination was the Place d'Itali where he planned to find a small hotel. After stowing his bag in the overhead rack, Logan observed a shady-looking character making his way to the seat behind his. He recalled reading somewhere that pickpockets in the Paris Metro were notorious. A favorite maneuver entailed sitting down behind the intended target and slipping a hand around the side of the seat to steal the victim's wallet. Logan tensed when the man sat behind him but then relaxed as he realized that he was probably overreacting. A moment later however, he felt the slightest tug at his pocket. He wasn't overly concerned because he never kept anything valuable in his outside pockets anyway, but still he was peeved by the brazenness of the thief.

When he felt the hand go deep into his pocket, he clenched it in a vise-like grip, turned part way in his seat and squeezed even harder, releasing the hand only after he felt it slacken. Looking over his left shoulder Logan could see the agonized look of shock on the man's face as the pain set in. His eyes were wide and he trembled as he surveyed his mangled appendage. *"Merde, merde, merde,"* he whimpered.

Other passengers on the car moved away from the man as he slumped in his seat. Logan decided to get off at the next stop rather than risk the possibility of the confrontation escalating. He stood up to retrieve his bag, then leaned over the man and whispered in his ear, "You piece of shit. Keep your hands to yourself next time." The would-be thief did not respond. Perhaps he didn't speak English. But his sullen, hangdog expression left no doubt in Logan's mind that he would think twice before he tried that stunt again.

Logan emerged from the Saint Marcel subway station onto Avenue de la Republique and walked two blocks before turning down a winding side street. Saint Marcel is noted for its seventeenth-century architecture and he decided to wander around there in search of a bed-and-breakfast rather than continuing on to Place d'Itali. It was still early and in all likelihood he wouldn't be able to check in until after three anyway. Walking by a bookstore selling foreign newspapers, he spotted the *International Herald Tribune* on display and went in to make a purchase. After paying for his newspaper, Logan continued down the street until he spotted a café. Inside he ordered a café au lait and a strawberry tart.

Logan unfolded his newspaper. The front-page headline above the fold caught his attention and caused him to catch his breath. "US President Warns Iran Military Option on the Table" followed by the subtitle "Israel to Take Out Iranian Nukes." Damn, he thought. If Israel or the U.S. made a preemptive strike on Iran, all bets would be off.

He felt a surge of despair as he considered the possibility that events might conspire to doom their plans for the IED facility. There was no way they could enter Iran covertly if the country was under siege. It would be a suicide mission. As passionately as he felt about destroying their target, he had to admit that it paled next to neutralizing Iran's nuclear ambitions. The last time the U.S. had taken on Iran with its military was Jimmy Carter's failed hostage rescue attempt. The Iranians had played that one to their advantage, eventually dooming Carter's presidency.

Logan felt someone standing next to him and looked up. His waiter was standing there reading the headline. "So, your president will fight with the Iranians?"

"Oh. No. I'm not American. I'm from Canada."

The waiter looked down his nose at him. "You are from Quebec? Perhaps you speak French?"

"No. My family is from Ontario. We live in Toronto."

"Hm. Just as well. The Quebecois do not speak real French and it would grate against my ears to listen to it."

Logan asked for his check, and when he had paid the bill strode out into the cold December air. Pompous ass, he thought to himself. Despite French attitudes of grandeur, Paris had always held a certain allure for him, perhaps because of his mother's French-Canadian roots. It would probably make for a great romantic getaway. He was startled that as he entertained that thought, an image of Zahir flashed into his mind. Pushing it aside he hurried on down the street. He had to keep moving. Standing still was driving him crazy.

Be patient, he cautioned himself. Tomorrow he would be in Kuwait. The team would be reunited and get to work finalizing their preparations.

Chapter 23

Colonel Ghabel strode into Kazemi Garrison. He'd been summoned to Tehran to discuss the Afghanistan proposal he and Major Samadi had been developing. Ghabel was initially surprised by the enhanced security evident around the garrison's perimeter, but then he recalled his conversation with General Salehi a week earlier during which the general had said that Iran was going to a higher state of alert in response to Israeli and American threats.

Bandar Deylam had been relieved of the enhanced security requirement because of the emphasis Salehi was placing on the IED program. No distractions, he had said. In the anteroom of General Salehi's office, his aide de camp, Captain Saatchi, greeted Ghabel.

"Colonel Ghabel. It's good to see you again, sir. Welcome back to Tehran. We were all sad to hear about your father-in-law. How are your wife and mother-in-law doing?"

"Thank you for asking, Captain. I spoke with my wife last night. She and her mother had just returned from the Hafteh commemoration at Hafez Cemetery."

"Oh, has it been a week already? Her father was buried in Shiraz? I had forgotten that they were from there."

"Yes, her father was a respected professor at Shiraz University."

"I had an uncle who was buried at Hafez Cemetery. He died in the summer of 1975 when I was in high school, and when we went for his burial I remember walking through the orange groves and thinking how peaceful the place was with all of its pavilions, pools, and memorials. We sat in a tea house there and had refreshments."

"Yes, it's very peaceful there. Speaking of the cemetery,

did you know they turned Quasem Khan Wali's tomb there into a library for Hafez scholars? It houses a special collection of over 10,000 volumes in honor of Hafez."

"No, I didn't know that. Anyway, it's a nice place, and that's a fitting tribute for our most famous poet. Please give my regrets to your wife and her mother."

"Thank you, Captain Saatchi. I will pass on your sentiments."

"Please have a seat in General Salehi's office. He was called away earlier this morning to meet with the Supreme Leader; I believe it has something to do with Afghanistan, but he asked you to wait."

"Of course." Ghabel walked into Salehi's office and took a seat. So none other than the Supreme Leader himself was meeting with the general to discuss Iran's Afghanistan posture, he thought. He felt a momentary thrill as he imagined Supreme Leader Khamenei reading their proposal for augmenting the Qods Force role in western Afghanistan.

Ten minutes later General Salehi breezed into the room. He appeared upbeat. "Ah, Colonel Ghabel. Thank you for coming up, especially with your family situation as it is."

Ghabel had come to attention, and saluted the general. "No matter, General. The burial and memorial service were well attended, and my wife is staying with her mother for a month."

"Please give them our regrets." Gesturing to a small conference table on the other side of the room, Salehi motioned for Ghabel to have a seat. Captain Saatchi had brought in a pot of steaming tea, Salehi withdrew Major Samadi's report from the satchel he was carrying when he entered the room.

"Colonel, I've just returned from a meeting with the Supreme Leader. I generally meet with him once a week, but he asked me to come over this morning especially to discuss Afghanistan. It seems he took a special interest in your proposal to step up our cooperation with the Taliban. He would like you to take it to the next level. That means he wants you to meet with some of their military leaders in Kandahar Province as soon as possible. You'll have to be careful though. You know we've had a rocky relationship with the Taliban. Going back to 1997 we almost went to war with them over that incident in Mazar-i-Sharif."

"You mean when their soldiers massacred nine of our diplomats and an Iranian journalist?"

"Ah, you remember that?"

Ghabel grimaced. "How could I forget? I was one of 200,000 soldiers massed on the border, getting ready to invade Afghanistan over that incident."

"I had forgotten, or perhaps I never knew that you were involved in that whole affair."

"Yes. I was a young captain."

"Fortunately, we were able to broker a diplomatic solution, and didn't go to war with them." Salehi glanced down at some notes he had made in the margins of the report.

"Khamenei cautioned me that this approach is politically very sensitive. On the one hand we have Karzai admitting in the open press that the Afghan presidential office receives bags of money from Iran. He even put a number on it, somewhere around a million dollars each delivery, which is probably about right. Now if we are seen to be openly supporting the Taliban, Khamenei is concerned that this could lead to unwanted friction within the Karzai camp and could jeopardize our relationship with him."

"Who are these Taliban military leaders I'll be meeting?"

"They're a number of Mullah Omar's fighters who are based in Kandahar Province. They're hardcore battle-hardened combatants. As you know, we already have two advisors in western Afghanistan working on a rudimentary level with the Taliban, but the goal here is to ratchet this cooperation up a notch.

"We want to enhance their capabilities by introducing more sophisticated IED bomb making techniques and advanced tactics. This will take their fighters beyond the basic skills we are now teaching them, and without question will make them more effective when they target the Americans. These commanders you will meet with should be in a position to accept our offer."

"Did the Supreme Leader welcome our proposal to target Shindand Air Force Base? It seemed logical to us since it's only seventy-five miles from our border and would reduce our logistical tail as we supply weapons and materiel to the Taliban forces on the ground," Ghabel said.

"I assume we also have good infiltration and escape routes in and out of Afghanistan from Yazdan. When Major Samadi and I were putting this together, we took into consideration that in addition to the U.S forces stationed at Shindand AFB, the International Security Assistance Force is there as well. There are many good targets for us to pursue."

"You'll be able to check out the logistics on the ground yourself. You'll be meeting one of our officers in Zabol tomorrow. He'll have more area familiarization and will also be the one to take you to the meeting with our Taliban friends. You won't have to overnight in Afghanistan though. It will be a quick visit in and out."

"What are our specific goals for the meeting?"

"I want to gauge the Taliban commanders' interest in enhancing their troop capabilities to better target the Americans and their allies in ISAF. If they express interest, you have my authority to propose some dates for training. Once you determine what their level of interest is, come back to me with some numbers for your training budget. Money is not an issue in this case. You'll have as much as you need."

"Good. I look forward to this development. I had one other question, General, before I go. What was your reaction to our report on the meeting with Al Adel, the Al Qaeda explosives expert, in Borazjan?"

"Thank you for reminding me. I meant to bring that up. Al Adel seems to be an accomplished young man, if not an ideologue. Too bad he was on ice for a year. His talents could have been put to good use. I like what you're trying to do with him. Keep it up and keep me up to date. If he works out, perhaps we can expand the Al Qaeda program and snap up some of the other detainees before they wander off and cause mischief elsewhere. I believe that's all I have for you, Colonel Ghabel."

Ghabel rose from his seat and retrieved his cap from the side table. "General, thank you for your support."

"You're welcome, Colonel." Salehi stood up and shook Ghabel's hand. "Captain Saatchi has the details for your meeting tomorrow. He'll give you your flight particulars and contact information. Good luck."

Early the next morning Ghabel boarded a C-130 military transport at Tehran's Mehrabad Airport, bound for Zabol in Sistan Baluchistan Province. The decrepit C-130, a four-engine turboprop designed and built by Lockheed, had been in the Iranian military's fleet since 1970. Some of these aircraft, such as the one he was on, were in their golden years, despite efforts on the part of the regime to optimize their performance.

Even as he entertained this thought the pilot came on the intercom to announce that they were diverting to Khatami Air Force Base in Esfahan because of an engine problem. After landing, the pilot taxied to a maintenance hanger and the passengers deplaned as the engines sputtered and then were still. Four hours later they were in the air again. A clogged fuel line had been the culprit.

It was noon when Ghabel landed at Zabol Air Force Base. His contact, Major Hassani, was waiting for him at the flight operations center. Without delay they boarded a dusty Safir Jeep and headed east out of the base.

"I was able to contact the Taliban commanders you'll be meeting to tell them about the delay," Hassani said.

"Where will we be meeting them?"

"About ten miles inside Afghanistan. We'll go off-road northeast of Zabol." Hassani pointed to a spot on the map. "There's not much out there except for wild goats and jackals. We'll be meeting them at an encampment I've used before. Here." He gestured towards a narrow valley surrounded by peaks. "It's in a stand of cedar trees in this narrow valley." Hassani looked at his watch. "We should be there in about forty minutes."

Chapter 24

When they reached the meeting site, Ghabel could see the Taliban commanders standing outside a dome-shaped *yurt* covered in black felt. They were a formidable-looking bunch, dressed in traditional attire and armed to the teeth. The encampment was set amongst gooseberry bushes and wild roses, and Ghabel mused over its rustic simplicity. The yurt had an air of permanency to it. It was sturdy, supported by bent struts held in place with a central ring that ran around its interior. Straight slats arranged in a trellis pattern shaped its walls.

The group entered through a door frame draped with a heavy felt flap. Inside a fire was blazing and dusty carpets strewn about provided warmth from the frigid ground.

Ghabel took his time sizing up the Taliban commanders as they arranged themselves around the fire and one of their subordinates bustled about preparing to serve them tea. They were Pashtuns, dedicated to a belief that incorporated strict adherence to the Koran and Sharia law. They were also driven by a fervent Pan-Islamic nationalism. Ghabel recalled that the Taliban had its roots in Kandahar and that General Salehi had said these commanders were close to the legendary Mullah Mohammad Omar, Taliban founder and spiritual leader.

The four commanders were not in uniform, but each wore a turban, a long dress-like garment, baggy trousers and leather boots. They had shed their lambskin coats as the yurt began to heat up, but kept their weapons close at hand.

After tea was served, Awalmir Khan, the senior commander for the Afghan contingent, spoke up. "Welcome to

Afghanistan, Colonel. I trust your trip was a pleasant one. I hope that you find our humble meeting place acceptable?"

Ghabel understood the commander's Dari with little difficulty. It was similar to Farsi, although he suspected that Awalmir and the others would be more comfortable speaking Pashto, their native tongue.

"Thank you, Awalmir Khan. I am most honored to be here." He raised his cup of tea in a form of salute to all four of them. "To your health, and the health of your families."

Ghabel observed the other commanders exchanging appreciative glances and knew that he had won at least initial acceptance by adhering to Afghan rules for hospitality. Sharing tea or food and expressing sincere concern for your counterpart's health were essential elements in the Afghan book of etiquette.

"We have worked with Major Hassani for some time, and have enjoyed the support that we receive from the Qods Force."

Ghabel looked towards Hassani as Khan spoke. They had discussed specific support Iran had been providing the Taliban over the years on their drive up from Zabol. "I know we've provided your fighters with some materiel support over the years, mostly small arms, ammunition and rocket-propelled grenades."

"Yes, and on at least two occasions that I am aware of, Qods Force officers have conducted training sessions in small unit tactics for our men. I myself attended one of these." Awalmir toyed with a strand from his thick brown beard.

"And I trust this training proved worthwhile?" Ghabel scrutinized the impassive faces gathered around the fire.

"Very much so. Do you remember the attack on Kandahar last year? We targeted the Governor's palace, various military installations and the police headquarters. There were few actual casualties, but our men demonstrated that we remain a force to be reckoned with. We controlled the entire downtown area of Kandahar for over thirty hours. It was the valor of our fighters that made this possible, but Iran's materiel support and tactical training certainly played a role in our victory."

"I'm gratified that we were of some assistance. I'm here today to suggest that we expand the level of cooperation between our two sides. This comes with the blessing of our Supreme Leader, who himself directed that I come to you with this proposal."

Awalmir and the others broke into Pashto. Ghabel spoke passable Pashto, but he did not let on that he understood their conversation.

"What can the Iranians hope to gain by this?" Awalmir said to his cohorts. "They're in bed with Karzai, who has been no friend of ours since we were blamed for his father's death in 1999."

"Well, weren't we the ones who carried out that attack?" another man asked him.

"No matter. That's ancient history. And besides, Karzai's also in bed with the Americans. He's playing both ends against the middle."

"Perhaps the Iranians are hedging their bets too, using us to make trouble for the Americans while at the same time making it more difficult for Karzai to maintain any credibility as a unifying force once security has been transferred to Afghan forces." This came from a steely-eyed combatant named Atal Khan. "We know within the Taliban political leadership there are those who want to deal with the American and Karzai. Time is running out, particularly if NATO forces do withdraw from Afghanistan as planned," Khan said.

"Yes, our political leaders want to cut a deal so that we're not left on the outside when the Americans do leave." This came from the youngest commander who up to this point had remained silent.

Awalmir looked at his fellow commanders. "We're a long way from any kind of agreement with Karzai or the Americans. There are constitutional matters to resolve as well as the issue of how the Americans are going to treat our brothers being detained at Guantanamo. But getting back to our original question, I'm uncertain of the colonel's ulterior motives, but, if they are offering to support our struggle with more weapons and training, I don't see the downside. Are you in agreement?" The others nodded their assent.

Turning to Ghabel, Awalmir smiled. "So it seems, my dear Colonel," he said, speaking in Dari again, "that we are all in agreement that we welcome the opportunity to expand our cooperation with Iran, and we look forward to working more closely with the Qods Force."

You lying sack of shit , Ghabel thought to himself. I don't trust you for a minute. Without betraying his understanding of their private discussion, Ghabel cleared his throat and raised his teacup in a toast to closer cooperation.

He spent the next hour briefing the commanders on Bandar Deylam's capabilities, emphasizing their development of new IED technology and their capacity for conducting advanced tactical training. They agreed to conduct an initial training class in Bandar Deylam in January. Major Hassani was charged with handling communications between the commanders and Colonel Ghabel.

As the meeting broke up and Ghabel stepped outside the yurt, he noticed sunlight reflecting off of something on the mountainside. Looking more closely he could see Taliban fighters ringed around the encampment. Ghabel's hair stood up on the back of his neck. He wasn't really surprised that Awalmir had his men deployed nearby to provide security for the meeting, but he felt outmaneuvered, certainly outmanned, and that wasn't something he was accustomed to.

The ride back to Zabol was uneventful.

"That seemed to go well." Major Hassani glanced in Ghabel's direction as he downshifted at a steep curve in the road.

"Do you speak Pashto, Major?"

"No. Why do you ask?"

"Do you remember when Awalmir and the others broke into Pashto after I laid out our proposal?"

"Yes."

"Well, I speak enough Pashto to get by, and my sense is that Awalmir and his cohorts are very politically astute.

They don't trust us. But that's all right because I don't trust them either. Some advice for you Major – watch your back. Remember that a snake can change its skin, but not its disposition."

As Hassani negotiated the jeep out of the curve he slammed on the brakes. Before them was a horde of Kuchi nomads crossing the road. Camels, horses and sheep converged in a raucous melee as they jostled each other to get out of the way. There were perhaps a dozen men and just as many women, with children ranging in age from infants to teenagers. The women's colorful scarves and the bright, coarsely woven camel bags shifting under the weight of winter provisions presented a vivid spectacle. Hassani and Ghabel watched as the throng left the road and turned onto an obscure bridle path snaking through the mountains.

"This is late for the Kuchis to be on the move," remarked Major Hassani. "They're a pastoral tribe, Pashtuns, who normally would get out of the mountains before the winter settles in and relocate to the Indus Valley in Pakistan. When the border between Afghanistan and Pakistan was closed in the early 1960s most of these nomads remained in Afghanistan, although some continued to attempt the annual border crossing into Pakistan."

"I wonder what's happening with this group?"

"Could be anything," Hassani replied. "They may have been in an area where there was fighting and decided to look for a safe haven. The Kuchis pretty much stay out of politics, although at one time they were highly regarded and favored by Afghan royalty. They're Pashtuns and so were Afghanistan's kings back in the 1800s."

When the last ragged child, swishing a branch at an errant sheep, had disappeared from view, Major Hassani continued down the rough mountain road to Zabol.

They reached the airfield a half hour later, giving Ghabel forty-five minutes before his flight to Bushehr was scheduled to depart. He and Hassani sat in the flight operations center sipping chai and going over their meeting.

"I know General Salehi is going to be pleased with our

progress, and I suspect the Supreme Leader will be as well. It's early though, and much work needs to be done before we can count it as a success. Remember, Major Hassani, a single rose blossoming does not mean that spring has arrived."

Ghabel bade Major Hassani goodbye and strolled over to the boarding area. Moments later he had settled into his seat, and the pilot was taxiing for take-off. As they lifted off and gained altitude, the pilot banked gently, towards the setting sun.

Chapter 25

Logan negotiated immigration and customs at Paris-Charles de Gaulle Airport without a hitch. He was much more comfortable in his Canadian alias now and answered the immigration official's questions without hesitation. He felt a sense of mild relief when the officer stamped his passport and waved him through.

"Logan. Logan Alexander!"

Logan nearly leapt out of his skin when he heard his name being called out. He looked around to see if the immigration officer had heard it too, but saw that he already had his hands full with a self-important windbag chiding him to speed up his processing lest he miss his flight.

Looking back out towards the concourse, Logan spotted the source of his anxiety, Dr. Pike Delaney, his Game Theory professor at the academy.

"Dr. Delaney. How's it going?" Logan put his bag down and grasped Delany's outstretched hand.

"Aren't you a sight for sore eyes, Logan. What are you doing in Paris?"

"Business. Got out of the Seals a few months ago on a medical issue, and I'm setting up a consulting business."

"Good for you. You know, I lost track of you after graduation. Of course, we heard about your injury in Afghanistan, and I knew you were back in the States in rehab, but I hadn't heard that you'd been discharged."

"Yeah. It was a big disappointment to me. Always thought I was going to be a lifer. They did a good job saving my leg in the field hospital over there, and the rehab folks at Walter Reed were awesome, but I just couldn't get my leg back to the point where it was 100 percent. So how about you?

What are you doing over here?"

"I've been up in Brittany for the past semester on an exchange with the Ecole Navale, the French naval academy. Still teaching and working on a new book. It's *Games People Play: Game Theory in International Conflict*."

"Well, did you get any insights into whether or not the French are rational decision-makers after all?"

Delaney laughed. "I can't say that I've developed any greater appreciation for French attitudes or their politics. But I will say this. The French are sophisticated thinkers. We used some current examples of complex foreign policy and military negotiations in the course, and I give them credit for being quite astute even if nationalistic to a fault." Delaney looked at the wall clock. "I'd love to have coffee with you and hear about your new venture, but we start boarding in fifteen minutes and I better get to my gate."

"Maybe next time. Nice catching up with you."

As Delaney hurried away, Logan's tension began to subside. Whew! That was a close call. How random was that, though? What were the odds he would run into someone he knew in Paris of all places? It was a good thing he'd rehearsed his cover story. While it was believable, the other thing he'd learned to do was to deflect questions and turn the conversation back to the other person as soon as possible. People love talking about themselves and what's going on in their lives.

Logan picked up his bag and looked for signs to Terminal 1. His Kuwait Airways flight was scheduled to depart from there in an hour. He hadn't found any direct flights to Kuwait out of Paris. They would be stopping in Rome, but he wouldn't have to deplane.

Eight hours later, Logan stepped into the arrivals area at Kuwait International Airport. It was hard to believe that he'd been here less than six weeks ago. He felt a moment of anxiety when the immigration officer pulled him into secondary, but then he remembered that Nayef had arranged for the team members' alias passports to be watch-listed, with instructions to the immigration officers to expedite their processing.

Without this assurance he never would have felt comfortable using alias documents to transit an airport he'd visited in his true name. With the sophisticated automation and facial recognition technology available in airports today, that would be foolish, especially in a modern airport. If you were off the beaten track in some poverty-stricken backwater you might get away with it, but even then, why take the risk?

His team had reservations at the same Crowne Plaza Hotel where Logan had met Nayef, his uncle, and Thamir Alghanim just weeks before. It was a five-minute drive from the airport and after Logan had checked in and taken a shower he started calling around to see who else had arrived.

Everyone had made it in except Zahir. Logan wasn't too concerned, though. With nine people traveling in from all over Europe, what were the odds that everyone would show up right on time? Logan told the team to rendezvous in his room at six. He wanted to have a short meeting with them before they got together with Nayef and Thamir. Just before five, Logan's room phone rang.

"Logan. It's me." Zahir's voice sounded travel weary.

"Hey, Zahir. When did you get in?"

"I just checked in. My flight out of Brussels was delayed. It was snowing and the control tower told our pilot that the storm system was moving north out of the area, so they boarded our plane, but then the weather suddenly turned worse. You couldn't even see ten feet in front of the plane, so they had everyone go back inside the terminal. We waited three hours before they cleared us for take-off."

"You must be exhausted. Everyone else is already here. We're going to meet in my room at six. We shouldn't run too late."

"OK. I think I'll take a quick shower first. I feel pretty grubby. See you then."

When everyone was assembled in Logan's room, he surveyed the expectant faces. "OK, listen up. Glad to see you all made it. Anybody have any problems traveling on your alias docs? Let me see a show of hands. No one? I'll tell you

a quick issue I had, for the lessons learned department."
Logan went on to describe his chance encounter with Doctor
Delaney.

"It pays to know your cover story backwards and for-
wards. I would have preferred not to run into anyone, but
in this case, no harm, no foul. Delaney is a smart guy, but the
key thing is that I didn't give him any reason to question my
story. If I'd been hemming and hawing, or didn't have my basic cover story down, it could've been a different outcome."

"I think the Europeans are way more laidback than the
guys at Homeland Security. I never felt threatened by anyone I came across." Francis Tyler looked around the room.
"Anybody else?"

"Seems like everybody did fine," Logan said. "No doubt
it helped that we had actual Canadian documents. It's not
like we were trying to get by on Nigerian passports or some
of those other fly-by-night passports you hear about. These
are the real deal. Good job, everyone. Before we get started, I'd like to take a minute to talk about what happened
to Gomez." Logan gave everyone a rundown of what had
transpired in London.

"We all need to be on our games 100 percent. We're going to get tired, and just like always we'll push through it.
That's what we're trained to do. I'm sure John was tired and
he just had a momentary lapse of judgment, forgetting to
look in the right direction and he got creamed by that double-decker." Logan shook his head.

"I've asked Norm Stoddard to replace Gomez as my number two." Logan looked in Stoddard's direction. "We talked
it over and Norm stepped up. If anything happens to me,
Norm's in charge."

Everyone nodded in agreement. Stoddard was a serious
player. The Seal from Burnt Cabins had four combat tours
under his belt and was well regarded in the tightly knit special operations community. There was no finer Navy Seal
than Norm Stoddard.

"We've got Nayef Al Subaie and Thamir Alghanim
coming in at seven to meet with us. Just in case you need

reminding, Nayef's family is bankrolling this whole thing and Thamir's in charge of the operations side of the Kuwaiti Intel and Security Service. They'll give us an update on anything that's come up in the last week, and get us squared away for our trip out to Failaka Island tomorrow morning."

A few minutes later there was a knock on the door. Nayef Al Subaie and Thamir Alghanim entered the room. Nayef spotted Logan from across the room and walked over to him. "Logan, my friend, it's good to see you here."

Logan smiled and grasped Nayef's outstretched hand. "Good to see you too, Nayef. Thamir. Let me introduce you to everybody."

After several minutes of informal chatting with the team, Nayef took Logan aside. "I thought there were going to be ten of you. Is somebody missing?"

Logan shook his head. "Yeah, we lost John Gomez in London." Logan proceeded to relate the events of the accident to Nayef and Thamir, who had sidled up to Nayef's side. Logan didn't try to sugarcoat the incident, and he was forthcoming about the near miss with Gomez's backpack and the alias documents.

Nayef was silent for a moment as the import of Logan's narrative was driven home. "I'm very sorry for your loss. That was indeed a close call. If the authorities had recovered Mr. Gomez's backpack we could have had a real crisis on our hands."

"Oh, it would've been the end of the line. We would've had to abort then and there. The police would've had documents for half the team, so those guys would've had to bug out at the first opportunity. That would've left only five of us to carry out the mission; too few to go forward with it. MI-5 would've been brought in and they would've been all over this. They have a lot of experience with counter-terrorism ops, so I'm sure they would've been talking to the Canadians right away, especially once they figured out those passports were fake. They would probably start looking at any and all Canadians in the UK.

"I'm pretty sure we could've gotten everyone out of England on our true name documents, especially if we had moved fast enough, but eventually, given enough time, I'm confident they would've been able to identify us."

"Nice job, Mr. Alexander." Thamir withdrew a cigarette from a gold case, lit it and inhaled. Slipping the case back into the breast pocket of his jacket, he continued. "I agree with your assessment. It would've been a puzzle for them, though. Even if they had captured the backpack they would not have been certain about what they had. The biggest break for them would've been that Mr. Gomez still had his true name passport on his person. Once they identified him, and discovered that he had an Army Ranger background, that would have been a red flag, and eventually it would have led them to U.S. military authorities.

"The passports are not traceable to Kuwait, so we would not have been implicated. The greatest challenge would have been what you, as individuals, might have said, assuming they eventually learned your true identities."

"We all belong to the admit nothing, take no prisoners school of training, so they wouldn't have gotten much out of us," Logan said. "Despite that, though, with enough time the Intel guys would be able to figure out our travel patterns and link us through our passports. It wouldn't take them long to figure out that we were up to no good.

"I don't know if they'd just let it go or go after us on false document charges. My guess is that we all would've been called in and given the third degree. And you can bet that our names would be entered into Homeland Security's databases and we'd be pulled into secondary anytime we travel in the future."

At Thamir's request, the team gave the two Kuwaitis a rundown of their training exercises in Arizona and California. Nayef had already heard most of this earlier from Logan but listened quietly until they were through. Both men seemed impressed by the progress the team had made exercising the scenario.

"We've made arrangements to get you over to Failaka Island tomorrow morning," Thamir told them. "I'll have a helicopter waiting for you on the military side of Kuwait International Airport. Your transport will take you directly to the hangar so you won't be seen boarding the aircraft and there will be no record of your having traveled there. There's a slight complication regarding our use of Failaka Island as a training site, but with discretion I think we will be able to manage this."

Thamir lit another cigarette before going on. "Our government is in negotiations with the U.S. military to give them land on Failaka for housing some of the troops coming out of Iraq. I don't think this arrangement has been finalized, but in all likelihood it shall be. We're going to permit the U.S. to augment its military presence in Kuwait by 15,000 troops.

"Outside of the army base there are not many people on the island. As a precaution though, I request that while there you limit your comings and goings to your compound and to the areas within Failaka Army Base, where you will be conducting your training."

"How about getting around to purchase supplies?"

"All of that will be provided for you. Besides, outside of the base, there is nowhere to buy anything. We also want you to be able to maximize your training time while there, Logan. At the compound we've arranged for a cook and a two-man char force to keep the place clean, do your laundry, etc. Fresh supplies will be delivered there as needed. You won't have any worries on that score. You'll have a vehicle at your disposal for getting back and forth and around the base.

"Out there, Colonel Al Fahad will be your point of contact, although he'll probably delegate day-to-day matters to his operations commander, Major Al Salman. His J-2 will provide you with a current intelligence briefing every morning, and his operations commander will support your operational requirements," Thamir said. "The colonel also has a little surprise for you that I think you'll find quite intriguing. Any questions?"

Logan looked around the room. "I've got one. Any chance we can get some more time with that man of yours, Jaber Behbehani? He's the one guy we know of who's been inside Bandar Deylam and who could be a real gold mine."

Thamir looked thoughtful for a moment before replying, "I'll do you one better than that. If you like, you can take Behbehani with you into Iran. He's feeling much better than he was when you met him last month. He actually volunteered for this mission."

Logan looked surprised. The last time he'd seen Behbehani, the man had barely been able to walk. He must be one tough little bastard, he thought. "Let me think about it. At a minimum, I'd like to continue debriefing him. Zahir speaks Arabic, so she'd be able to handle that unless you want Behbehani's handler there too."

"As you wish. He's comfortable meeting with you. We don't need to be there. Just let me know if you do decide to take him with you." A few minutes later Nayef and Thamir said goodnight and left.

Logan looked around at the faces in the room. Despite the inevitable jet lag, he could feel their energy. They were only two weeks away from prime time. "Everybody get a good night's sleep. We have an 0730 pick-up out front tomorrow morning. It should only take us five or ten minutes to get to the airport from here and it'll be a quick chopper ride to Failaka Island."

As everyone was filing out the door, Logan caught Zahir's attention and motioned for her to stay behind. When the others had left he closed the door.

"I just wanted to see how you're doing. I was thinking about what you said at breakfast the other day. I miss Cooper, too. Not a day goes by that I don't think about him. He was my little brother. Millie and I always felt kind of protective towards him because he was so sick when he was a little kid." Logan shook his head and ran his hand through his hair.

"Our family's always been close and we have each other for support. But for you, with Gomez gone and your family not accepting you, you haven't had anyone to lean on. I just want you to know that as far as we're concerned, you're family. Heck, I think Mills already thinks of you as the sister she never had."

Zahir walked over to Logan and embraced him. She rested her cheek against his chest for a moment and then looked into his eyes. "Thanks, Logan. You don't know how good that makes me feel."

"If you need to talk or anything just let me know. I'll be here for you." A moment later she was gone.

The next morning the team assembled in front of the hotel. Their Mercedes mini-bus was double parked near the valet waiting area. A placard in the front window read simply "Campbell Party." The ride to the airport felt like a death-defying dash through snarled traffic. At one point Logan observed an irate driver jump from his car waving a tire iron in pursuit of a motorcycle that had cut him off. Leaning on the horn and weaving through an endless procession of slow moving vehicles, their driver managed to deliver them to the military airport on time.

The crew at the flight operations center was ready for them. After brief introductions, their crew chief led them over to a Sikorsky S-92, a four-bladed, twin-engine, medium-lift helicopter. Following a short safety briefing, they lifted off.

"Look, there's Liberation Tower." Zahir pointed to the 1,200-foot spire with its two distinct disc-shaped pods. "It was supposed to be called the Kuwait Telecommunications Tower, but while it was being constructed Kuwait was invaded by Iraq and building stopped until after the war. When they finished it in 1993, they decided to call it Liberation Tower in honor of their liberation from Iraq."

"Aren't you a font of knowledge?" Logan grinned at Zahir.

As they paralleled Kuwait City's Corniche, Logan pointed out Green Island, a manmade retreat connected to Kuwait's mainland by a causeway. "That's a big park and amphitheater. Apparently the in place to go on the weekend around here."

Their pilot turned east and climbed to two thousand feet. Failaka Island lies a scant twelve miles east of Kuwait City. In antiquity, the Greeks garrisoned troops on the island. During the fourth century BC, the Greek town of Ikaros became an important maritime trading center and even after they left two hundred years later, evidence suggests that the island maintained some prominence in maritime commerce throughout the region.

In more recent times Failaka Island had been a popular tourist destination for Kuwaitis, and it had even harbored a smattering of full-time residents. But during the first Gulf War, the Iraqi military relocated these families to the Kuwaiti mainland, mined the beaches, and converted the island to a military garrison. Even though the Iraqis were expelled in 1991, twenty years later the island had failed to regain its former renown.

A moment later the pilot announced their imminent arrival. Looking out his window, Logan could see a triangular-shaped expanse no more than fifteen square miles in area. It was flat, with a trifling hill interrupting the landscape at the far west end of the island. Three minutes later they landed. Logan felt his pulse quicken in excitement. They were here. They were on Failaka Island. Let the games begin.

Chapter 26

Major Al Salman bombarded Logan with a staccato stream of Arabic, pausing only when he saw the confused look on his face. The team had deplaned and was milling around in the flight operations center. Zahir elbowed her way to the front of the group and answered the major's question in Gulf Arabic.

The lean, hawk-faced officer visibly bristled at having to deal with a woman, but upon realizing that she was the only Arabic speaker amongst them, reluctantly turned his attention to her.

"Major Al Salman is the Chief of Operations for the battalion," Zahir said to the team. "He extends a welcome to us on behalf of Colonel Al Fahad, the base commander. The major would like to take us over to our quarters in a little village called Az Zawr so we can get settled in. After that we'll come back over here, process through security, get a tour of the base, and then see where we'll be working. All of our gear is already stored over there."

She looked back at the major as he clarified a point. "It's in a converted warehouse. Then at two o'clock we're scheduled to meet with the J-2, followed by a brief meet and greet with the colonel."

They piled into an Army 4X4 and departed the base, which by Logan's reckoning was situated in the northeast quadrant of Failaka Island. Fifteen minutes later, after driving through a barren stretch of crumbling roadway, distinguished solely by a neglected archaeological ruin and pockets of devastation, the team arrived at the village of Az Zawr. The invading Iraqi Army had seized many of the buildings on Az Zawr in 1990 and used them for target practice, reducing most to rubble.

Those buildings still standing had not completely escaped the Iraqi barrage; they were pockmarked with bullet holes, and many had taken direct hits from mortar rounds. A National Bank of Kuwait branch office on the main street sat in a state of complete ruin, its windows blown out and its interior pillaged.

Major Al Salman turned down a side street, drove fifty yards and then pulled up before a walled compound that miraculously appeared unscathed in comparison to the destruction they had just witnessed. Stepping out of the vehicle, he beckoned the others to follow suit. Zahir continued to interpret for him.

"This is where we'll be staying."

"How come this place is still standing?" Norm Stoddard stood with his hands on his hips, surveying their bleak surroundings.

"This compound was the Iraqi commander's headquarters on Failaka during the war. The Iraqis bolted when the Americans liberated Kuwait, so they didn't take the time to gut the compound. This all happened over twenty years ago. Not much has changed around here since then."

Major Al Salman's eyes hardened. In Arabic, he said, "I had family members living on Failaka Island when Saddam Hussein's forces crushed our defenses. The Iraqis relocated everybody to the mainland when they swept in like a tidal wave. After the war nobody wanted to come back. There was nothing left for them."

Zahir continued translating his words. "It seemed that was all going to change three years ago when Parliament approved a new development plan for Kuwait. They identified over 1,000 projects, some of them so-called mega-projects, and said they would spend $125 billion on this. One of the mega-projects was for Failaka Island. The developers say they're going to build twenty hotels, a golf course, marinas and more. I'll believe it when I see it."

Logan whistled in appreciation. "That's some serious money. It's kind of hard to envision it the way the place looks now, but if the government is committed to investing those kinds of resources it would be a game-changer."

Moments later they were standing inside the walled compound. What had been nondescript mud walls on the outside gave way to alabaster walls inside. Ornamental tiles were set into the plaster, creating a rich mosaic. A short corridor from the entryway led to an interior courtyard dominated by a small pool and bubbling fountain. Blooming rose bushes added a splash of color and an expanse of grape vines wove a leafy ceiling across the terrace. Several bedrooms and common rooms opened up to the center.

A portly Kuwaiti man waddled over to where they were gathered. His name was Faran, the team learned. Faran would do most of the cooking, and a couple of manservants, Hamad and Yassin, would clean the place and take care of the laundry."

Faran nodded a greeting and then spoke quietly to Major Al Salman as Zahir interpreted. "He says to let him know if we have any food allergies or special preferences. Also he would like to know at what times we wish to take our meals. The dining room is over there. It's also possible to set up a table here on the terrace if we wish to eat outside, weather permitting."

Logan looked at Faran as he replied. "Please tell Faran that we will not be much trouble. We are very pleased that he, Hamad and Yassin are here to make our stay comfortable. If we could plan on having breakfast at around seven o'clock and then have something prepared to take with us for lunch, we can eat that on base. Unless we're doing night training, we could probably plan to have dinner around seven o'clock."

Faran nodded his understanding after Zahir had finished translating. The team then split up and spent the next ten minutes familiarizing themselves with the property.

A moment later Tony Barbiari let out a muted groan from the direction of the bathroom. When they wandered over to where he was standing, the source of his distress became obvious. There was no Western-style toilet in the bathroom.

Instead, it was equipped with a squat toilet, a water faucet and a plastic pitcher with a curved spout.

"Two tours in Iraq and I never had to use one of them things. I don't even know where to start."

Zahir looked amused. "OK. You have to squat down over the hole. If you don't have good balance or your thighs can't handle squatting, support yourself against the wall. But when you squat you have to be careful about your aim or else you'll be sorry. Also there's no toilet paper here. You have to use that water pitcher next to the squatter. Pour water into your left hand and clean yourself. When you're done just give your rear a flick with your left hand to get the extra water off. Easy."

Barbiari looked dubious and the Kuwaitis grinned as they realized the source of his dismay.

Ten minutes later they were back in the 4X4. Before heading back to the base Major Al Salman gave them a tour of the island. They drove southeast towards the water.

"All of these beaches were mined by the Iraqis. After they were expelled it took us months to clear the beaches of all the mines. As you can see, they destroyed most of the buildings on the island, but they left some of the key infrastructure intact."

"What infrastructure?" Logan looked around at the destruction and wondered what the major meant.

"Water and electricity. We get fresh water and electricity from the mainland. There's a pipeline for the water, and submarine power cables on the northwest coast tie into Kuwait City's power grid."

"How about waste disposal?" Logan shaded his eyes from the sun.

"Another gift from our Iraqi brothers. They pretty much destroyed the sewage system before they left. So far it hasn't been completely repaired, but we've patched it up so that it meets our needs for now."

"There's hardly anyone around. Does anyone live here full time?" Makes Montpelier seem like a metropolis, Logan thought to himself.

"Aside from the base, not really. Some of the people who used to live here come over occasionally to check on their property. Many people also like to fish off the coast, but they need special permits for that. Mainly because we conduct live fire exercises on the north end of the island and we don't want anyone getting hurt."

An hour later they had completed their tour and were back at the base. Major Al Salman took them into base security where the MPs had access badges prepared for each team member. Captain Nazari, Chief of Security, gave them a standard security briefing. He pointed out that only the Base Commander, Major Al Salman, the J-2 and he were briefed on the team's mission. Even they did not know what the team's ultimate objective was, though.

If team members got any questions from anyone else on the base their cover story was that they were part of an advance team evaluating future training needs of the Kuwaiti Army. Following their briefing, Major Al Salman finished showing them around the base.

The base had originally been built by the Americans after the first Gulf War, the team learned. It was designed to accommodate several thousand troops, but only a small battalion of about five hundred Kuwaiti regulars served here now.

Leaving the flight operations center, Major Al Salman turned left and drove two hundred yards to a complex of buildings. "This is the Battalion Headquarters Building and Administrative Offices. You'll be coming back over here later to meet with the J-2 and Colonel Al Fahad." Kuwait's black, green, red and white flag hung limp atop the headquarters building.

Their tour continued with Major Al Salman pointing out enlisted and officers' living quarters, the post dining facility and the PX. Turning left onto a newly resurfaced macadam road, they drove for several minutes and came to a firing range. A quarter of a mile west there were several warehouses. Major Al Salman pulled up before one of the corrugated structures and they all got out.

"This is where you'll be working. Everything on your equipment list is stored inside, but you should complete an inventory as soon as possible to make certain everything you ordered is there. Let me know if you are missing anything, or if you think of something else you need. This building is also outfitted with an air-conditioned briefing room, so you'll be able to use that as your base of operations. This warehouse is off limits to our troops so you'll have all the privacy you need. Still, we've alarmed the warehouse and outfitted the doors with security locks." He gave Logan the keys and typed in a code to enter him into the security system.

Just then a Jeep turned down the road fronting the warehouses and pulled up next to the major. "Ah, my ride is here. Unless you have any questions for me I will leave you to your work. The 4X4 is assigned to you for the duration. Please plan to be at the headquarters building at two o'clock for your Intel brief. I'll be there to introduce you to the J-2 and then take you over to meet Colonel Al Fahad."

After Major Al Salman had left, Logan and the others trooped into the warehouse. Several shrink-wrapped pallets stood in the middle of the room. "OK. Let's break these down and inventory everything."

Two hours later Logan looked up from his checklist. "I think that's it. Thamir's people did a good job getting everything on the list. Weapons, ammo, magazine pouches, demolitions gear, field communications set, desert camouflage clothing and boots, night vision goggles, GPS, compass, body armor, backpacks, first aid kit, vests, rigs, hydration systems, flashlights, tools, Zodiac Futura Commando F470, scuba tanks. Anybody think of anything we're missing? No?"

He checked his watch and saw that it was a quarter to two. "We need to get over to the J-2 briefing. Let's lock this place down."

Ten minutes later they rolled up to Battalion Headquarters. Major Al Salman was waiting for them at the main entrance. "Please follow me." He took the stairs to the second level and walked part way down the corridor before turning into a conference room on the right.

Sitting at the conference table was Major Wassem, a reed-thin wisp of a man who evidently suffered from ill health. His pallor, hacking cough and dissipated countenance made him better suited for the infirmary than the briefing room. His handshake was limp and clammy to the touch, yet his voice had an unusually rich timbre as he welcomed the team to Failaka Army Base.

"Welcome. I want you to know that I am at your service during your stay with us. I will leave it to you to determine if daily Intel briefings are desirable. While I do not have the need to know your mission, I can better tailor the briefings to your requirements if I have a clearer sense of your objective. I know that you're going to be operating inside of Iran, on the Gulf Coast between Bushehr and Bandar Deylam.

"There are Navy and Air Force bases in and around Bushehr, the nuclear facility south of there and then of course there's Kharg Island," he said. "I tend to doubt that a small force such as yours would be going into any of those heavily fortified areas. The only military target that I am aware of in the vicinity of Bandar Deylam is an IED research facility and training camp run by the Qods Force. Would it be safe to say that area is of interest to you?" Major Wassem peered over his glasses as he waited for a response.

Squirrelly bastard, Logan thought to himself. I suppose it's unrealistic to think that we could be tasking their J-2 with requirements and not expect him to figure out what we're up to. Still it's all about plausible deniability. We don't have to confirm it for him. "I think we just leave it at that. The whole stretch from Bandar Deylam to Bushehr is of interest to us."

"Well, then, as you wish. Shall we begin?" He dimmed the lights and turned on an overhead projector connected to a laptop computer.

"I'm going to assume that you possess a certain level of background information on the Iranian military, their capabilities, vulnerabilities etc. However, if that assumption is incorrect, I am prepared to address those issues with you in some depth." Major Wassem studied the faces around the conference table.

"No? All right then. What we'll concentrate on this afternoon is several recent developments which I assess are a result of the increased political rhetoric directed at Iran by the United States and Israel."

Wassem clicked on a folder and overhead imagery depicting the Strait of Hormuz was displayed. "Iran has a fleet of small boats, many of which have been converted so that they can fire short-range missiles. The Iranian Revolutionary Guard Corps Navy controls these assets. We've seen a fairly significant up-tick in patrolling activity by these craft in and around the Strait over the past week."

He clicked the next slide. "In addition, Iran has a class of midget submarines, the Ghadir-class subs that can be used for covert operations, such as mining the Strait." Using a laser pointer, Wassem highlighted Kharg Island. "The Navy has a hovercraft fleet based on the island, but we've seen some of their Ghadir-class subs showing up there as well. We don't know what they're up to, but they could be preparing for mine-laying operations if their leaders decide to close the Strait."

"Has Iran ever actually closed the Strait of Hormuz?" Logan leaned forward in his chair and looked at Major Wassem.

"No, although there have been many threats to do so over the years. When international tensions rise, as in the case of international pressure on Iran to curtail its nuclear program, the Iranians typically counter by threatening to close the strait."

"Could they actually pull that off?"

"The experts I've spoken with say that it wouldn't be that hard. Basically they would mine the strait and declare it closed." Major Wassem leaned back in his seat. "Of course, many would consider that an act of war, given what's at stake."

Returning to his presentation, Wassem spent the next

thirty minutes pointing out the locations of Iran's mobile Shahab-3 ballistic missile batteries along the Gulf Coast. "We've been able to determine through signals intelligence that these missile batteries are on a heightened state of readiness. I would characterize their actions as a defensive ploy, again resulting from international tensions over the nuclear confrontation. Are there any other questions?" Major Wassem looked at his watch.

"If not, it's three o'clock. Time for your meeting with the colonel." He rose from his seat and turned on the lights. "I have hard-copy imagery for the entire coastal area that you identified as being of interest. It's two days old. Since you have secure storage over in your work spaces, you may take it with you."

"Thank you, Major. That was very helpful and the imagery will facilitate our planning." Logan took the portfolio of imagery from Wassem and shook his hand.

When the team stepped out of the conference room they found Al Salman waiting for them. "This way, please." He guided them back down to the first floor and into a suite at the end of the corridor.

According to the bio sheet that he had read, Logan recalled that Colonel Al Fahad was a highly decorated career Army officer. Just forty-five, he had distinguished himself during Operation Desert Storm, and had enjoyed a rapid rise through the ranks following the war. As a young second lieutenant in 1990, he was completing a military exchange program at Sandhurst, when four Iraqi Republican Guard Mechanized and Infantry Divisions accompanied by an Iraqi Special Forces Division, blitzed into Kuwait.

Al Fahad had finagled an assignment to the UK's First Armored Division, subordinate to what would become the Army Central Command in Iraq. Over several weeks he and his comrades distinguished themselves in action against Republican Guard troops in Iraq and by late February 1991 they were leading the third-phase allied advance into Kuwait. Not to take away from the colonel's military prowess was the fact that his rise to prominence had not been inhibited by his marriage into the ruling Al Subaie family as a young man. He was one of Kuwait's elites.

Al Fahad rose from his desk and came around to welcome them. He spoke with a posh British accent, but his eyes were twinkling and his smile was warm as he greeted the team. "Ah, Mr. Campbell. It's so nice to have you all here." Nodding to the others he continued. "Nayef speaks very highly of you. We had a memorial service for a nephew two days ago and I spoke with him at length. He shared with me some details regarding your operation. It's very ambitious, and not without risk. But of course you knew that when you put forward your plan."

"Colonel, thank you for making it possible for us to train and launch from here. It's a calculated risk, no doubt. My team's got a lot of experience on the ground. Iraq, Afghanistan. A couple of the guys were even in Somalia a few years back. Everybody's going into this with their eyes wide open."

"I think most of the current action is south of Bushehr City," Al Fahad said. "The IRGC has forces massed around the Strait and their readiness levels down there are higher than normal. As Major Wassem probably told you, their naval assets and mobile ballistic missile batteries have been active in that area, but we haven't seen nearly the same level of activity anywhere else." Colonel Al Fahad turned to his desk and picked up a report.

"I have a little surprise for you. This is a SIGINT report that just came in this morning. I don't think Major Wassem has even had time to read it, but you should find it interesting."

Logan took the report and scanned it. It detailed a conversation between an Al Qaeda bomber by the name of Mustafa Al Adel in Iran and Ibrahim Al Asiri in Yemen. Al Adel was telling Al Asiri that he had just been released from house arrest in Iran and had been approached by the Iranian Qods Force. He was planning to relocate to Bandar Deylam soon and would be in touch.

Logan looked up from the report. "This gets more and more interesting as we go along."

"Indeed it does, Mr. Campbell. Indeed it does."

Chapter 27

"Well, that pretty much sums it up." Colonel Ghabel stubbed out his cigarette and looked at Major Samadi. The two Qods Force officers had just completed a surprise inspection of the IED Research and Training Facility. It was the day after Ghabel's trip to Kandahar Province in Afghanistan to meet with the Taliban commanders, and he had just finished summarizing his impressions for Samadi.

The major wheeled the dusty Safir 4X4 utility vehicle he was driving into the Administration Building parking lot and turned off the engine. "So do you trust these Afghans? From the way you described him, Awalmir Khan is a crafty bastard."

"Tahmouress, never underestimate your adversary. Our relationship with these Taliban commanders is a marriage of convenience, both for them and for us. I'm under no illusions about enjoying their trust or respect. I think Khan and his cohorts would just as soon cut our throats as look at us. Still, they seem to have some level of confidence in our comrade there, Major Hassani. Obviously this trust has been built up over time. Hassani's been in and out of Kandahar Province for a couple of years now."

"What's our next move?"

"Khan is going to vet what we put on the table with his boss, Mullah Omar, even though Khan has already tentatively agreed to send a team of fighters to us in January for advanced tactical training. I don't expect him to back away from this. Omar will see the value added of our training. He'll be intrigued by the opportunity to strengthen Taliban military capabilities against coalition forces."

"So Hassani's on the hook to provide specific dates, number of fighters, and so on?"

"Yes. We don't have a direct link to the Taliban commanders. It's probably better that way. With a single point of contact they won't be able to play us off of one another. It also will bolster Hassani's status with the Taliban. He'll continue to be seen as the point man for all Qods Force operations in Kandahar Province."

As they entered the Administration Building, Ghabel's orderly, Sergeant Yavani, called out to him. "Colonel, it's General Salehi's office calling for you."

"Coming." Turning to Major Samadi, he said, "Let's stay on top of this, Tahmouress. Meanwhile I want to go over a couple of items that came up on our inspection. Check back with me in fifteen minutes."

"Yes, sir."

Ghabel hurried into his office and told Sergeant Yavani to transfer the call to his desk. Captain Saatchi asked him to hold while he transferred the call to Salehi's secure phone.

"Colonel? Salehi here. I trust you made it back to Bandar Deylam without incident? Look, I know that I told you we could wait until you submitted your written report on your meeting with the Taliban, but we just had a call from the Supreme Leader's office. It seems he's following this activity very closely and is looking for a read-out on your meeting yesterday."

"Thank you for calling sir." Ghabel recounted the results of his meeting with Awalmir Khan and the other Taliban commanders. "We'll have to see how this plays out. For now though, they seem receptive to the idea, and we have established a tentative time frame of January to offer them a course in advanced tactics."

Ghabel divulged his feeling of mistrust of the Taliban commanders, giving an account of his eavesdropping on the Pashto-language conversation between the four Afghans.

There was a moment of silence on the other end. "I agree with your assessment, Colonel. There's been no end of bad blood between Iran and the Taliban over the years, although

Hassani's done a good job of gaining their confidence since he's been there. Just stay on top of it. If you would get your report up to us first thing I would appreciate it. I'll notify the Supreme Leader's office that it's on its way. In the meantime I'll provide an interim verbal brief based upon our conversation today. Good job."

After he had hung up, Ghabel leaned back in his chair and allowed the warmth of General Salehi's praise to wash over him. The general was not one to casually sing the praises of his subordinates, making his accolades that much more cherished. "Sergeant Yavani, could you let Major Samadi know that I'm ready for him now?"

"Yes, sir, right away."

Within a couple of minutes, Samadi appeared at Ghabel's office door. "Sir, you mentioned that you want to go over the inspection results?"

"Yes, Tahmouress. Come in, please." Ghabel and Samadi had initiated the inspection first thing that morning, beginning at the warehouse behind the Administrative Building. Per protocol they had entered the building unannounced and shouted "freeze" to the personnel working inside. Then they had inspected the premises, taking note of the infractions they had observed. They worked their way around the base in the same fashion throughout the rest of the morning.

"Two items jumped out at me that we must put straight right away, Tahmouress." Ghabel referred to a sheet of handwritten notes in front of him.

"Let me guess. The three crates of open ordnance in the warehouse and the unsecured classified reports in Captain Amanpour's desk drawer."

"Tahmouress, are you reading my mind?"

"No, sir. Those were just the most egregious violations we found. I'm less concerned about the classified reports in Amanpour's desk drawer. I mean it's not good OPSEC to have classified information sitting around the office, but we are on a secure military installation after all. No, I was more concerned about the lax handling of the ordnance. We have established procedures for a reason. The C-4 was sitting right next to a box of blasting caps and detonation cord. It must be separated from the other materiel to prevent an accident."

"I couldn't agree with you more. Give Captain Amanpour a verbal warning. I believe this is the first time he's had a security violation. Also, remind everyone who has access to classified information about the secure storage policy. On the ordnance issue, I want to come down harder. That was sloppy. That level of disregard for procedures could get someone killed.

"I want you to issue written reprimands for all involved. Also, I want each of those men to receive remedial training on the proper handling and storage of ordnance. Finally, I want to document this in everyone's annual evaluation. Unless we see measurable improvement, no one is getting promoted this year."

"Yes, sir. I'll see to it. If you have a minute I'd like to give you an update on a separate matter – the Al Qaeda demolitions expert we met with last week."

"Mustafa Al Adel?" Ghabel put his inspection notes aside and turned his attention to Samadi. You know, I mentioned Al Adel to General Salehi when I saw him a couple of days ago."

"What was his reaction?"

"He was very supportive. He even suggested that if our initiative with Al Adel works out we might turn that into a pilot program for enhanced cooperation with Al Qaeda."

"You mean, tapping into some of the other detainees in Iran?"

"Precisely. But I digress. You were talking about Al Adel. Have you contacted him since our meeting in Borazjan?"

"Yes. We met in Bandar Deylam two days ago. I had done some research on housing options for him, but there was little available. I did locate a family with a vacant room for rent. I checked them out. They're merchants – an older couple with adult children. Nothing negative came out of the background check on any of them. I took Al Adel over to look at the room, and he's already moved in."

"That was quick."

"He's eager to do something. I think a year of house arrest has left him fidgety. He misses all the action. Anyway, I had him come in yesterday to meet Captain Amanpour and some of his people."

"Oh? Any first impressions from Amanpour?"

"He said Al Adel is the real deal. We had devised a kind of test for him. The idea was to show him an IED package that we were supposedly about to deploy. But, unbeknownst to him, the IED had a subtle modification so that, if deployed, it would fail."

"And?"

"It took him maybe two minutes to figure it out."

"Well, that's encouraging."

"It looks as though he might work out. One thought occurred to me, though. I wondered if it might boost his motivation if you were to give him an official welcome. He's down on the bombing range with Sergeant Major Tehrani right now, getting an orientation. I thought perhaps we could just drop by there rather than making a big production out of it."

"All right, let's go." On their way out Ghabel stopped at Sergeant Yavani's desk. "Have you finished typing up the memorandum from my trip?"

"Yes, sir. I just finished it."

"Tahmouress, give me five minutes to review this and then we'll head out." Ghabel pored over the memorandum, editing a couple of sentences and correcting punctuation. He handed it back to his orderly and asked him to make the changes before sending it Eyes Only to General Salehi.

When Ghabel and Samadi reached the firing range a few minutes later, they could see the Al Qaeda bomber in spirited conversation with Sergeant Major Tehrani. Walking up to them, Ghabel clasped Al Adel's outstretched hand. "Mr. Al Adel, welcome to Bandar Deylam."

"Colonel."

"Major Samadi tells me that you're getting settled in and have been meeting our people."

"Yes. Everyone has been very helpful. Even that little test that Captain Amanpour designed for me."

Ghabel and Samadi feigned ignorance. "What test?" Ghabel hoped that the surprised look on his face would register as genuine.

"Oh, come on, Colonel. A rank beginner wouldn't have made the wiring mistake on that IED package. I'm certain that Captain Amanpour had something to do with it, perhaps to see how much I've forgotten over the past year," he scoffed.

Ghabel looked at Major Samadi with raised eyebrows. "Yes, well, perhaps. It seems that you haven't lost your touch. What are your initial impressions?"

"For me, one of the biggest differences is having the facilities to field-test the IED's. When I was in Iraq and Afghanistan, we were always working out of a safe house or an apartment one of the brothers had rented. We never had the capability to field-test anything. We would just build these bombs and deliver them to the IED teams. There was always a short-fuse requirement." Al Adel laughed at his play on words. "I'm certain that some of our failures could have been avoided if we had had facilities like this to work out the kinks."

"It's true. One cannot underestimate the value of these facilities for our program. We're the premier IED research and training facility in the Republic. We have the highest levels of support, both from the political leadership and from within the IRGC. We want for nothing." Ghabel studied Al Adel's face.

"You can build great bombs, but ultimately if the brothers screw it up, what's the point?" Al Adel said. "Yesterday, when I met with Captain Amanpour, I had a chance to review several tapes from recent operations. I was particularly interested in the one you mentioned when we met in Borazjan – the Ramadi operation."

"Oh? Did you learn anything?" Ghabel offered Al Adel a cigarette and lit it for him.

Al Adel inhaled deeply and paused before replying. "You recall when we met in Borazjan I talked about the Emir's vision to establish an Islamic worldwide Caliphate?"

Ghabel nodded his head in the affirmative.

"I learned Bin Laden's manual for Jihad by heart," Al Adel said. "In his *Military Studies in the Jihad Against the Tyrants,* Bin Laden said, 'Islam is resolute against the heathens and heretic rulers; it does not know the dialogue of Socrates, the ideals of Plato, or the diplomacy of Aristotle. Islam only knows the language of bullets, the ideal of assassination, violence and devastation, and the diplomacy of the machine gun and cannon.'"

Al Adel flicked his cigarette onto the ground and crushed it with his boot. "These foreign fighters you're training don't show that level of passion for Jihad. They're ciphers."

Ghabel took his time before reacting. "So essentially you're saying that these fighters today don't have the stomach for Jihad?"

"It may be that. It may be that the brothers are exhausted from waging war for all these years with no end in sight. But I think the overriding truth is that with Bin Laden gone, there is no one offering a strategic vision for Al Qaeda."

"So what do you think the solution is?"

"We have to keep driving home the Emir's message. I'll bet there are young Jihadists out there who haven't even read Bin Laden's manual."

Ghabel looked thoughtful. "We're a research and training facility. We're not equipped to delve into political indoctrination, nor is it our role. But if you want to bring an element of that to the teams that come in for training, you could probably pull it off. You would have credibility with them." They talked for a few more minutes and then Ghabel and Samadi left Al Adel to continue his orientation with Sergeant Major Tehrani.

Riding back up to the Administration Building, Ghabel stared out the window. He shifted his gaze back to Major Samadi. "It seems General Salehi was right when he said that Al Adel appears to be a bit of an ideologue."

"A bit? He's a fucking lunatic."

"Perhaps. But, Tahmouress, for now he's our fucking lunatic."

When they returned to the Administration building, Ghabel checked in with Sergeant Yavani.

"You had two calls while you were out, Colonel. Your wife called, but she didn't leave a message. Also, First Sergeant Ghorbani's widow is trying to reach you. She's having trouble processing her insurance claim. It seems the army has lost Sergeant Ghorbani's military records, and they are not being very helpful. She keeps getting the runaround. The insurance company won't do anything for her until they have his paperwork."

Ghabel cursed to himself. Those fucking camel drivers! Ghorbani gets blown to smithereens doing his job and some bean counter is pissing on his widow. "Thank you, Sergeant Yavani. I'll see to it." Ghabel placed a call to the IRGC headquarters personnel office in Tehran and after being transferred to three different desks, was finally able to locate Ghorbani's records. They had not been misplaced, but were being held in a classified area because of his work at the secret Qods Force facility.

Ghabel instructed the clerk to produce an unclassified version of Ghorbani's service record and to send it to Ghorbani's widow immediately. He put the clerk on hold while verifying with Yavani that the woman's address of record was correct. Once that was finished he had Yavani place a call to Ghorbani's widow.

"Hello? Eleni? Colonel Ghabel here. Sergeant Yavani told me that you had called. How are you doing? How are the boys?" Ghabel looked at the clock on the wall and saw that it was already three-thirty. Where had the day gone?

"Ah, Colonel. Thank you for calling back. It's not so good. My boys are not handling their father's death very well. You know they were very close. They worshipped him."

"I'm sorry for your loss. We miss him here too. Listen, I've located your husband's records. They're in Tehran. Copies of everything will be delivered to you this week. On behalf of the IRGC please accept our apologies for this mix-up."

"Thank you, Colonel." Eleni Ghorbani gave a convulsive sigh and then began to weep.

Ghabel felt his throat constrict and then got his emotions under control. "If you need anything, please do not hesitate to call. Let me give you my personal cell phone number."

Next Ghabel tried Azar's number and reached her on the third ring. "Azar, I'm sorry that I missed your call earlier. Tahmouress and I were outside conducting an inspection."

"It's all right – I just wanted to hear the sound of your voice." Her voice sounded strained.

"Are you all right? How is your mother?"

"We are fine. There was some trouble in a mosque near the university this morning."

"I haven't seen any news today. What's going on?"

"A bomb exploded in the mosque."

"What! Were there any casualties?"

"Seven dead and over 100 people injured."

"My God! What's happening?"

"The mullah there is known for his weekly sermons against the Wahabists and the Bahais. Some are saying that it is their supporters who did this. Then I heard one other man in the bazaar saying that it was probably militants from God's Brigade. I'm afraid, Barzin!"

"Now, now. Everything will be fine. The police will find the perpetrators and punish them. We should expel those damn Sunni Wahabists and send them back to Saudi Arabia. As for the Bahais, I find it hard to believe they could muster support for something like this. They've been banned from worshipping in Iran a long time. Why don't you come home? Bring your mother with you."

"We can't. We must be here to celebrate the Cheleh."

Cheleh, Ghabel mused. The forty-day commemoration of his father-in-law's death was two weeks away. He felt a slight twinge of guilt that he would not be in Shiraz to support Azar and her mother, but he didn't see how he could take time off. With the new Taliban initiative, their work with Al Qaeda, and the nationwide alert, he couldn't justify taking leave.

"Be careful then, if you must stay. If you can, avoid going to the bazaar for a few days until this settles down." They talked for several more minutes and then said goodbye.

Afterwards, Ghabel sat staring at Azar's picture, pondering what she had just told him. Usually Shiraz was quiet. Of course, there was that time a few years ago when God's Brigade had exploded a car bomb next to an IRGC bus in downtown Shiraz. A dozen troops had been killed and many more were injured in that attack. He pursed his lips. Bastards. May they burn in hell.

Chapter 28

"What do you think, Norm?" Logan wiped his brow and took a sip of water from his canteen. He and Norm Stoddard were squatting in the shade of the warehouse on Failaka Island Army Base.

Zahir had just escorted Jaber Behbehani, the Kuwaiti asset who'd been inside the Iranian IED training camp, over to his ride to the ferry terminal. It was the third time in the past ten days that Logan had debriefed Behbehani, and the question he had just posed to Stoddard was whether or not they should take him into Iran.

"I think it's a no-brainer, Logan. I mean, he's the only one who's been inside that facility. We can debrief him all day long but it's not the same as having him right there with us when we go in."

"I know. I just don't know if we can trust him. His motive for going back is to get even with Ghabel for the beating he took. He might lose it."

"Let's be honest, Logan. Behbehani isn't the only one with a grudge against the Qods Force. Everyone on this team is looking forward to taking those bastards down."

"You've got a point. But the difference is we're trained professionals. We can put our personal feelings aside until after it's all over. We don't let our feelings affect our judgment on the ground."

"True that. But think about what Behbehani's been through. That story about him agreeing to sit in a Kuwaiti jail for months after the Kuwaitis wrapped up his foreign fighter cell so nobody would think he was cooperating with the police; going into Iran to identify where the foreign fighter IED teams are being trained. I mean, this guy's got cojones."

"Let me think about it. I'm starting to think it might not be a bad idea."

Logan and Norm stretched and then walked back into the warehouse. Logan looked at his watch and was surprised to see that it was already twelve o'clock. "Time for lunch. Let's see what Faran made for us today."

The portly Kuwaiti had turned out to be an excellent chef. Cooking in the traditional Bedouin style over an open charcoal flame, he'd turned out a steady stream of mouth-watering dishes. Today Faran had prepared *machboos*, a mutton stew served on fragrant rice.

As had been their custom since they'd arrived a week ago, the team held a working lunch. Their mission this afternoon was to scout out the best insertion point for their infiltration along Iran's coastline. Using the overhead that Major Wassem had loaned them, they pored over a five-mile stretch of coast north of the port of Bandar Deylam.

"What are the coordinates for Bandar Deylam?" Stoddard leaned forward to get a better view of the port. "I need to put them into this GPS unit."

"30.050791 latitude by 50.162891 longitude." Logan squinted as he read the numbers off the map legend. "Look at this." Logan pointed to a spot on the map north of the port city. "Before we came over here I was doing some research on these caves along the coast. Most of them are salt caves. There's this really famous one off the south coast of Iran on Qeshm Island. I wonder if this one here is like that?"

"Oh, I remember reading about those caves." Zahir looked up. "That big one you're talking about is called the 3 N. Some Czech cavers found it in the 1990s and then worked with Shiraz University for over ten years to map it out. There ended up being dozens of interconnected caves stretching out for several miles."

"Isn't it supposed to be the biggest salt cave in the world?"

"Something like that. These caves are supposed to be totally different from limestone caves. I remember the article I read saying that rock salt comes up from the ground and then when it rains it corrodes these salt cylinders that have been formed, and you end up with these unique karst formations."

"So for our purposes next week, it doesn't matter if it's limestone or salt. What does matter, though, is tides. When we were back home I looked at tide data for the Gulf and it's pretty complex. But the Department of Hydrography at Iran's National Cartographic Center is kind enough to model tide predictions online.

"On December 15, when we'll be going in, Bandar Deylam will be at low tide, about three feet." Logan poked his finger at the spot on the map. "This looks like as good a spot as any to land."

Stoddard picked up from there. "So the idea is we vector in towards that cave on our mother ship, offload a couple of miles offshore and then after we get to shore, conceal the Zodiac inside that cave. A three-foot low tide will allow us to get in and stow the Zodiac, do our thing and then retrieve it a couple of hours later."

"What's the cover for action for the mother ship?" Delray directed his question to Logan.

"We're going to have two boats in play, because one boat coming in at that hour and then turning right around and departing two hours later would look strange. You might be able to pull that off if you were simulating a ferry run scenario, but at that time of day, and the fact we won't have any other passengers on board, makes that pretty weak.

"So here's what I've been thinking. A private yacht is going to depart for Bandar Deylam early on the morning of the 14th. They're going to be coming from the south, not Kuwait City. They'll overnight in Bandar Deylam. Thamir tells me that they have maritime assets that go into Iran all the time so this will look normal. That boat will be our extraction vessel early in the morning on the 15th."

"What are we going to be using for our insertion?" Blackjack Wozolski, the Seal from Princeton, spoke up.

Logan pulled a couple of photos out of a manila folder and passed them around the table. "This fishing trawler is another Kuwaiti Intel asset. They use it in the Gulf to monitor Iranian naval operations. It has a pattern of calling at Bandar Deylam a couple of times a month, so its presence there on the 15th won't arouse any suspicions. We'll launch the Zodiac here." Logan pointed to a spot about two miles off the Iranian coast.

"Delray's going to stay aboard the trawler so he can transfer to the yacht once they're in port." Logan passed around another set of pictures depicting the yacht.

Delray spoke up. "The only tricky part I envision will be switching boats without attracting any attention from the Iranians. At that hour it should be quiet so I'm thinking I'll be able to pull it off without heating things up."

"You'll be documented with Kuwaiti seaman's papers for flash purposes if anyone questions you," Logan pointed out. "But that introduction to Arabic that you took at Monterrey a couple years ago won't get you too far, so try not to talk to anybody if you can help it."

Delray gave him a rueful smile. "Oh, don't you worry about that. My lips are sealed." He made a zipping motion across his mouth.

Logan collected the photos and looked around the table. "I've got the two boat captains coming in tomorrow morning. We're going to brief them on their part of the scenario to make sure everyone's on the same page. It'll also give the yacht captain a chance to eyeball Delray. What do you think?"

Stoddard spoke up. "The maritime piece looks pretty solid. But how about actually getting from where we cache the Zodiac, onto the base? I know there was some talk about using transportation assets the Kuwaitis have over there, right?"

Logan stood and paced back and forth in front of the group. "The Kuwaitis offered us one of their assets, an Iranian who owns a long-distance trucking company in Bandar Deylam. Most of his business involves hauling cargo inland from the port. Their idea was to have him leave a truck for us here off the road, close to where we'll be dropping anchor." He pointed to their landing spot on the imagery map.

"How would he explain that to the police when all hell breaks loose? I'm assuming it wouldn't take the Iranians very long to make the connection between this trucking guy and what happens at the base." Stoddard appeared dumbfounded by the proposal.

"My thinking exactly. Well, their idea was to have him call the police after we're back on the mother ship to report the truck stolen. I didn't like it. It still implicates him and even though Thamir says this guy's a vetted asset, I didn't like the idea of one more person knowing when and where we'll be. Thamir hinted that this guy has a hard-on for the Qods Force and is super-motivated to stick it to them."

"Why's that?"

"The way Thamir told it, the guy's son was fulfilling his military service obligation last year. He was assigned to a Qods Force unit in Shiraz. It turns out this kid was gay and when his chain of command found out about it they did a number on him. They tried making an example of him. He was ostracized in front of everyone. Apparently he couldn't take the humiliation and killed himself. Shot himself in the head. He was only eighteen years old."

"No fucking way!"

"Yeah, so you can understand why his old man feels the way he does."

"Man, that's fucked up." Barbiari joined the conversation. "Guess the Iranians never heard of 'don't ask don't tell.'"

"I don't know if they did or not." Logan let out an exasperated sigh. "I do remember a couple of years ago when their president was giving a speech at the United Nations and he said that Iran didn't have any homosexuals. Everybody laughed at him. It was ridiculous. The Iranians are in their own little world. But you know, even at home it's not like 'don't ask don't tell' was some kind of enlightened policy DOD came up with."

"Yeah, until 2011," Barbiari said. "Remember when Congress repealed the policy?" He looked around the room. "There was this guy in my unit in Iraq who was gay and got kicked out in 2009. It was just wrong. Calvin Simpson.

He was one tough bastard. We were in a firefight in Iraq a couple of years ago and one of our scouts got shot in the leg and couldn't walk.

"Simpson carried that poor SOB for almost a mile before they sent in a chopper to get us out. You know, before I served with Simpson, I'd never even met a homosexual, at least not that I knew. I mean, it wasn't like I was a gay-basher or anything, but we just didn't run in the same circles. I'd serve with Calvin Simpson again in a heartbeat."

Stoddard held his hand up and broke in. "All right, guys, we got sidetracked. So let's get back to the transportation issue. If we don't get the vehicle from the guy with the trucking company, how are we going to make it from the beach to the base?"

"I'm just thinking we hump it, Norm." Logan walked back over to the front of the room and stood next to the map. "It's a little under three miles." He traced an imaginary line on the map with his finger. "We can get off the road almost as soon as we stash the Zodiac and come in cross-country through here. There's almost nothing out there."

"How long do you think it would take us to walk it?"

"I don't know, thirty, forty-five minutes max. We'll have more options coming back. We could use vehicles from the base to get back to the Zodiac. Behbehani gave me a good idea of what's in their motor pool. The only down side I can think of is it'll stick out like a sore thumb once we're gone. When the balloon goes up, and they start trying to figure out what happened, the bad guys will hone in on that truck. They may start checking all the boat traffic that's been in and out of Bandar Deylam. At least if we're on foot there's a fig leaf. It wouldn't immediately point to a water landing.

"Let's think it through," Logan went on. "If everything goes according to plan, we'll be in and out of the target in say, thirty minutes. The base isn't that big and except for a skeletal security detachment, everybody lives off base."

Zahir raised her hand. "What about if they're running a training program? We know that the foreign fighters are housed on the base."

"Good question. So far there's nothing in the Intel indicating they'll be training anyone that week."

"How about that piece of SIGINT Colonel Al Fahad showed us the other day?" she continued. "You know, the one about the Al Qaeda bomber? What's his name? Al Adel? If he's moving to Bandar Deylam it's probably because the Qods Force wants to use him to help train their foreign fighters."

"Could be. Maybe they're getting ready to bring in some foreign fighters. When Wassem read that report the other day he said that Al Adel and Al Asiri's names rang a bell, so he did some checking around. Turns out both those guys are heavy hitters inside Al Qaeda. There's a bounty out on both their heads. CIA wants to nail Al Adel especially because he was the mastermind behind that 2009 attack in Afghanistan that killed seven CIA officers."

Stoddard let out a low whistle. "I hope that bastard's there, Logan. I'd like to take him down."

Logan sat back down in his chair. "Getting back to the question of land transportation. Time on target is going to be critical, especially after we hit the base. We're not taking any prisoners, so anybody that's in there is going down. After we've secured the area we'll have two missions. Collect as much Intel as we can, and destroy that place. I don't want a frigging building left standing.

"We'll time our charges to detonate once we're back on the yacht and out of the area. Even if they go off earlier, I don't think it would get anyone's attention. They're used to stuff blowing up there at all hours."

"The longer those charges are sitting there, the greater the risk of something going wrong. We can probably save ourselves thirty minutes by using one of their trucks," Stoddard said. "We'll be on the yacht and on our way back here forty-five minutes after we leave the base." Stoddard stood up and stretched. "I think the benefits of using the truck outweigh the negatives. Here's another thought. What if someone gets injured when we go in and isn't mobile? We'll need transportation to handle that."

Logan paused for a moment as he thought it through. "All right, let's leave it at that. We'll plan to hike in and use one of their trucks to exfil out of there. OK, everybody. Let's wrap it up. We've got a busy day tomorrow. We're meeting those two boat captains down at the ferry port at seven o'clock."

Chapter 29

Early the next morning the team drove their 4X4 to the heavily damaged ferry port on the island's northwest coast. Overnight the two vessels had ridden the high tide into port and were tied up at the dilapidated dock. The anchorage did not wear its neglect well. Dredging operations in the channel had ceased during the Iraqi occupation and afterward, never resumed. As a result, the inlet leading to the docks was slowly filling in with silt, compelling boats to arrive and depart on the high tides.

The team spent the next two hours touring the two boats and talking with the captains. The Ocean Dreamer was a sixty-nine-foot cruiser and with its two inboard diesel engines was capable of cruising at thirty-three knots per hour. The less elegant, but decidedly sturdy, Gulf Pearl fishing trawler was a seventy-five-foot steel-hulled freezer shrimper.

Sitting aboard the Ocean Dreamer, Logan led the briefing, with Zahir translating into Arabic. He outlined the scenario beginning with their early morning departure from Failaka Island aboard the Gulf Pearl on the 15th.

"Captain, what time do you recommend we leave Failaka Island to assure a three-thirty a.m. arrival here?" Logan indicated a point on the map north of Bandar Deylam Port.

Captain Al Shayah, a swarthy seaman, whose creased skin and gnarled fingers bespoke decades of labor on Gulf fishing vessels, stroked his chin. "If we're loaded up and ready to go, we should plan to depart here no later than midnight." He rose and consulted a tide table sitting on the chart desk. "High tide is at eleven-thirty that night, so conditions will be favorable for our departure then. How long do you think you'll need to load all of your gear?"

"We'll have everything down here at eleven. It shouldn't take us more than half an hour to get all of our stuff on board, and that will give us an extra half-hour cushion."

"I have a four-man crew, so we can get everything on board quickly."

"So, once we get to this point," Logan pointed to the spot on the chart, "we'll be going in the rest of the way in our Zodiac while you continue on to the port." He pointed to Delray. "He's going with you all the way so that he can get on board the Ocean Dreamer. Is there much going on at the port at that hour?"

"No. It will be very quiet. In fact, he will be able to get onto the Ocean Dreamer and no one will be any the wiser." Captain Al Shayah looked in the direction of the Ocean Dreamer's skipper, Captain Al Watan, who nodded his agreement.

"Do you have legitimate business in Bandar Deylam?"

"Yes. I've been going in there for years. I'm delivering a shipment of shrimp that morning so everything will look quite normal."

Logan glanced over at Captain Al Watan. "Do the two of you ever have any contact with each other when you're over there?"

Al Watan, who was slim and refined looking, arched his back with feline grace. "No. In fact, we would make every effort not to be in port at the same time." He paused a moment.

"Having your man move from the Gulf Pearl to the Ocean Dream links our two boats in a way we've successfully avoided up until now. But it seems to be an acceptable risk, mainly because at that hour there is hardly anyone about. We'll be waiting for him, and get him below decks right away, where he should remain until we are out of the port. As I understand it, we should be at the target location by five-forty-five a.m. Is that correct?"

"Earlier is better. We just want to make sure that we don't raise your profile by having you there so early that you have to wait for us."

"I think we'll manage just fine, Mr. Campbell."

"So, Captain Al Watan, you're coming up from Bushehr Port on the 14th, right?"

"Yes, that's correct. I have a crew of two and we'll be carrying one passenger, a wealthy Kuwaiti businessman who has legitimate business in Bushehr City and in Bandar Deylam. Telecommunications."

"I assume he'll know something about all of this?"

"When it becomes necessary. In fact, this is his yacht, which he allows our friend Mr. Alghanim to use from time to time."

"I see. Well, gentlemen, I think that pretty much covers it. Does anybody have any questions?" Logan scanned the expectant faces sitting around the Ocean Dreamer. No one did. After Al Shayah and Al Watan had raised anchor and drifted off on the high tide, the team boarded their 4X4 and made their way back to the base.

"Nice job with the interpreting, Zahir." Logan gave her an appreciative glance.

She flashed a smile. "Gulf Arabic isn't too challenging. Now, if it was North African Arabic, we'd be in trouble."

Logan scanned the faces of the team as they drove onto the army base. "Four more days, guys, and then it's show time. We're ready for this now. I've been thinking about a quote from Thomas Paine when he wrote *The American Crisis* in 1776. It goes something like this:

"'These are the times that try men's souls. The summer soldier and the sunshine patriot will, in this crisis, shrink from the service of their country; but he that stands it now, deserves the love and thanks of man and woman. Tyranny, like hell, is not easily conquered; yet we have this consolation with us, that the harder the conflict, the more glorious the triumph. What we obtain too cheap, we esteem too lightly: it's only dearness that gives everything its value.'"

Chapter 30

"All right. Let's do it!" In the dim light, Logan studied the eager faces of the team members pressed together on the deck. It was almost midnight and they had just finished loading their gear aboard the Gulf Pearl.

Logan, the last of the group to board, had barely cleared the dock when the four crewmembers began hauling in lines as they prepared to get underway. The trawler backed slowly away from the ferry port, swung to its starboard side, caught the current, and began to churn into the Gulf. The diesel engines throbbed, a reassuring, resonant pitch that intensified into a throaty roar as the captain opened up the throttle and set a north by northeast course.

Once they cleared the northern tip of Failaka Island, the lights from the army base were the only sign of human activity. As the island receded in their wake, midnight's black pall enveloped them.

"We're about three and a half hours out, so if anybody wants to try and get some shut-eye now's probably a good time to do it." Logan leaned back against the bulkhead and went through a mental checklist of their operational plan. They had rehearsed it to perfection and he felt a sense of anticipation as the trawler cut through the Gulf waters.

He heard the whispering of soft-spoken Arabic and could just make out the shape of Jaber Behbehani in conversation with Zahir. Logan had decided to bring the young Kuwaiti along, and in the short time Behbehani had trained with them, he had proven to be an adept student.

Logan drifted off, but awoke to the sound of Captain Al Shayah's voice. He was talking to Zahir and gesturing toward the stern of the trawler. The captain returned to the wheelhouse as Zahir stood and made her way over to where Logan was resting.

"Captain Al Shayah says we're only fifteen minutes from the coordinates you gave him."

Standing up and looking aft, Logan could just make out distant lights to the south. "That must be Bandar Deylam over there." He pointed south and held his gaze for a moment. "Let's get everybody assembled near the stern. Get your gear together. Delray, you and Wellington break out the F470. Jones, grab hold of that scuba tank over there and let's get this thing pumped up."

Ten minutes later the Futura Commando F470 was fully inflated. Captain Al Shayah eased back on the throttle and the Gulf Pearl glided to a stop. Gentle waves lapped at the prow, rocking the trawler as the team readied to hoist the Zodiac off the stern. Within minutes their craft was in the water and team members had clambered down the Gulf Pearl's stern ladder, stowed their gear, and had taken low-profile positions in the Zodiac.

As they pushed away from the larger vessel and picked up speed, Logan glanced back and could see the Gulf Pearl angling away from them towards Bandar Deylam Port. Delray stood at attention on deck and snapped off a salute as they pulled away.

* * *

Colonel Ghabel awoke feeling groggy. He snapped the light on in his office and looked at the clock on the wall. Three a.m. As base commander, he seldom pulled evening security duty, but with Azar still in Shiraz, and the additional workload stemming from their redoubled Afghanistan initiative, he had started sharing some of the burden.

Also, the foreign fighter team from Iraq was due in sometime later that morning for training. Their new instructor, the Al Qaeda demolitions expert, Mustafa Al Adel, had begun sleeping in the student quarters as he worked overtime to revamp the curriculum. He was also working on a segment he would personally lead on Al Qaeda's political ideology.

Ghabel turned off the light and rolled over onto his side. Things were going well. His relationship with General Salehi had never been better, and a number of the initiatives he had put forward were coming to fruition. Maybe when the next round of promotions were announced he would get his star. He mouthed the words to see how it would sound. Brigadier General Ghabel. Nice, he smiled to himself as he fell back asleep. Azar would be proud.

Norm Stoddard put the Zodiac on a southeast heading, and began angling the boat in towards shore. The engine emitted a muted growl as it powered the inflatable through the waves in the direction of their beachhead. The team members straddled the gunwale and spray doused them as they took wave after wave head on. Logan could feel a surge of adrenaline as they neared the shore and sensed rather than saw the same level of anticipation in the others.

Ten minutes later, paralleling the coastline about two hundred feet offshore, they searched for the entrance to the salt cave. "There." Logan pointed straight ahead.

Stoddard aimed the inflatable towards the opening and ran it up inside the rocky shelter. The cave was more spacious than it had appeared on the imagery. There was ample room to stand, and as Logan shined his flashlight onto the walls, he could see several sturdy karst columns that would provide secure tie-downs for the inflatable. After they had secured the boat and gathered up all of their gear, Logan took the point. Using hand signals he instructed everyone to move out.

They were about twenty feet below the road, and after navigating a rocky path climbing away from the beach, they emerged onto a coastal highway. It was deserted at that hour, and as the imagery had depicted, there were no manmade structures within miles. A quarter moon, sharply etched against the night sky, seemed to hang, almost like an ornament, above them. Ambient light from the moon and the star-filled sky lit their way.

Before crossing the highway, Logan took a reading from his compass. "Zahir, ask Behbehani if any of this looks familiar to him."

Zahir questioned the diminutive Kuwaiti in Arabic. "He says that he's been on this road before. When he was here the last time, Ghabel's men drove his team to the facility along here." Behbehani continued to talk and pointed to the northeast along a line similar to the one Logan had identified. "If you go cross-country in this direction, you will come out near the main entrance to the IED facility."

"OK. No talking from here on out. There's nothing out here and sound carries pretty far."

The team moved at a steady clip through the rocky terrain. Their month of desert conditioning and training was paying off. Skirting thickets of brush and date palms, their path was largely unimpeded. Their stealthy movement spooked a wake of nesting buzzards whose flapping wings and shrill calls disrupted the quiet night.

Forty-five minutes later they were approaching the training facility's main gatehouse. According to Behbehani, usually only two guards were on duty in the evening. Logan signaled to the Ranger from South Carolina, Kyler Jones, to secure the gatehouse. Logan watched as Jones inched forward on his stomach to within thirty feet of the structure.

The door was open and Logan could hear the voices of two men conversing. Shifting slightly, he could see the two Qods Force soldiers leaning against the door frame, talking. Their weapons were propped up against the wall.

Jones slipped off the safety on his AK-47 and sighted down the barrel. He tapped a head shot into each soldier. Neither of them had time to react, although there was a look of surprise, and then shock on the second guard's face as his buddy's head exploded next to him. The noise suppression on the AK-47 was effective in masking the sound of the short burst, the only noise being the impact of the soldiers' bodies crashing to the ground.

Logan and the others rose as one and rushed the gatehouse. Jones cleared the room as Wozolski and Stoddard dragged the bodies of the two dead soldiers into the enclosure and out of sight. Logan signaled Jones to remain behind to secure the entrance as the others moved onto the base.

The Intel and Behbehani's description of the facility had been spot on, Logan decided. Getting his bearings he could see the research and administration building a hundred yards in front of him. Behind it was the warehouse and motor pool. Across from a dusty parade ground was the classroom and student quarters.

Logan signaled Tyler and Wozolski to cover the classrooms. He directed Stoddard and Barbiari to the warehouse behind the Administrative building. Wellington's mission was to cut power to the base and take out its communication center, after which he was to secure a vehicle from the motor pool and then take out the range control facilities at the bombing range. Logan, Zahir and Behbehani took off at a medium trot in the direction of the research facility.

Tyler and Wozolski moved at a fast clip towards the classroom. It was quiet at that hour and only the sound of their boots on the road and their labored breathing broke the stillness of the night. Entering the classroom, Tyler swept his AK-47 180 degrees from left to right. It was empty. "Clear."

Seconds later they pushed their way into the single-story barracks. As Wozolski entered the room there was a strangled shout from the far end. Mustafa Al Adel had just emerged from the bathroom and was hitching up his pants. As he spotted the two men, the dim light bulb above his head flickered out.

Al Adel rushed towards one of the bunks about twenty feet away, but Wozolski, whose night vision goggles provided a clear image of the Al-Qaeda bomber despite the enveloping darkness, cut him down mid-stride with a single burst from his AK-47. Al Adel slumped to the floor, a neat bullet hole drilled into the socket where his left eye had once been.

Searching the nightstand next to the bunk, Tyler scooped up Al Adel's cell phone, wallet, several DVDs, and a number of notebooks with diagrams and writing in Arabic. "I don't know if this sucker was Qods Force or not. There aren't any military uniforms in here, just civvies," he whispered.

"Maybe he's one of those foreign fighters Behbehani was talking about." Wozolski took Al Adel's wallet from Tyler and flipping through it, saw that it contained a photo ID. After securing the wallet, he withdrew a ruggedized SLR 35-mm camera from his pack and photographed the body and the interior and exterior of the two buildings. He returned to the barracks, knelt by al-Adel's corpse and removed a sample of his hair and nail clippings, which he deposited into two separate plastic baggies. "If this guy is on anybody's watch list, this stuff will be good for forensics. We've got his DNA and some kind of photo ID."

Wozolski keyed the tactical radio and spoke into the microphone. "Team Alpha, this is Team Bravo. Do you read me? Over."

Logan's quiet voice responded immediately. "Team Bravo, Team Alpha reads you loud and clear. Over."

"Team Alpha, our objective is secure. One hostile down. Moving on to Phase Two."

"Roger that." Logan smiled as they breached the Administrative Building. So far so good.

"Alpha, this is Charlie. Over." Wellington's voice came across as a whisper.

"Go, Charlie. Alpha reads you loud and clear. Over."

"OK. Power's cut and the land-line is out. Heading over to secure a vehicle."

"Roger that. When you get the vehicle, go down range and see what you can do with their range control facility. Take it out."

Wozolski and Tyler set to work rigging the classroom and barracks with explosives. They unpacked several blocks of C4 plastic explosive, blasting caps, det cord, fuses, time delay circuits and thermal batteries. They had twenty-five minutes to wire the place and get out of there.

Ghabel awoke with a start. He had been sleeping fitfully since he had awakened at three o'clock. He turned on the light but there was no response. Cursing, he pressed the night mode light button on his digital watch and squinted in the dark to make out the time. Just after four. He had been dreaming that he had heard the sound of gunfire, but that was impossible at this hour.

Rising, he moved to the entryway opening onto the main corridor and pressed his ear against the door. There was a faint rustling sound in the corridor. Alarmed, Ghabel went back to his desk and picked up the phone to call security at the main gate. The phone line was dead.

Chapter 31

Logan, Zahir and Behbehani slipped through the main corridor of the Research and Administrative Building. There had been a BMW sedan parked in the lot outside, but there was no sign of life as they began moving through the building. Logan wondered who the Beamer belonged to. His mind was racing as they turned down another corridor leading away from the labs. They had caught a break not having to deal with any foreign fighters, he thought.

He knew from the Intel and what Behbehani had said, that the foreign fighter cells were usually no more than eight guys. Not a deal-killer if there had been a group but it sure would have complicated their lives. Logan gestured towards the other two to fan out. They needed to clear the building before they could do anything else. He was half-way down the corridor when he heard the sound of scuffling and Zahir's panicked scream.

"Help!"

Logan turned around and raced back in the direction Zahir had gone. Reaching the corridor he could see her wrestling with a wiry Qods Force soldier. In a split second Logan took in the fact that the man wore the rank of colonel, had short curly hair and just the shadow of a beard. Ghabel. He was a perfect match for Behbehani's description of the Qods Force officer.

Where the hell was Behbehani? Searching farther down the corridor he noticed an office door slightly ajar and could just make out the shadowy outline of the little Kuwaiti inside the door frame. Logan didn't have a clear shot at Ghabel without risking injury to Zahir.

Ghabel had disarmed Zahir and had her in a headlock,

with his service pistol pressed against her jaw. "Who are you?" he demanded.

His eyes swept back and forth and he spotted Logan down the hall. "Come out! Now! Or I'll kill your friend." Ghabel tightened his grip on Zahir and pulled her against him. He pressed the pistol into the fleshy part of her neck.

Logan stepped into full view pointing his weapon at Ghabel.

"Put your weapon down," Ghabel shouted. "Kick it over there or I swear by God I'll kill her! Do it!"

Trembling, Zahir translated Ghabel's demand.

Logan's mind raced. He couldn't risk playing chicken with Ghabel. Zahir's life was at risk. From what Behbehani had told him, he knew that Ghabel was a ruthless bastard who'd no doubt make good on his threat. He placed his AK-47 on the floor and kicked it away.

Ghabel relaxed his grip slightly on Zahir. "Now, come closer and get down on your knees."

"All right, easy. Don't shoot."

When Logan had complied with his order, Ghabel stared at him. "She is Persian, but you, I'm certain, are not. Your accent sounds American, but how can that be? Are you American?" How did you get here? More importantly, why are you here?"

"We know all about your little research facility, Colonel." Logan gave him a cold look. "You're going down."

Ghabel started to laugh. "But this is absurd. Look at you. I'm going to let you watch me kill your friend, and then I'm going to kill you. But first you're going to tell me who you're working for and how you got in here."

"It doesn't matter. Iran is finally going to be exposed for what it is, a rogue terrorist state." Logan spat the words out.

"Perhaps I must convince you that I am serious." Ghabel grabbed hold of Zahir's hair. "Take off your clothes!"

Zahir cringed and began to shake.

"Now!"

Zahir hesitated and Ghabel tightened his grip on her hair. She gave Logan an imploring look and then deliberately began to remove her clothing. She paused as she stood there in her bra and panties, and Ghabel prodded her with his pistol. "Those too."

Zahir's head slumped in embarrassment and fear as she stood there naked before the two of them. Ghabel pulled her closer to him, pressing the pistol into her neck and then released his hold on her to reach around and squeeze a nipple between his thumb and forefinger.

Zahir gasped in pain and tried to pull away but Ghabel only squeezed harder.

Logan watched in rage. He wanted to tear Ghabel apart. Anything to protect Zahir.

"So now, Mr. American. Will you tell me who you are?"

There was a movement down the hall and Jaber Behbehani came into view. The slight motion caught Ghabel's attention and he shifted his gaze away from Logan to Behbehani. Recognition set in, and in that instant of confusion, Logan made his move.

Lunging forward he rolled and came up just in front of Ghabel. Zahir had turned slightly away from her tormenter, and in one fluid motion, Logan withdrew the fixed blade dagger from his ankle sheath and thrust it into Ghabel's gut.

Ghabel gasped and staggered back, releasing Zahir. Logan pushed her aside and rushed his foe, who was doubled over in agony, gripping his stomach with one hand and waving the pistol with the other. He aimed the pistol at Logan and as he was about to pull the trigger, a burst of automatic fire from Behbehani's AK-47 cut into the Qods Force colonel. Logan kicked the pistol away from Ghabel, who now lay crumpled on the floor.

Crouched in shock, Zahir began to shake. Logan walked over to her, pulled her up and held her until she had calmed down. "Are you all right?"

She nodded slowly.

Behbehani walked over to the corpse on the floor and nudged it with his toe. Averting his gaze from Logan and Zahir, he walked down the corridor.

Logan stooped to pick up Zahir's pile of clothes from the floor and handed them to her. "Why don't you take your things in there and get dressed." He gestured towards Ghabel's office. "We'll finish clearing this building and then Behbehani and I are going to start in the labs down the hall and collect as much stuff as we can. You could start in here. Grab anything that looks important; files, memo, computers, drives, whatever."

They worked efficiently over the next twenty minutes. Stoddard and Barbiari reported in, advising that they had met no resistance and that the warehouse area was rigged to blow in an hour. Logan directed them to move to the Research and Administrative Building to help the others lay their charges.

Wellington called in to report that he had secured a truck and had rigged the range control facility to detonate in one hour. He got back into the vehicle and drove it up to the main building.

It was still dark when they finished inside. They scooped up everything they had collected, took it outside and loaded the truck. As expected, the warehouse had yielded little of interest, but the labs and administrative building had been a treasure trove. They had found IED prototypes, schematics, reports, computers, memos and correspondence.

It turned out that Ghabel had been a bit of a hoarder, retaining reams of correspondence, and Zahir, scanning several memos, said that there were many memos from General Salehi. There was even a concept paper for attacking coalition forces in Western Afghanistan using the Taliban as surrogates.

"Guys, great job. We dodged a bullet in there, literally." He recounted the scrape with Ghabel, and clapped Behbehani on the shoulder. "If Jaber hadn't come out when he did, there's a good chance Norm would be leading you guys back to the boat. All right, let's get out of here before this place blows."

Wellington stopped at the gatehouse to pick up Jones and they sped away from the facility. There was tension in the air, because they were by no means out of harm's way. Still, there was some joking and a sense of relief that they had executed the mission with no injuries or loss of life. Ten minutes later they were back at the salt cave. After everyone had gotten out of the truck, Wellington eased it off the road and down an embankment so that it was not visible from the highway.

"All right, let's move out," Logan said quietly. The water level in the cave had not changed perceptibly, and it only took them a few minutes to stow everything, and cast off. As they pulled out of the cave, Logan noticed that one of the pressurized air chambers had lost air and was deflated. His throat tightened as he considered the possibility that they might end up in the water.

"Wellington, over here with the scuba tank. We've lost pressure in this chamber."

"Damn." Wellington slid over to where Logan was kneeling and hooked up the scuba tank line to the valve on the faulty chamber. There was a reassuring gush of air, and the chamber began to fill.

"They make these things now so that if one chamber goes you don't lose the whole shooting match. They've got interconnected baffles and valves, what Zodiac calls a connected air value system. We'll be all right." Wellington gave a thumbs-up to the others.

Logan checked the time. It was five-thirty-five, about ten minutes until their rendezvous with the Ocean Dreamer. Stoddard put them on a course towards the rendezvous point. Logan pinched the tear-resistant material of the damaged chamber, but felt no slack. It was holding air. Ten minutes later Logan saw Delray's light signal from the deck of the yacht, two short flashes and one long.

A moment later they were alongside the sleek pleasure boat. Delray tossed them a line and they pulled in close and began to hand up their gear. After everyone was on board, they muscled the Zodiac onto the deck and began to deflate it. As they were stowing it, the Ocean Dreamer picked up speed and began to pull away.

"Man, I'm glad to see you guys. Everything go OK?" Delray gave Jones a high five and looked around.

"We had a couple of tense moments. Four dead guys on their end, including the base commander. Let's go inside and we'll debrief." Logan and the others walked into the chart room and he was surprised to see Nayef Al Subaie sitting at the chart table conversing with Captain Al Watan. Nayef walked over to Behbehani, spoke to him in Arabic and then embraced him. He then went over to Logan and grasped his hand.

"Nayef. What are you doing here?"

"Logan. Congratulations. The Ocean Dreamer belongs to the Al Subaie family, and we do legitimate telecommunications business in Iran." His voice caught, however, as he spoke the next words. "Jaber Behbehani is my son." Turning towards Behbehani, his eyes glistened as he gestured. "I'd like you to meet Hamid Al Subaie."

Logan and the others were open-mouthed as Jaber, now Hamid, spoke to them in perfectly accented Oxford English.

"Sorry for the deception. I'm actually an officer of the Kuwaiti Intelligence and Security Service. I've been under cover as a foreign fighter for two years and we were close to identifying this IED facility when my father met you, Logan. As part of the ruse I had convinced my cousin Mohammad that I shared his views about Jihad, and joined him and the other Kuwaiti foreign fighters when they traveled to Bandar Deylam for training. You know the rest of the story."

As Hamid Al Subaie finished his story there was a muted explosion and then a succession of loud booms. Logan and the others rushed out to the deck. Day was just breaking, and as they looked back towards the receding Iranian coastline they could see plumes of smoke rising above the area where the IED facility had been.

Logan caught Zahir's eye. He walked over to her and put his arm around her shoulder. "This one was for Cooper, Zahir."

Zahir leaned her head against Logan, and then looked up at him. "For Cooper and all of the men and women who've died or been injured by the Qods Force and the terrorists they support."

Chapter 32

"Welcome back to the United States, Mr. Alexander." The U.S. Immigration official handed Logan his passport and waved him into the international arrivals area at LaGuardia Airport. Logan took the passport and smiled his thanks. It was good to be home. He'd only been gone for three weeks, but it felt like a lot longer.

The return to Failaka Island aboard the Ocean Dreamer following their assault on the Iranian IED facility had passed without incident. Logan had kept looking back towards the Iranian coast as they beat a path through the Gulf waters to the safety of Kuwait. He'd half expected to see Iranian naval vessels pursuing them, but all had remained quiet.

Once back on the island, they'd secured their weapons and the Iranian materials in the warehouse, and then returned to the villa for some much needed rest. Then, later that evening, refreshed, they had feasted on another one of Faran's sumptuous creations.

The next morning most of the team had packed their personal belongings and headed for the airport in Kuwait City. They were slated to take separate flights back to Europe, and conduct a document exchange with Thamir's man in London before retrieving their true name passports and continuing on to their U.S. destinations. Zahir and Logan planned to spend three more days on the island reviewing and cataloging the material they'd collected. It had been bittersweet saying goodbye to everyone. They'd all grown close over the past couple of months.

Logan and Zahir had driven to the warehouse that first morning. Zahir was going to compile an inventory of everything that they'd collected, and then was going to begin systematically reviewing it. Logan had left her there to get started while he had driven over to base headquarters for an out-brief with Colonel Al Fahad. He had waited only a couple of minutes before being shown into the colonel's office.

Al Fahad rose from behind his desk and grasped Logan's hand. "Well done, Logan. I had a few minutes with Nayef and Hamid yesterday before they went back to Kuwait City. They seemed very pleased with the ways things went."

"It was pretty smooth. We had a tense moment when things got out of control. That Qods Force colonel, Ghabel, got hold of Zahir's weapon and had us in a tight spot for a few minutes. If Hamid hadn't reacted when he did, it could've been a very different outcome."

"Hamid told me that four of the facility's men were killed. Aside from the colonel and a couple of his security guards, the other one turned out to be a major player. Do you remember that SIGINT report I showed you on Mustafa Al Adel?' Well, that was *the* Al Adel, the Al Qaeda bomber who was on the CIA's list of high value terrorist targets."

"No kidding! Now I remember. You briefed us on that SIGINT intercept of Al Adel calling one of his buddies in Yemen to tell him he had been released from house arrest. He said he was going to be moving to Bandar Deylam and would be working with the Qods Force. That name rang a bell last night but I didn't put two and two together until just now. Damn. That's amazing we got him."

"It was him all right. CIA is going to be really happy when they get the news. So what's your plan going forward?"

"Thamir and I talked about this a few weeks ago. We came up with a three-pronged approach to exploit the Intel. The CIA has the best Intel distribution in the world. Thamir is going to make copies of everything that we collected and then he'll request a high-level meeting in Washington, probably with the director of the National Clandestine Service.

"He'll give the director a copy of everything, and basically just say that Kuwait acquired it through a third party, to remain unnamed. All of this will be non-attributable to Kuwait when CIA shares the Intel with its allies."

"So then, CIA will be able to verify all of this?" Al Fahad removed a cigar from a humidor on his desk and offered one to Logan. Both men lit up.

"Yes. They'll task the NRO to get some new imagery of the facility and they'll confirm that it's been destroyed, if they haven't already. They also have linguists, analysts and forensics scientists who will be able to exploit this material pretty quickly. CIA will want to know who the source is and they'll probably put a lot of pressure on Thamir to spill the beans. But the deal is no attribution. We don't need some Al Qaeda or Qods Force whack job looking for revenge if our identities come out, and then trying to track us down. And Kuwait sure doesn't need Iran gunning for it over this."

Logan paused to relight his cigar. "Second, there are a lot of different angles we could pursue, based on an initial reading of the material we collected: Iran's IED program; their cooperation with the Taliban; the Qods Force program with Al Qaeda, etc. Our goal going in to this was to expose Iran's role in training foreign fighters and putting IEDs into the battlefield, IEDs that have maimed or killed thousands of U.S. service members, and civilians like your nephew."

"How're you going to do that?"

"We'll cull through everything. There's enough information to do a major story on Iran's role in this whole thing. We're going to make copies of all the IED-related material and then reach out to a major newspaper, probably *The Wall Street Journal*. They'll have to agree to deal with us on deep background so as not to expose our role."

"What makes you think they'll agree to that?"

"Oh, I have no doubt. This is going to be one of the biggest stories of the year. They're going to have enough material to do a series on Iran's program. And it's not going to get buried on page ten. This will be front page above the fold."

"And you mentioned a third prong?"

"*Al-Jazeera*. Thamir told me that he has a media asset who will get the same story to *Al-Jazeera*. Same deal.

Non-attributable to Kuwait or my group. It's important that the Arab-speaking world, Iran's neighbors, see this coming from a media source they trust. If it only appears in the Western press, they'll dismiss it as a fabrication. Have you seen any reaction from the Iranians yet?"

"Actually, the airbase at Bushehr put up some aircraft forty minutes after your charges at Bandar Deylam blew. I think it was about 0500 hours. Iranian forces around the country also raised their alert status around then, but we haven't seen anything else out of the ordinary."

Logan thanked Colonel Al Fahad for his generous support and bid him good-bye. He returned to the 4X4 and drove back to the warehouse. When he went inside, he found Zahir slumped over her desk. She raised her head when she heard him come in, and he could tell that she had been crying.

"Zahir, what's the matter? Are you all right?"

She choked back a sob and pointed to a DVD case sitting on the desk next to her.

Logan walked over and picked up the DVD. Zahir had affixed an English language label on the outside. Ramadi, Iraq, October 3, 2011. Logan felt his throat constrict and his pulse quicken. He knew that the foreign fighter IED teams filmed their attacks to use later on for propaganda purposes. He realized that what he was holding in his hands was in all likelihood a film of the attack that had killed Cooper.

He didn't trust his voice, but managed to choke out, "Did you watch this?"

"I couldn't bring myself to watch it by myself."

"We need to do this." Sitting down next to her, Logan slipped the DVD into the disc drive on the computer. He tensed as it began to whir, and then a grainy image of a U.S. military platoon retreating down a narrow street came into focus. The sound of gunfire could be heard and shouts from the soldiers as they made their way down the street.

"Look, there's Cooper." Zahir reached over and held Logan's hand. Her face was strained as she watched the screen. Cooper was leading the retreat and had just turned around to signal the men behind him to tighten it up. Suddenly there was a loud explosion and Cooper was thrown violently to the ground. He twitched and convulsed for a moment before he was still.

A lone figure rushed up and dropped to the ground next to him. It was Zahir. She whispered into Cooper's ear, cradled his head and rocked back and forth. Around her the other platoon members sought cover, but it had suddenly become very still. The only sound was Zahir's distraught cries. Then there was nothing.

"I don't remember anything after that." Zahir's voice sounded dull. "Gomez got me back to our unit and I was out of there within twenty-four hours. It was all like a bad dream."

She raised her head and looked into Logan's eyes. Tears began to well up and Logan moved his chair closer to hers so that he could hold her. They clung together like that until her tears had subsided and she wiped her eyes.

Logan and Zahir worked together for several more hours before they decided to call it a day. When they got back to the villa, they had a quiet dinner. Nayef had smuggled in several bottles of Argentine Malbec, and after Faran had finished cleaning up the kitchen and had bid them goodnight, Logan and Zahir retreated to the courtyard with two glasses and a bottle. It was beginning to cool off and Logan went inside to grab a fleece blanket off the couch.

"I didn't really get a chance to thank you for what you did yesterday." Zahir took a long sip from her glass and then leaned back on the couch. She looked up at the grape arbor and then shivered as the air began to cool off. She pulled the fleece closer and then reached for the bottle to pour herself another drink. "It was so stupid of me to let Ghabel get my weapon."

"It turned out all right. I'm just glad Hamid was there to finish him off." Logan held out his glass and Zahir splashed some more wine into it. She wandered back into the kitchen for another bottle and when she returned she sat down next to Logan and drew up the blanket to warm them both.

What he didn't tell her were the mixed emotions he'd experienced when Ghabel had held her hostage. The sudden fear that she would be injured or worse, killed; his uncontrolled fury when Ghabel had forced her to disrobe and then had violated her by touching her; but mostly the intense longing he had experienced when he had seen her standing there naked, beautiful and vulnerable.

Sensing his torment, Zahir raised her eyes to his. Logan leaned down to her and their lips brushed against each other, at first in tender exploration, his mouth caressing hers. Then their tongues met, softly probing, as he tasted the wine on her breath. Logan felt the fire of Zahir's passion and it ignited suppressed longing in him.

She unbuttoned his shirt and he slipped his hands into her blouse, caressing her firm breasts. They explored each other's bodies, unknown but in some way familiar. And when they were naked beside each another they were consumed with passion. They began to move in rhythm, joined in ecstasy. And then their longing gave way to a sensation of oneness, and there was nothing but the two of them melting into one, emptying themselves out until there was nothing left and at last they lay spent against each other gasping for air.

After a moment of silence, Zahir turned on her side to face him and Logan brushed the hair away from her face. Her eyes searched his and he bent down to kiss her lips.

He pulled back and studied her face. "I wasn't expecting that to happen."

"Are you sorry that it did?" Zahir reached for his hand.

"Are you kidding? You're incredible. I think I'm only just now beginning to realize how I feel about you. We got off to a rocky start in Montpelier, but over the past two months I've just come to feel that you are this really incredible woman. I love you."

Zahir buried her face in his chest and whispered, "I love you too, Logan." Afterwards they drifted off, wrapped in each other's arms only to awaken at midnight.

"Let's not give Faran anything to gossip about," Zahir whispered. She kissed him on the lips and began pulling together her clothing. Logan reached for her but she wriggled away and went to her room, looking back at him as she closed the door.

Logan lay there for a while, staring at the leafy ceiling. He had not felt so complete in a long time.

In the morning they had breakfast in the courtyard. There was no awkwardness between the two of them, although they made an unspoken effort to conceal their newfound passion for one another from Faran and the others when they arrived. In the 4X4 on the way to the Army base they had shared an embrace and Logan had desperately wished that he could pull over then and there and make love to her.

It had taken the full three days that they had allotted to plow through all of the material they had collected. When they had finished cataloging everything, Thamir sent a courier over to the Army base to transport the material securely back to Kuwait City. It filled four pouch bags and would take the Kuwaiti Intel and Security Service a couple of days working around the clock to make duplicate copies; one for him, one for *Al-Jazeera*, one for CIA, and the original for their archives.

The morning of their flight back to Paris, Logan and Zahir had met briefly with Thamir, Nayef and Hamid in Kuwait City. The Kuwaitis had been ecstatic over the success of the operation and had decided to give each team member $100,000 for their participation. The money would be funneled through the same offshore front company that Ali Al-Sabah had set up to manage their expenses. Logan planned to make certain that besides the others, Gomez's family got his share.

Nayef promised to have Logan's copies of everything delivered to Millie's apartment within days. Thamir mentioned that he had been in touch with the CIA and was scheduled to fly to Washington early the next week for a special meeting with the director of the Clandestine Service.

Later, at the airport, Logan had felt a sense of relief that the mission was over, except for wrapping up some administrative loose ends and setting up an appointment with the

Wall Street Journal. He and Zahir were on the same flight back to Paris, but would then split up to retrieve their passports in London. They had held hands on the flight to Paris, and had reluctantly parted ways as they caught their flights to London. Logan had pressed Zahir to him and kissed her before they had parted.

Logan snapped back from his daydream. He had a one-hour layover before his connecting flight to Boston, and decided to give Millie a call. She picked up on the third ring. "Hey, Mills. It's your long lost brother reporting in."

"Logan!" Logan had warned Millie not to say anything on the phone, but her excitement upon hearing his voice was palpable. "How was your trip? When will you be home?"

"I just got into LaGuardia and I have another flight out of here in about an hour. So you can tell Ryan that his days of solitude are about to come to an end."

"Oh, he doesn't care, Logan. You're welcome to stay with him for as long as you want." So –"

Anticipating her question, Logan cut her off. "So, Mills, maybe we can have dinner at your place tonight. Lots to talk about." They chatted for a few more minutes until Logan heard Delta announcing that they were boarding his flight.

Later that night in Millie's Stillman Street loft, Logan, Zahir, and Ryan sat with Millie in the living room. The mood was somber as Millie and Ryan had listened with rapt attention to Logan and Zahir's account of the operation in Bandar Deylam. Zahir had just recounted her discovery of the Ramadi tape depicting Cooper's death.

Millie sipped her drink and looked at Zahir with newfound respect. Then she turned her attention to Logan. "How are you going to reach out to the *Wall Street Journal,* Logan? Do you know anyone there?"

"No, but I've followed a couple of their foreign correspondents, the ones who have been covering Iraq and Afghanistan. I'm just going to make a cold call to the Journal to set up a meeting with them in New York. If they're interested I'll hand everything over to them, and then off the record, give them as much detail as I can about what we did there. I'll also let them know that the CIA and *Al-Jazeera* will have copies of everything and they may want to reach out to them to manage how the story plays out."

"Are you sure that they'll be able to keep your name out of it? I don't know if you've broken any U.S. laws, but like you said, the Iranians and Al Qaeda are going to be looking for revenge."

"They're professionals. I think this is going to be so big that they'll pull out all the stops to make sure nothing derails it." He raised his glass. "This one's for Cooper."

"For Cooper." One by one they raised their glasses to toast the absent brother, lover and friend.

Chapter 33

Logan's meeting with the *Wall Street Journal* got off to a slow start but it had ended on a high note. Beth Stoner was the paper's chief foreign correspondent and she had readily agreed to meet with Logan in New York on December 20.

Logan had reached out to her because she was a Pulitzer Prize-winning author who had a reputation for being passionate about her work. Her recent series of articles on the Arab Spring had garnered the *Journal* new accolades and she was working with PBS on a soon-to-be-released documentary on Afghan war orphans.

Ms. Stoner was mousy haired, slight in stature and intense. Their mid-town rendezvous at a diner on West 44th Street was initially strained.

"So let me get this straight, Mr. Alexander. You expect me to believe that you led a group of former Special Forces Seals and Rangers into Iran with the objective of taking out an IED research facility *cum* foreign fighter training camp?"

"That's right."

"I just find that highly improbable. I mean, look what happened to Jimmy Carter when he tried to send Delta Force operators into Iran back in 1980. Eight members of that team died."

"That was different. Operation Eagle Claw called for deploying helicopters into Tehran off of an aircraft carrier. We didn't have that kind of a challenge. The facility we were targeting was in Bandar Deylam and was relatively easy to access from the Gulf."

"But you have to admit that it sounds far-fetched."

"Look, I know you're a professional, and you probably

get all kinds of kooks calling in with fantastic stories. I'm going to leave something with you. You can take it back to your office and look at it, and then give me a call."

Logan handed her a manila envelope. Inside was a copy of the Ramadi tape and photos they had taken of the base. There were also grisly photos of the Al Qaeda bomber, Mustafa al-Adel. The Kuwaitis had been able to transmit the video file and still photos to their office in New York and these had been hand-delivered to Logan's hotel just that morning.

Logan had barely returned to his hotel when he had a call from Beth Stoner. "Deal," she said. "This is going to be big, though, and my editor wants to meet you." They set a time for later that afternoon at the newspaper's Avenue of the Americas offices.

Gary Paulson, a balding, fifty-something New Yorker, stared at Logan for a full minute before speaking. "We've checked you out, Mr. Alexander, and we've looked into your story. We'll agree to your request to do this on deep background because we recognize the risk you'd be taking if your identity came out. I'm going to have Beth travel to Boston so that you can spend the necessary time to walk her through the entire operation. She'll work out of our Boston offices for a week.

"I imagine it's going to take some time to fact-check everything, but I would like to get the first piece out no later than two weeks from now. That'll be just after New Year's. I don't want *Al-Jazeera* to scoop us on this. I'm going to send a Farsi linguist with her to translate everything you have. And, Mr. Alexander," Paulson nodded his head slightly and smiled, "you called it right. This story is definitely front page above the fold."

Logan had received a call from Nayef shortly after that, telling him that Thamir's meeting with the CIA had gone well. Predictably, the National Clandestine Service director had tried to get Thamir to reveal the identity of the team that had conducted the raid, but Thamir resisted the pressure and the team's identity was secure.

Nayef had told Logan that the Kuwaiti courier would

deliver full copies of the Iranian materials to Millie's apartment on Wednesday, and Logan had been there to receive the delivery. Gary Paulson had arranged to have a driver at Millie's later that afternoon, and everything had been transferred to the Journal's custody.

For the next three days Logan worked at a fever pitch with Beth Stoner, whose reputation for being a workhorse proved to be well founded. No wonder she's so good at what she does, Logan mused to himself on the last day as he said goodbye and headed over to Zahir's new East Boston loft.

The Bennington Street property Zahir had bid on had fallen through, but just after their trip to Arizona she'd found a new condo on Porter Street that she'd liked and her bid had been accepted. It was a duplex penthouse loft with incredible twenty-two-foot ceilings and oversized windows providing a panoramic view of the city. Zahir had given Millie power of attorney to close on the loft while she was traveling, and Logan had been helping her move in this week.

Zahir opened the door and brushed a wisp of hair back from her face. "Hi. How'd it go today?"

Logan embraced her. "I think that's the end of it. Beth said she might have some follow-up questions for me, but for now they have everything for the first piece that they're going to run. It will take them a while to go through the rest of it. Beth was pretty pumped up when she came by Millie's the other day and saw everything we had."

Logan looked around the loft. It had been transformed in just a week. Persian area carpets covered the bamboo wood floors and modern furniture gave the place a contemporary but understated elegant feeling. Logan wandered over to the fireplace and noticed that Zahir had arranged several family photos in silver frames on the mantle. He examined one closely. "This guy looks familiar."

Zahir looked at the picture Logan had pointed out. "Oh, that's my great-uncle."

"Who is he?"

"He died a few years ago, before I was even born."

"I'm sorry. Who is he?"

"The Shah. The Shah of Iran."

Logan didn't react initially, but then Zahir's meaning hit him. "You mean *the* Shah of Iran?"

Zahir squirmed and looked away. "It was a long time ago. He died in 1980, just before I was born. My mother is his niece."

Logan whistled and shook his head in wonder. "But wasn't he like royalty? I mean the Shah was considered a king, right?"

Zahir sighed. "My mother's side of the family is wealthy, and my uncle took good care of all his nieces and nephews. I'm sorry that I never got to meet him. Growing up in the U.S. it always meant a lot to me that he had tried to change the role of women in Iranian society. He was pro-Western, but in the end his government was corrupt and he was forced to leave the country."

"So all of this?" Logan made a sweeping gesture around the apartment.

"I have money, Logan, a lot of money." She sighed again. "It's not important."

"OK. Now that we've cleared that up, I came over to ask you to come up to Vermont with us for Christmas. Mom and Dad always do a big New England style Christmas. You know, we go out in the woods and cut down a tree, go on sleigh rides, go to midnight mass. Ryan's coming up with Millie."

"Are you sure? I don't want to intrude."

"Zahir, I'm as sure as anything. Besides, Mom and Dad have been asking when they're going to see you again."

"Have you said anything to them?"

"About us? No. But that'll be as good a time as any." He walked over to where she was standing and put his arms around her. She wrapped her arms around his waist and leaned her head against his broad chest. Logan rested his chin on her head. "I love you." He paused and then asked her the question that had been burning inside him all week. "Zahir, will you marry me?"

She raised her head and looked into his eyes. A tear trickled down her cheek as she whispered, "I love you too, Logan Alexander. And, yes, I will marry you." She stood on her tiptoes and took Logan's face between her hands. She kissed him lightly and then pulled back.

Chapter 34

They got an early start for Montpelier the next morning. Millie and Ryan would be driving up later that afternoon. Logan had purchased a pre-owned BMW X5 SUV earlier in the week and he was pleased with the way it handled. It purred as they left Boston traffic behind, and began climbing into the Green Mountains. They stopped in Concord, New Hampshire, for hot chocolate, stamping their feet to shake off the snow after they made their way from the rear parking lot into Flo's Diner on North Main Street. Flo was known all over southern New Hampshire for her gourmet dark hot chocolate. She served it piping hot in white ceramic mugs, crowned with whipped cream, grated cacao beans and a sprinkle of cinnamon.

"Yum. This is good." Zahir leaned back in their booth and surveyed the diner. An eclectic clientele swarmed around the potbelly stove in the main dining room; bankers in wool three-piece suits, students on winter break, and skiers. Normally there would be hunters warming their hands by the fire, but hunting season had ended for the year on the 15th.

"Look, Logan." Zahir tilted her head in the direction of a TV that was playing FOX News.

Logan looked in the direction she had indicated and could just make out what the announcer was saying. "And this just in. The Arab-language newspaper, *Al-Jazeera*, is reporting that the Al Qaeda bomber, Mustafa Al Adel, wanted for masterminding the 2009 terrorist attack in Khost, Afghanistan, that killed seven CIA officers at Forward Operating Base Chapman, has been killed. *Al-Jazeera* is reporting that Al Adel, who, up until recently, had been under house arrest in

Iran, was killed in a pre-dawn attack at a Qods Force training facility. We must warn you that the image we are about to display is graphic."

Seconds later the grisly image of the dead Al Qaeda bomber that Wozolski had snapped in the darkened military barracks in Bandar Deylam appeared on the screen. "We'll have more on this breaking story as it develops."

Logan allowed himself to breathe again. "That was quick. Thamir's media asset didn't waste any time putting that story out there. Heck, the Agency may have decided to leak it to *Al-Jazeera*. It would have to be demoralizing for Al Qaeda to know that another one of their top guys had bit the dust."

Snow crunched underfoot as they walked back to the car. The far end of the parking lot was empty so Logan gunned the SUV and spun a U-turn on the ice. Zahir screamed and clutched his arm as he laughed. He eased the car back onto Main Street and headed north towards Montpelier.

Two hours later, Logan wheeled into the driveway of his parents' home. He hadn't seen them since Cooper's funeral two months earlier, and although they knew he had been up to something, he had spared them the details of the recent Iranian operation lest it be an added burden at an already difficult time. Lise was quiet, although she gave Logan a fierce hug and took Zahir's hand as she led them into the family room. Harry clasped Logan in a bear hug and kissed Zahir on the cheek.

Logan and Zahir sat next to each other in the warm family room as Logan recounted their exploits over the past two months. He spoke for over an hour, interrupted occasionally by a request for clarification from Harry. Otherwise, Lise and Harry were silent as the import of what Logan had revealed sank in. When Logan had finished, Harry rose and walked over to where they sat. Helping Zahir to her feet, he embraced them both in a bone-crushing hug. Lise joined them and they stood together for a moment.

"There's one more thing. Zahir and I are going to get married."

Lise gasped and turned to Zahir. She held her by the

shoulders, and searched her face, then pulled her close. "I'm so happy. You'll be like my second daughter. Does Millie know?"

"Not yet. Logan just asked me last night." Zahir glanced sideways at Logan. "It was a surprise."

Harry pumped Logan's hand and kissed Zahir. "Congratulations, you two. We're very happy for you." Harry looked at his watch. "I have a live tree picked out over at old man Seaver's Tree Farm. I was thinking of going over to cut it down if anybody is interested in tagging along."

"I'll go with you, Dad. Zahir, do you want to come?"

"No. You two go. I'll stay here and help your mother."

Logan and Harry drove the five miles to Seaver's and walked out into the woods. "That was something you and your friends did, Logan. I'm really proud of you. Nothing's going to bring Cooper back, but when this story comes out, if it brings attention to Iran's role in this whole IED thing that'll be something."

He located the ten-foot Fraser fir that was tagged with his name and he and Logan used a crosscut saw to bring it down. They lugged it back to Seaver's yard, and Seaver's sons strapped the tree onto the roof of Logan's SUV.

"I'd like to see the UN do something. A lot of times things get bogged down in the Security Council because the Russians or Chinese take a contrarian position. I don't see how anybody can ignore what the Iranians are doing now." Harry climbed into the passenger seat.

"We'll see."

As they approached the house, Logan pointed to the drive. "Hey, there's Millie's car. She and Ryan must have made good time." As they brought the tree in through the back patio, Logan could see Millie and Zahir hugging each other. Millie turned to Logan as he came into the family room.

"Logan! Why didn't you tell me?" She poked him in the arm and laughed. "Congratulations! We have our own little surprise." She flashed the diamond on her left hand. "Ryan proposed this morning just before we left."

Everyone started talking at once, laughing and sharing

congratulations. Lise disappeared into the kitchen and re-appeared a few minutes later bearing a tray with six champagne glasses and a bottle of Veuve Clicquot.

"This is for new beginnings, for your new lives together. May you be as happy in your marriages as we have been in ours." She raised her glass and her eyes brimmed with tears of joy.

The week flew by, filled with the warmth of Christmas in New England. Cooper's absence left behind a wistful, almost melancholy, feeling to the holiday, but yesterday's tears had given way to fond remembrances and even laughter at memories from times past.

The day after New Year's, Logan rose early and went down to Striker's General Store on Elm Street. They carried a selection of national and international newspapers, and he was anxious to see if the *Journal* story was out. His throat tightened as he approached the newsstand and stood before the *Wall Street Journal*. Taking it in his hands he read the headline – "Iran's Secret War: Qods Force Reign of Terror." Logan scanned the article. It was some of the best reporting he had seen from Beth Stoner.

In her opening paragraph she explained that this was the first in a four-part series that would expose the Qods Force role in designing, manufacturing and exporting improvised explosive devices to terrorist groups around the world. The article went on to describe a recent commando-type raid against Iran's preeminent IED facility and training camp. Photos depicting IED devices, secret Qods Force documents and the ruins of Bandar Deylam's IED Research Facility and Training Camp were startling in their clarity. Logan purchased four copies of the paper and returned home.

He and Zahir planned to drive back to Boston after breakfast. Logan gave a copy of the paper to Harry and one to Millie. As they perused the article, they shook their heads in wonder at what Logan, Zahir and the others had accomplished. When they were finished reading, Millie and Zahir changed the subject and began talking about having a double wedding in Montpelier in the spring, after Zahir's baby was born, which was four months away.

After they had packed the cars and said their goodbyes, Logan pulled out onto Main Street and then turned down Lincoln Avenue.

"Where are you going?" Zahir asked.

"I thought we'd stop by St. Augustine's and visit Cooper's grave. I have something I want to do."

Logan pulled into the cemetery and he and Zahir got out of the car. It was cold, in the high-thirties, but the brilliant sun lit up the blue sky and was just beginning to melt the ice clinging to the bark on the bare trees. Logan and Zahir walked over to Cooper's grave, and Logan bent down to wipe the snow from the headstone. They stood there in silence and then Logan leaned down to place a copy of the *Wall Street Journal* at the base of the headstone.

Zahir gave a little gasp, and clutched her stomach.

"Are you all right?"

"I felt him move just now. The baby just moved."

Logan put his arm around her and drew her close. "I've been thinking about what we should call him. What do you think about Cooper?"

She looked up at him and her face softened. "Cooper. Cooper Alexander. I think that's perfect."

THE END

Purchase Cooper's Revenge online at
http://coopersrevenge.com
or from your favorite bookseller

CPSIA information can be obtained at www.ICGtesting.com
Printed in the USA
LVOW060849131112

307084LV00001B/4/P